Nicholas F. Feodoroff

A COSSACK GALLOPED FAR AWAY

**An autobiography of
American Cossack's Ataman**

Fort Ross, Inc.
New York
1998

Nicholas V. Feodoroff
A COSSACK GALLOPED FAR AWAY

An autobiography of
American Cossack's Ataman

Copyright © Fort Ross 1998
All rights reserved
ISBN: 1-57480-032-9

Cover photo: Bruz Crowson

Published by
Fort Ross Inc.
229 Riverdale Station
Bronx, NY 10471
U.S.A.

Fort Ross Inc. does not necessarily share the views of the author; neither does it bear any responsibility for the accuracy of the dates, names and other historic facts mentioned by the author. Nevertheless, Fort Ross Inc. considers these colorful reminiscences as a very informative, important, and sometimes thrilling evidence of the Russian (especially Don Cossacks') history.

DEDICATION

I dedicate this book to the Emperor of Russia, Nicholas II, and to his August family; they were all massacred by the Communists.

I dedicate it to my parents who made me healthy, both mentally and physically, and provided me with a righteous, stoic understanding of life; to my teachers at the gymnasium; and especially to the professors of the Columbia University School of Engineering (New York) whose warm friendship towards me, a Russian student and later as faculty member, kept me going.

Nicholas V. Feodoroff.

12/12/ 1997

ACKNOWLEDGMENTS

For years numerous friends asked me to write about my "adventure" - my life. Only now at a very advanced age have I been able to accomplish this task.

I am very grateful to all my Russian and American friends whose support kept up my morale.

I am especially grateful to John C. Taylor for refining my English and editing this book.

I would like to express my sincere thanks to Norman J. Shumaker, Jr., Miss Nadia Karnov, and Miss Barbara Lewis for their support and valuable suggestions in preparing the manuscript. Thanks deeply to the ITEM Sumter, S.C. Photographer Bruz Crowson, and Mr. Ruiss Weinberg for their excellent article about me published around my 94th birthday.

N. V. FEODOROFF

TABLE OF CONTENTS

Chapter 1
CHILDHOOD

I was born on November 30, 1901, in my grandmother's house on *khutor* (farm) R., located in the lower reaches of the Don river valley. Later people told me that it had been a very cold night, a severe frost "painted" pictures on the windowpanes. The temperature was 25 degrees Centigrade below zero. Besides that, there was a snowstorm. The wind created snowdrifts. My grandfather was out; he was in Rostov on a business trip. But he knew that his beloved daughter was going to give birth, so he hurried home in that terrible weather. (The distance between Rostov and our khutor was about twenty miles.) As soon as I arrived in this world, the door opened and my grandfather came in. A violent gust opened the door wide, and the cold air rushed into the house. I screamed. (Many years later my family told me that my life would be very stormy.) I tried to avoid meeting my grandfather for a couple of years, but then I was reconciled with him. He won my heart with his fluffy mustache, excellent candies, and jokes. Unfortunately, our friendship did not last long; soon my grandfather passed away.

His death came unexpectedly. It was summer, and my parents, sisters and brother stayed at my grandmother's. Once we had our breakfast in the yard. It was nice weather with a tender, warm wind rustling through the foliage, freshening the air with the breath of the Don. My grandmother's two-story house stood on the bank of the river. As was the case with all the houses in that area, it was built on piles; the first floor was approximately seven feet from the surface. The Don used to overflow in the spring, and would cover the surroundings with water. At first the water came from the lower reaches; the northeastern winds moved the water up the river; then came the flood from upstream from the melting snow. Sometimes the flood reached the twelve foot mark. Motor boats and skiffs glided easily between the houses during the floods, and the fishnets were cast directly from the front porches. In addition to the house, my grandmother had a bungalow, a cattle shed, a stable, and other buildings.

So, on a beautiful summer day, when all of us were sitting in the shadow of the trees and having our breakfast, my grandfather told my grandmother that he would go to his room. He went away; my grandma, having whispered something to my mother, went to see him. She returned in a couple of minutes, said something to my parents, and ordered us children to be quiet and not speak loudly because our grandpa had become ill. Later we found out that, in accordance with an old custom, grandpa kept a coffin under his bed. On that day, sensing the approach of his death, he went to his room, summoned his remaining strength and put on his dark suit, lay down in the coffin, and soon fell into an eternal sleep—the sleep of the just. He had confessed and received the Eucharist several days before his death.

As for my early childhood, I remember that I could read and write when I was three-and-a-half years old. My mother was my first teacher, and she was the first and the last to receive my letter—the letter of love. I kept that letter in the small pocket of my pants, but I did not know how to pass it to her. I thought about it all the time, and then it came time to wash my pants. My mother found the letter, but she never told me about that. I found out, by chance, that she kept it in a special box.

Around that time I tried to "swim." The annual flood was exceptionally high. I remember a big boat moored to the front porch of my grandma's house, where my family came for the Easter season. The ice in the lower reaches of the Don started to break in April. It was accompanied by a deafening roar as if hundreds of cannons were firing simultaneously. Huge blocks of ice, three or four feet thick, were breaking, mounting each other, creeping out on the banks from the river channel which became too narrow for them, and making gigantic ice-blocks. It was necessary to dynamite these ice-blocks to provide room for the ice floe and save the houses which were standing too close to the river from destruction. That grandiose, fantastic scene lasted for several days—days filled with anxiety for the people. At the same time the flood started.

A big boat docked at my grandmother's front porch, and my father and brother sat in it. I, too, strived to get in the boat, but, for some reason they did not want to take me. At that moment when the boat was pushing off, I escaped from my mother's arms and jumped into the boat. The old man who owned the boat did not lose his wits and managed to take me out of the water; I was saved and taken away from the front porch. My first attempt at "swimming" was a fiasco.

In summer we children used to swim in a small river. When we grew up, we went to the opposite bank of the Don, which was gently sloping, and splashed there. Once I almost drowned, but my resourceful brother saved me. My brother and I (I was about seven years old, my brother about ten) went to the opposite, sloping bank of the Don in a small canoe. We approached the opposite bank, and I thought that it was not deep there and dived in the water; but, oh gosh, I could not touch the bottom! I emerged on the surface and started to sink again (I could not swim at that time). Then I heard my brother shouting, "Breathe some air and dive!" I managed to "take in" some air and dived. Then I emerged, this time closer to the bank, but still it was too deep. I repeated the "exercise", took in as much air as possible and dived, pulling my arms and legs toward the bank. I repeated this maneuver ten times before I reached the place where I could stand on my feet. That lesson taught me to be cautious and never hurry. Sure, sometimes it is necessary to make decisions quickly, and then instinct functions. I had to make a quick decision on a couple of occasions, but I'll describe these events later. The main result of that day was that I learned to swim. I swam slowly, but I could stay in the water for a long time, and I knew how to pause for a rest while swimming.

I have always liked animals since my childhood. People had plenty of chicken, geese, ducks, guinea fowl, and turkeys in the yard of every khutor. Sheep, cows, horses, and dogs were everywhere. What didn't they have! My grandmother had a big kitchen garden behind her house, as well as a big garden and a flower bed in front of and at the side of the house. Her flower bed was famous for its roses. They had gardens and kitchen gardens on almost every piece of property, and everybody had his melon patch where they grew watermelons, melons, squash, cucumbers, potatoes, and so on. Behind the melon fields (which are called

bastany in the Don area), the reeds were standing in a thick wall.
They were straight and tall—about seven meters (twenty-three
feet) in height. Local people used the reeds as firewood and as a
good construction material.

The reeds occupied a great deal of space, many acres of
land, in fact. Their thickets stretched along the shores of the Azov
Sea in the area of the mouth of the Don. These were real
jungles——thickets which stood in a dense, impenetrable wall. A
person who got into that thicket was at risk of never getting out.
But what a rich variety of life was hidden there! In some places
the thicket was cut by narrow, clean and deep streams, teeming
with fish and crayfish. Meadows, stretching away from the banks
of those countless streams, were full of wild strawberries and
blackberries. There one could find wild honey and peanuts.
Certainly, large numbers of fowl were found there, including
swans, hens, ducks, geese, wild turkeys, as well as numerous
varieties of small animals. It was truly a living ecosystem.

Nature was generous to that land, and the people living
there appreciated its wealth and protected it.

Between khutors R. and 0. were several mounds, the
remnants of the Mongol invasion. I used to dig there and found
copper arrowheads. I gave my finds to my father who made a big
collection of the objects found in the mounds. I remember a
legend devoted to the mystery of the mounds.

So it was; so it will be. The pagans can never conquer the
Quiet Don. It was a very hard time for the people of the region.
The pagans invaded the lands of the Don, and later they occupied
Orthodox Russia. They set the towns and villages on fire. The
pagans grabbed a great deal of loot and put many Cossacks to the
sword. The pagan leaders set up their tents on our native land
which was soaked with blood. There were seven tents for the
seven strong men who were the leaders of the pagans. They
divided the loot and quarreled with each other. When it came
time to divide the icon of Saint Nicholas, the Welcomer, which
had golden mountings covered with precious stones, they were
completely at odds with each other, and the level of their
quarreling reached new heights. Each of them wanted to get the
icon, so they decided to split the precious object into seven parts.
But as soon as they split it and took the parts away, their tents
were turned into mounds, and these mounds, in turn, covered the
seven pagans. They are still sitting there waiting for the Judgment
Day.

The vile hordes of the seven pagans ran away in terror. Blue flowers grew up in the steppes, and the Cossacks took heart. Now one can hear moans from under the mounds. And the songs, devoted to God, rise to the skies above the mounds. These are the souls of the slain Cossacks singing Glory to God. Oh Don, our Father...You, the chivalrous Cossacks.

I used to wonder how peanuts came to grow in the Don region. The answer is simple; they were introduced by the Mongols.

Since childhood I have liked to fish. We fished with fishing rods, nets, etc. Early in the morning, at sunrise, our father, accompanied by my brother and me, went to the bank of the Don and threw the line. The line hadn't yet touched the surface when a young carp (*kaborozhny*) swallowed the bait.

Usually after sitting for fifteen to twenty minutes, we caught five or six big carp. Nothing compares with the beautiful scene of the "playing" fish; a carp jumps from the water, and water droplets shine like thousands of tiny crystal clear diamonds in the morning sun.

There were plenty of fish there, as well as other creatures of nature. We children caught birds with our bare hands. We did it in this manner: in autumn, during the process of mowing, the birds gathered to peck the grain around the sheaves. We set up a net around a sheaf, and a goose or a duck was entangled in it. As I remember, we never killed the birds. After catching them, we let them go free. That was our fun.

Early in my life I remember Easter. I was dressed in a new suit. The day was clear and warm. Walking in the yard, I came across a hen's nest. Wishing to become acquainted with the surrounding world, I went to the fence which enclosed the pond. Climbing over the fence, I discovered goose nests full of eggs. I decided to surprise my mom by bringing her some eggs. Then I hit upon the idea of putting them inside my shirt, because my pocket was too small and could contain only one egg. In order to get home, I had to climb over the fence again. I climbed successfully, but while hanging on the other side of the fence, I lost my balance, bent, and crushed the eggs. Sticky fluid ran down my body, soaking through my brand new suit. I felt sorry for myself, my suit, and the eggs. But I was really upset by the thought that I could not bring the gift to my mother. Mother rebuked me, took off my suit, and bathed me. That was the second "fiasco" of my childhood.

Being seven years old, I was sent to school where I studied until I was ten. We had a three-year school in our *stanitsa* (large Cossack village). After graduation and a short period of training, children could enter middle school or take technical or vocational courses. My father decided to send my brother and me to a classical gymnasium named after Ataman Count Platoff located in Novocherkassk. I usually spent the summer at my grandmother's khutor R. Her neighbor was an old man and I used to gather berries and catch crayfish with him. During several hours spent in the reed filled streams, we caught more crayfish and more berries than we could carry. I especially remember the night watch. To go for a night watch means to pasture horses. Sometimes it was held on the distant steppe; sometimes the event would be held in a melon field. Grown-ups hobbled the horses and let them go and feed. Then they showed us how to make a fire. We boiled *conder* (a sort of millet porridge) and baked potatoes. If there was a river nearby, we caught some fish for the fish soup and some crayfish. It happened that we cast a net and dragged it back half-filled with crayfish. The same thing happened with the fish such as tenches, carp, ruffs, and so on. Sometimes it was not easy to drag such a heavy net.

Sitting by the fire and watching the boiling food, the old men shared memories of their adventures, losses and victories. I have heard a lot from our Cossacks who were veterans of the RussoTurkish and Russo-Japanese wars. They told about the courage of commanders and fellows-in-arms. Of course, the storytellers did not portray themselves in a bad light. I remember how one of them said that he was an expert shot. He told us how he hunted wild geese and killed a dozen geese with a single shotgun shell. We children believed the stories the adults told us; that's why we regarded the storyteller seriously. But most of all I liked the tales about the exploits of Count Platoff, General Baklanoff, and other heroes. Certainly they sang a lot of Cossack songs by the fire.

The summer nights in the Don Region are clear and warm. Billions of stars were sparkling in the skies; the moon was shining, and its beams were silvering the mirror-like surface of the water. Nature, as if enraptured by the mysterious charms of the night, remained peaceful and silent. Once in a while the mystic charm of the night was interrupted by a horse's snort or by a bird's cry.

During the supper the assignments were made to determine who would watch the horses and the fire, and gradually everything became silent. A deep sleep overcame the kids; the old men, too, fell asleep, tired after a long day. Sometimes an owl's hooting or the scream of a rabbit torn by a fox could be heard. And again a divine silence fell over the land—the silence of a warm southern Russian night.

It is impossible to forget that wonderful country—Russia, Imperial Russia—the country of freedom and Orthodoxy. My best memories are connected with the holidays. I want to tell, especially, about Christmas and Easter.

People started to fast several weeks before Christmas. They were not allowed to eat meat and eggs. Fish was permitted on Wednesdays and Fridays only. There was no noisy merrymaking or singing of secular songs. On Christmas Eve, people fasted the entire day and when the first star, the load star of the Magi leading them to the crib of the Newborn, appeared, people gathered at the table to eat from the restricted menu for the last time. The dinner as a rule consisted of fish soup or lean borscht, a pie with rice, potatoes, cabbage or fish, fried fish with garnish, and *uzvar* (stewed fruit). After a quiet dinner, both the young and the old started decorating the Christmas tree. Then the kids went to bed, and their parents distributed the gifts.

We, the children, usually did not sleep that night, waiting for the morning impatiently; then we could have fun, go skating, sing, jump, and so on. The idea of receiving gifts also gave us no rest.

I remember Christmas dinner in our house where we dined on borscht with meat, a goose, and a roast piglet with an apple in its mouth. For dessert we had pies and candies. This was not a luxury meal; the same dishes could be found in every house. A goose cost three or five kopecks at the market; a dozen eggs cost one kopeck (sometimes the owners gave eggs free of charge); a lamb cost seventy-five kopecks. Besides that, every household had more than enough poultry, pigs, and cows.

On the first day of Christmas, the children went to sing Christmas carols. We were singing in the yards, and they gave us *varenyky* (curd or fruit dumplings) and kopecks. Once my friend was given a portion of freshly cooked dumplings, bit one of them and burned his tongue. "Uncle!" he shouted at the owner of the house, "the dumpling is too hot! I have burned my tongue!" "Put it in the snow, little boy, and then put it in your mouth with the snow; it will be all right," responded the owner, smiling. Often the owners put the equivalent of a dime in the dumpling. The child who got it was considered to be lucky, but he told everybody that he almost broke his tooth.

On the first days after the New Year, people also had fun; they arranged races and fancy riding events. All Russia was celebrating the holiday. Easter was an especially joyous occasion. Easter follows the Great Lent, during which no songs could be heard except for church liturgical singing; everything was strict and mournful. Men repaired horse harnesses, prepared for the spring sowing and fixed the buildings. Women were occupied with their households, spun thread from sheep wool, and wove cloth. But then came Easter. Easter cakes were baked, eggs were decorated and Easter sweet cheesecakes (*Paskha*) were made. Each woman wanted to boost about her cakes, and in some houses they baked cakes with a height of one meter (three feet, three inches). During the last week, we fasted and attended divine services. The lessons at school were canceled during the Holy Week. We fasted very solemnly, and when we received the Eucharist, we congratulated each other as part of the Holy Sacrament. We regarded that ritual with great respect.

We did not sleep at all on a night before Easter. We were too excited, waiting for the change from meekness and silence to celebration. We were waiting for tasty food to be served because we were already tired after seven weeks of Lent, despite the ability of our moms and grandmothers to cook very appealing Lenten dishes. The scent of Easter cakes from the kitchen filled the house. The scene around a church on the night before Easter where the Easter cakes were sanctified was very beautiful. The cakes with burning candles, surrounded by decorated eggs and bacon, were standing around the church all night long. They were standing in two rows with a passage between them. The congregation and the priests made a triple round of the church with icons and banners approximately a half an hour before midnight. Everybody was standing at the church door exactly at midnight. The door was closed. Then the priest knocked at the door; it opened, and the good news was announced from the church which was filled with light. "Christ is risen!" All the people answered: "Indeed, He is risen!" After that the morning service began, and then—mutual congratulations. Every parishioner approached the priest; they congratulated each other, and the priest received an egg. In his turn, he gave an egg to a parishioner. (An egg is a symbol of eternal life.) Then the cakes were sanctified, and the parishioners went home. Sometimes people celebrated the break of Lent in the parish house. The bells were ringing constantly.

I liked to watch how carefully people were carrying sanctified cakes with burning candles. In the darkness of the night, hundreds of lights were taken to people's homes from the church.

Easter dinner was extremely joyful. The common feeling of joy, arising as a result of participation in a celebration of a great miracle and the coming spring, was supplemented for us children with a knowledge that now we could have fun, frolic, and do whatever we wanted.

So at the dinner, first of all, we ate a piece of food that had been sanctified at the church including cakes, *paskha*, eggs and bacon. That dinner was as rich as Christmas dinner. The only difference was the presence of a lamb instead of a piglet. We had noodle pudding and uzvar for dessert.

Orthodox Christians in Russia had remarkable rituals. During the forty days after Easter people greeted each other with the words: "Christ is risen," and kissed each other three times. Even enemies could not evade the ritual. The Tsar would visit a prison and greet the prisoners. Another custom was to visit friends and employers and supervisors. The employees visited their superiors, greeted them and received gifts (usually money). The bells were ringing throughout the day. It seemed that the air of the villages and towns was permeated with the sound of chimes. Some bell ringers were genuine virtuosos. They could perform the Russian anthem, tunes from Tchaikovsky's *1812 Overture*, and other melodies. It was nice and merry to listen to the chimes—the fragrance of blossoming life. That was Russia; that was my motherland.

I spent three years at primary school. After graduation my father prepared me for the entrance examinations for gymnasium. My principal was Victor Genrykhovich Granjean. Quiet, tender and always ready to help, he was like an elder brother and a father to us. I always remember him with a special warmth from the bottom of my heart. It is a pity that the Revolution forced us to part so early. The classes lasted from nine in the morning until noon, and from one to four in the afternoon. All the volunteers could join the chorus, or the orchestra, or a certain circle: historical, geographical, literary, etc. I joined the orchestra and the chorus. But in order to be enrolled in the orchestra one had to choose a musical instrument and learn to play it. I chose a cornet and soon could play the notes and make my instrument sound in accordance with the notes. I was enrolled in the orchestra. My teacher of music in the gymnasium was the Counselor of State Feodor Ivanovich Popoff. His main place of service was at the Military School—the Cadet Corps named after Emperor Alexander the Third—where he taught music and singing. In the gymnasium he directed his assistants who were musicians from the Army Orchestra. They taught us how to play musical instruments and made an orchestra of us.

I was enrolled at once. I used to sing in the treble clef since my childhood. I learned the anthem, *God Save the Tsar, If Glorious*, and *The March of the Preobrazhensky Regiment*. These were the first musical pieces that I could play well. When the elder cornetist graduated from gymnasium, I took his place in the orchestra. My namesake, Nicholas Apryzhkin, was the second cornetist. I "rose up the hill" and at the ball of the graduates of the eighth grade I had to play *Spanish Bolero* playing a considerable section of the piece solo.

We studied diligently. We were promoted from one grade to another. I remember that two days before the graduation ball the rehearsal was taking place on the second floor. My timing was off. I had to make a phone call to my parents, but the telephone was on the first floor. I came downstairs, started to speak to my father, and all of a sudden—oh, gosh!—I heard the orchestra playing *Bolero*. I rushed headlong to the assembly hall and saw our dear Feodor Ivanovich coming to my chair to make a signal for me to start the solo. And I could see his face when he beheld my empty chair. I should mention that a conductor is not supposed to approach a musician personally to remind him to start, but I was very small, only four feet, and it was not easy to see me behind the violins. Out of respect to the first cornetist, Feodor Ivanovich broke the conductor's etiquette. The orchestra stopped playing. Feodor Ivanovich made a helpless gesture, and at that moment I appeared. He looked at me for about a minute, then said softly and distinctly, "Sit down and play." The rehearsal continued. The graduation balls, with our performance as the main event, was a great success. Later the skill of playing cornet happened to be very useful for me.

All my life I have cherished the memory of Emperor Nicholas II, who visited Novocherkassk on the occasion of the three-hundredth anniversary of founding of the House of Romanov. In 1913, the Tsar was welcomed by the Ataman of the Don Region and representatives of different strata of the city. A solemn Divine service took place which featured prayers for the Emperor's health, and a parade was held. Then the Emperor visited a Military yunker School *(a yunker school in many ways resembled an American service academy),* a cadet corps, and our gymnasium. Of course, we welcomed him with the anthem and then with *The March of the Preobrazhensky Regiment.* The Emperor approached the orchestra and patted me and my namesake, the second cornetist, on our heads. That sign of special attention was easy to explain; we were the smallest members of the orchestra. I can never forget the blue eyes of the Emperor, full of kindness. They were shining with calmness, tenderness, and a father's affection. The director of the gymnasium, Feodor Karpovich Floroff, greeted the Emperor. In his short reciprocal speech, Tsar Nicholas told us about the importance of science, and advised his to study diligently. I remember his words, "Russia needs you. Study!" I don't remember the details of the speech; I was too charmed by the sound of his soft, quiet voice. It reminded me of a murmuring brook.

I don't remember how many days the Emperor stayed at Novocherkassk. I know that he visited the nearby villages and cities such as Rostov-on-Don, Azov and, certainly, Taganrog. I remember very clearly his visit to stanitsa Elizavetinskaya, the largest fishing stanitsa. As it happened during His Majesty's visits, he was welcomed by the Ataman and Cossack representatives, as well as the priests. A dinner was served after the Divine service. The tables were crammed with food such as *balyk* (cured fillet of sturgeon), fresh sturgeon, black and red caviar, herring, the famous Don trout, crayfish, jellied fish, and pies filled with crayfish, fish, cabbage or meat; in addition, fish soup, borscht, meat dishes, and all kinds of desserts had been prepared. All the food was cooked and served by women from Cossack stanitsas. The tables were a hundred meters long (three hundred and thirty feet), accommodating three thousand people at a time where they could share the joy of meeting the eminent quest.

After resting, the next day the Emperor went to watch fishing where he was served a special fish soup. The old Cossack, grandfather K., was a great master of cooking fish soup. The Emperor liked the fish soup very much, and he thanked the cook who soon received a special thanksgiving medal for his hospitality. One of the tragic pages of the history of our Don is connected with that medal. The Cossacks from stanitsa Elizavetinskaya told me the end of the story in 1918. Now I want to tell it to you.

It was a clear, quiet summer day in 1914. The sun was shinning pleasantly, the air suffused with a strong fragrance of summer grass. The villages and khutors along the Don river were buried in green gardens and foliage. It seemed that everybody was having a quiet afternoon dream. Kids were playing near the water, making sand castles; ducks and geese were sitting on the water, motionless like porcelain figurines. Nothing could be seen from the sides of the houses (they were obscured by green trees), and only a small landing pier showed that the dwelling was nearby. In my mental travels to the past, I often see that pier and a tall, strong man going in the direction of the houses. A fifteen-year-old girl is running to him, joyfully hanging on his neck. This is his daughter. My brother and I are watching him from afar. We have been waiting for that man for a long time; he is the inspector of the Don River game preserve, and we came to him to request permission to hunt and fish during summer vacation. While he was out, we made friends with his daughter, a nice girl named Ada. Her laughter was so sincere and joyful! Peter received permission to hunt and fish, but I only to fish.

"I am very sorry," said the inspector, "but you, Nicholas, are too young to own a gun. This is the law, though we learn to handle firearms since our childhood, according to the old Cossack custom." Then he called his daughter. "Ada! Be a good hostess, and treat us to a cold watermelon. We'll be waiting for you at the flower garden, in the summer-house."

Ada brought a large tray with a big sliced watermelon. It was sweet, juicy, and cold, and we ate it with pleasure. The inspector asked us if we knew good places for fishing and hunting. We only knew that all the places here were famous for fishing and hunting. "Then I'll give you a guide," the inspector said. "He is a real specialist in hunting and fishing. When would you like to start?" We were eager to go, so we asked if the guide could accompany us early in the morning at five in the morning. "Let's try to settle it," the inspector said. "Ada, go and entertain the quests. I'll go to 'Daddy' and ask him if he could help us tomorrow."

Everything happened to our satisfaction. In the morning we met an elderly man on the bank of the river. He greeted us with a smile. In the boat he introduced himself, "Vasily Kedroff. But everybody calls me 'Daddy,' though I am not married and have no children. You may call me that. And who are you?" Peter told him our names. "Oh yes, I remember Vladimir Feodoroff very well. Are you his grandsons?" asked "Daddy." "He was a very nice person; he passed away too early. But let's go to a good fishing place."

We floated in the direction of one of the Don's branches. In half an hour, "Daddy" suggested we cast the lines. Yes, he was a real expert. Literally in half an hour we caught eleven carp, weighing from twelve to eighteen pounds each. That was more than enough, and we decided to stop fishing and go hunting. When we were fishing we looked closely at "Daddy." His hair was absolutely gray, though he was not old. He was limping heavily, the result of a wound he had received in the Russo-Japanese War, and he used a crutch for assistance. He spent all his life at his khutor. Coming back from the war as an invalid, he realized that he was limited in his choice of occupation, so he started fishing and hunting. Nobody was as skilled at hunting as he was. He never hunted or fished for money, and gave all his trophies to his neighbors as gifts. He received some gifts in return, such as vegetables, bread, milk, etc. And what an excellent cook he was! Fish soup, crayfish and ducks were especially tasty when he prepared them, and "Daddy's" baked fish was famous far beyond the neighborhood. Very often he had visitors who wanted to taste fish soup and other exotic delicacies. When the fishing crews were organized, local fishermen invited "Daddy" to accompany them, and he was a cook for their crew. Besides that, he was a matchless storyteller, describing events that had occurred in the Russo-Japanese War (he had seen a lot). Whatever—it was very interesting to be with "Daddy."

"Daddy" smiled at our delight over the fish we caught. "It's a pity you were not here when I was a child. At that time there was really an abundance of fish, though now it's not bad. Your grandfather came here with a big group of people. They arrived in boats—"oaks." Each "oak" was thirty feet long and fifteen feet wide with a net measuring 4,000 feet in length and 100 feet in width. When the net was dragged to the bank, it had about three tons of fish. Once it caught a *beluga*. When we pulled it out, it was as big as a cow. It had more than seventy pounds of caviar. Oh, yes, your grandfather was a good fisherman."

We remembered our grandfather vaguely; when he died I was a baby. "Daddy" told us a lot about him. In particular, he told us one of grandfather's stories.

Many years ago, here on the banks of the Don, lived a childless couple. The husband was quiet and docile, and his wife was ruling the house. One could hear her commanding voice all day long, telling the husband to do the next task; go, bring, watch, make, and so on. Once in the evening she ordered her husband to bring a calf from the opposite bank of the river where it had been grazing on rich grass since morning. The old man took a boat, crossed the Don River, put the calf in the boat and started rowing back slowly. Having reached the middle of the river, he saw a strange picture: a roller of water was approaching him like a wall; fish were jumping and playing in front of it. Fish were jumping and splashing, cutting the water, and raising thousands of emerald droplets in the evening air. The old man was stupefied with astonishment; he saw a similar water wall moving from the upper reaches, and two gigantic shoals of fish were moving to meet each other. The fish were so abundant that they raised the boat, causing the boat to rock, and the calf jumped out, doomed to drown. But instead of drowning, it jumped and jumped on the fish until it reached the bank.

The old man found plenty of fish in his boat. He reached the bank in a daze, caught the calf and brought him to the barn. His wife reproached him in a scolding manner because he had almost drowned the calf. And when the man proudly brought her the fish from the boat, she scolded him because there were too few fish.

Later my brother and I, reading books by Professor F. I. Shcherbina, found the confirmation of that story. That year fish were amazingly abundant in the Don and Kuban regions. Feodor Ivanovich Shcherbina described, as well, a case where a soldier on horseback who was crossing a river in the Caucasian mountains was knocked out of his saddle by a fish shoal.

That abundance was a result of the harmony between the lives of the people and nature. Everybody took care of his household and the surroundings, knowing that the natural resources would be inherited by his sons and grandchildren.

We turned to the brook from the main channel of the Don. There were plenty of brooks. All of them were full of fish, crayfish and wild ducks. We frightened away the flocks of geese and ducks, which soared up in front of the boat. We were paralyzed, amazed by the beauty of untouched nature. "Daddy" possessed an extensive knowledge of all the breeds of birds and their habits. He told us hunting stories tirelessly. Soon we found a clearing and decided to stay and have breakfast. "Daddy" decided to cook our fish. My brother and I brought some dry branches and made a fire. "Daddy" fetched a pail of water, scaled the fish, put them in the pot, added some herbs, threw in some millet, and soon breakfast was ready. Oh, it was such a beautiful breakfast! "Daddy" was a magician. Gulping the fish soup, we forgot about everything so tasty was this dish. I have tried all kinds of food during my life, but I would never exchange "Daddy's" fish soup for French or Italian delicacies. I remember its fragrance even now, and I see "Daddy's" contented, squinted eyes before me.

After tasting the wonderful soup, we stretched out with pleasure on the grass, and "Daddy" took a small package out of his pocket. It contained a silver cross and a golden medal. "Daddy" received his St. George Cross for heroism during the Russo-Japanese War, and Emperor Nicholas II personally presented him with the medal. He repeated several times that the medal was sent to him by a special order of the Tsar. "You have seen the Emperor? Did you talk to him?" My brother and I were excited. "Not only have I seen him and talked with him, but I treated him to our Don fish soup. You have tasted it today. Do you like it? That means I am not a bad cook. It occurred in 1913. The Emperor visited the lands of Russia on the occasion of the three hundredth anniversary of the establishment of the House of Romanov.

"The inspector of the game preserve received a letter telling him to allow the fishermen to get some fish in the most forbidden places of the Don. Having read the letter, the inspector ordered the fishermen to go fishing. Three men and I were ordered to cook a dinner—three times bigger than usual. We understood that a very important reception was going to take place.

"After dragging the net out of the water, we chose the best fish, and started cooking. However, the inspector did not answer our question about the quests. By noon a motor boat was moored to the bank, and several persons in uniforms greeted us. We recognized the Ataman of the Don Army and several atamans from the stanitsas. But we could not believe our eyes—the Emperor was among them! I had only seen his picture, and now I was standing near the Russian Tsar. The Emperor approached each of us and greeted us. Coming up to me, he noticed that the fingers on my hand were missing, and he asked me about that injury. I answered that it was the result of the War of 1905; I was wounded in my hand and right knee. But it did not hinder him from working. Plucking up my courage, I declared, 'Your Imperial Majesty, let me offer you and your companions freshly prepared Don fish soup made from fresh fish.' 'Thank you,' answered the Emperor, 'but if everybody accepts your invitation, there would not be enough fish soup for you.' 'We have cooked more than enough today,' I replied. The Emperor smiled.

"I spread a raincoat on the grass, took a bowl with porridge and another with fish soup, and put them in front of the Tsar. After he was seated, all the others sat down for breakfast. I gave a bowl filled with porridge and a large bowl of fish soup, containing a whole fish, to everybody. To my great satisfaction, the Emperor asked for a second helping. Having finished the breakfast, he came up to me, thanked me and said, 'Never in my life have I eaten such wonderful soup and fish.' Others also thanked me. Soon the eminent quests left, and later I received a package with my name and address on it. A stamp was in the top left corner which read, 'House of Romanov, St. Petersburg.' Having opened the envelope, I almost fainted. There was a golden medal and a letter thanking me for my courage displayed during the Russo-Japanese War.

The medal on "Daddy's" palm was shining under the rays of the sun reflecting the happy face of a plain Russian man—a patriot and the real master of Russia.

The war, fatal for Russia, started in 1914. The Russian government appealed to its people to donate gold, silver, and copper in order to help the defenders of Russia. Everyone gave whatever he had. "Daddy" Vasily donated his St. George Cross and the medal. The local committee accepted it, but the area committee decided to return it to "Daddy" with a letter of gratitude.

The Communist Revolution broke out in 1917, and later the Civil War, the most terrible of all wars. Life became very hard; everybody had to look for food. Bad fortune did not spare "Daddy." His neighbors were helping him as much as they could, but he was growing old quickly; his old wounds were getting worse. The curse of Bolshevism was spreading on Russian territory swiftly, taking away hundreds of thousands of lives, the lives of the best people. Death came from hunger, massacres, and the brutality of the concentration camps.

The Communist gangs often came to khutors and stanitsas to take away the food—the so-called requisition. They grabbed everything, including grain, vegetables, cattle, valuables, gold, and money. One day a Communist gang came to khutor R. and burst into "Daddy's" house. "What do you need?" asked "Daddy." Instead of answering, one of the bandits struck his face, pushed him to the floor, and said hoarsely, "Where is your gold?" "I have no gold," answered "Daddy," wiping the blood from his face. "You are lying! You have the golden medal!" Another bandit wanted to hit "Daddy", but "Daddy" eluded him and the bandit bumped against the wall, which caused the lamp on the wall to fall down and go out. It became dark, and "Daddy" managed to run out of the house; he ran to the river as fast as he could. The Communists followed him, shooting in the darkness. He almost reached the boat when a bullet overtook him. "Daddy" fell in the river, and the Don swiftly covered his body.

Several days later people found his body. They took him to a church for a funeral service. "Daddy" was a very religious man, but it was difficult to find a priest, because the Communists had killed many of them. At that time the Communists temporarily had abandoned the area, and it was possible to bury "Daddy" according to the Orthodox ritual. A priest was found in the neighboring khutor. According to Orthodox ritual, the priest and the people bid farewell to the deceased after the funeral service. Then the priest reads the last prayer and puts the paper with its text under the hand of the deceased. When the priest took "Daddy's" hand, he saw the golden medal grasped in it. He looked at the face of the deceased; it seemed he was smiling. The priest placed the paper at his side, and the coffin's cover was closed. The medal remained with "Daddy's" body. May the memory of God's servant Vasily live forever!

◆

◆   ◆
◆

I often came to stanitsa Elizavetinskaya in the summer. Here, on the sloping bank of the Don, the fishermen had their *tonya (a tonya is a place where the sweep-net of the fishermen is usually cast. The cast-net is also sometimes called a tonya.)* I always tried to get there at noon. At that time the fish soup and the millet porridge were ready. Everybody was having dinner. When they saw me, the Cossacks always said, "Did you bring a spoon and a bowl?" I never took a spoon and a bowl. A Cossack rebuked me gently, took his fine rye bread with a thick crust, sliced the end of the loaf, took the middle away (now it looked like a boat), placed a whole fish and porridge there, and gave it to me. The fish soup was made from specially selected fish. It was taken from each tonya at a rate of one fish weighing three or four pounds for each fisherman, and several extra fish for "uninvited" guests like me.

Sometimes fishing turned into an exciting game. Here beluga got into the sweep net. What a great deal of excitement, noise and rush occurs to prevent the gigantic fish from escaping from the net while the men drag it to the bank successfully! Once I saw the fishermen dragging out a beluga; it was as big as a cow lying on its side. Its weight was a thousand pounds.

But summer fishing was not as much fun as fishing in winter. In winter the Don was ice-bound. The ice was one meter (up to three feet) thick. After the most severe frost, the Epiphany frost, the fishermen started to fish from large ice holes (one by two, or three meters or larger). (*Fishing from ice-holes was called races; races lasted for only two weeks.*) The fishermen got rich during that time. First they cut ice holes. On a certain day the fishermen from the nearby stanitsas and khutors gathered there. The number of people reached a thousand. They came in low, wide sledges, known as *rozvalny*, and drove on the ice in horse-drawn sledges. The ice sagged but did not break. The fishermen had high boots, because water was up to their knees on the sagging ice. They inserted a net under the ice and soon dragged it out full of fish. Fish went to the ice holes to obtain some fresh air and got caught in the net. Having dragged out the net, the fisherman put the fish in the sledge and urged the horses with his catch to the market in Rostov. The catches were big. One sledge, full of fish, brought its owner more than a hundred rubles of profit. At that time the average worker's wage was twenty-five kopecks per day, and a qualified joiner received five kopecks per day.

Having sold the fish, the fisherman went to a tavern to cheer up. Then he went shopping to buy gifts for his wife and kids. The Cossacks told a story about a fisherman who brought his gifts home. His wife tried on a dress, then the shoes. She scolded her husband and said, "What is the matter with you? You have held my feet so many times, and you don't know their size?" The next day, the Cossack corrected his mistake.

On the next day he went fishing again, making an even greater profit from his catch. The winter fishing season lasted two weeks. Then the fishing stopped. I should mention that one could buy a small house with the proceeds from the season's catch.

Every fisherman made salted fish with carp, bream, etc. Everybody had at least two *shaplyks (a shaplyk is a half of a barrel, one meter in diameter and two-thirds of a meter in depth.)* One contained salted herring (the summer catch); another contained the winter catch. There was plenty of dried fish in every house—enough for several years' consumption.

The Don's fish fed not only the Don area but a sizable part of Russia. During the spring flood, the fish went up the river from the preserves. Water not only flooded the lower lands, but carried fish, filling the flooded lands with fish. Many cured fillets of sturgeon were hung from the eaves of the house, while the barrels were full of salted herring. When the flood was over and the rivers came back to flow within their banks, a lot of fish remained in small lakes in low-lying places. Surely those fish were caught, too.

The Don river was very rich and was known as Don Ivanovich. A Cossack is the Don's master and son who takes care of its purity and productivity. Not without reason they name him in Cossack's songs, "You, our benefactor, Don Ivanovich."

Women used to catch crayfish. While their husbands were fishing, the Cossack women filled their baskets with selected Don crayfish, and carried them on board steamships traveling to the market in Rostov. A captain ordered the women to put the baskets with the crayfish in the hold. Approaching the Rostov pier, he called loudly, "Women with crayfish, go ashore!" The Cossack women hastily took their baskets from the hold and carried them to the noisy Rostov market, adding to its variety and abundance.

As I have mentioned already, our family spent its summers at khutor R. at our grandmother's. A priest with two sons lived at that place too. His older son was the same age as my brother Peter; the younger was my age. The older boys had their common interests and spent their time together apart from us. They studied at the gymnasium, spent the summertime together, hunted birds, and took singing lessons from our local teacher of Russian and Don regional history. They entertained themselves, learned to ride horseback, swam in a shallow stream which ran through our khutor, rowed in a boat on the Don river, and so on.

Once my friend suggested that we travel on the Don in a large boat called an "oak." So we decided to begin the adventure. I suggested constructing a sail using a blanket; we made a mast and started sailing. It seemed to us that we could steer a big boat with the help of a blanket. And, indeed, in spite of our youth, we were very determined. When a strong wind prevented the boat from moving, we rowed to the shore, got out of the boat, and dragged it by a rope. In this way we navigated about twenty miles down to the mouth of the Don.

My uncle was the manager of the estuary port of the Don. He inspected all the vessels coming to the Don from the Sea of Azov. His work was very strenuous because many merchant ships from Turkey, Greece and other countries were constantly arriving. So my friend and I went to meet my uncle. He and his wife gasped with surprise. How could it happen that two ten-year old boys, without their parents' knowledge, had made such a long journey? My uncle sent an urgent telegram to my parents. Before we went home, we spent two wonderful days enjoying our rest in the Don's wildlife preserves. My uncle showed us how to hunt waterfowl. We made a circle of reeds and inserted standing reeds in it, thus making a small, floating reed island. My friend and I crept into it. There were plenty of birds in that area. When a flock of geese or ducks sat on the water near us, we approached them by hiding on the floating island. Curious birds came up to us, and we caught them by their legs. We caught them, and then set them free.

Having come home, we received a serious tongue-lashing. I can still remember those words.

The second case of my unwarranted absence occurred in winter. My father went to the "races" (ice-hole fishing). I wanted to accompany him, but he said that fishing during the "Epiphany frosts" occurred during the coldest time in winter. Indeed, the temperature was below twenty degrees centigrade (-2 F). But as soon as he left, I put on my clothes and ran away to the place where the people were fishing. The ice was sagging under the weight of thousands of people, horses, sledges, and various types of equipment. The ice was like a mirror, covered with water and very slippery. I could not stand on my feet, fell down and slid toward the ice-hole. I don't remember which Cossack saved me from drowning in the ice-hole. Somebody called my father, and I was taken home in a sledge immediately. While we were driving, my clothes were covered by a thin ice crust. My grandmother bustled around me, took off my clothes, prepared hot water, bathed me, put warm clothes on me, and had me drink a hot broth and raspberry tea. Thanks be to God, not only did I survive but I did not even catch a cold.

My father returned in the evening. We had a peaceful dinner, then he called me to his room and scolded me. My father had never beaten me, but his words burned into my conscience and soul worse than punches.

I remember another incident which could have ended my life. My brother and his friend went hunting wild ducks who fed in numerous "ponds" which were actually reed pools created by the river. I wanted to go with them, but they did not take me because I was underage. After they departed, I took a rifle and went hunting by myself. I went far away in the reeds and saw a duck in the pool. Having taken aim, I fired. It looked like the water was tinted with blood. A hit! But the duck dived and emerged again even farther away. It was getting away from me! I fired again. The duck dived and emerged once more. Hurriedly I come close to it and fired again. But I pulled the trigger too hastily, for the rifle was lowered at too great an angle causing the muzzle to be in about an inch of water. As a result, the recoil was terrible and I fell down into the pool. My shoulder was sore, but that was not the worst. A pack of wild dogs was waiting for me on the bank. I did not notice them in the excitement of hunting.

The situation was desperate. I had no more cartridges, and I was sitting in the water. I could only set my hopes on God's mercy. And it happened so. My brother heard the shots and decided to find out who was shooting. My brother and his friend came in time. They shot two dogs, and the others ran away. I got a scolding from my brother. I have never hunted alone since then.

Time was passing quickly; I had no time even to think about hunting because of my responsibilities.

It happened in December of 1914. I went to my gymnasium. It was the last day before Christmas. I decided to go skating on the Don after the lessons were completed, and I went to my grandma's khutor. Certainly I did not say a word about my intentions and I covered the skates with a notebook in case my father checked to see if I had everything necessary for my lessons. The classes were dismissed after noon. I put on my skates, and "flew" to my grandmother who lived down the river. With the arrival of darkness the full moon provided light. One could read a book printed in boldface type. I had warm clothes on me, my mood was excellent, and the ice was perfect—no ice holes, no unfrozen patches of water.

But approaching the khutor, I fell into icy water up to my waist. The problem is that the waves on the Don have froth, which stays alongside the bank. It freezes in winter, but not solidly, making the fringes of the ice by the bank very fragile. I happened to skate in that area. The temperature was about -15 degrees Centigrade (5 F). When I came to my grandma's house, my clothes were all covered in ice. My grandmother opened the door and saw a short (I was less than four feet in height), ice covered man. She could not believe her eyes, and was rendered speechless. The ice covered man was her grandson! But I happened to be lucky in that case, too. My grandmother took off my clothes, bathed me, gave me hot raspberry tea, and covered me with a woolen shawl. My strong constitution saved me again. I was in a lot of trouble at home for my unauthorized absence, with the predictable consequences taking place.

It seems strange, but all kids are the same in their urge toward adventure. The adventures are the same, too. For example, my father had a beautiful orchard containing various varieties of fruit trees—apple, cherry, pear, apricot, and so on. But we did not like our own fruit, and helped ourselves to the products of other people's orchards. I left a part of my pants in a dog's fangs, barely having been able to climb over the fence, but my thirst for adventure could not be eradicated. We also had our own melon patch which produced a good crop of melons and watermelons. We were growing thin-peel Astrakhan watermelons and thick-peel Don watermelons. Housewives made excellent, tasty candied peel in a sugar syrup. But the best dish made from watermelons was *nardeck* which could be described as watermelon honey or molasses. And what nice melons we had! In particular, the Persian or musk melons were fragrant sweet and juicy. But it seemed that we children were short of our own melons; we liked to steal from the neighbors. Once I asked my neighbor, who was carrying a cart of watermelons to market, to give me one. He said, "take one." Naturally, I chose the biggest—about twenty pounds. The old man laughed, "You have greedy eyes."

Nature in Imperial Russia was very rich. I could not find many things that were growing in the Don Region anywhere else in the world—and I have seen a lot of the world.

Chapter 2
FIGHTING YOUTH

It was 1914. The horror of World War I especially effected the Cossack areas, since the greatest part of the Imperial Cavalry consisted of Cossack units. All Cossacks from nineteen to fifty-nine years old were mobilized, and the households were left without the presence of husbands and sons. Working hands were needed, and the recruiting of apprentices in the middle schools began; they were to be used to help harvest the melon fields and make hay at the khutors and stanitsas. Almost everybody at our gymnasium enrolled for field work, and soon several groups were involved in harvesting the crops. Our group was composed of boys who were twelve to thirteen years old. We were sent to stanitsa Egorlytskaya and were housed at the local school. The Ataman told us that the Cossacks and Cossack women would come in the morning and take us to work. We received milk with bread and went to bed. In the morning I awoke because somebody pushed me. I opened my eyes and saw a man with a gray beard and smiling eyes. "Wake up, little boy! Oh, you are a good-for-nothing." I got up. I was really short and got used to remarks like that.

The old man chose seven boys and took us home. He had a root cellar, a stable, a cow shed, and an underground crop storage facility. He lived with his wife and daughter who was about twenty-two years old. They met us cordially, showed us their household and the place to sleep in the stable in the hay, gave us water to wash our faces and seated us for breakfast. There was plenty of food, including milk, fried eggs with bacon, and pound cake with watermelon honey. After breakfast, the old man told five of us to stay and took two boys back to the school. He said that he had too many workers. Later I was informed that the old man had been watching us while we were eating. Those who ate a lot and quickly were chosen because they were identified as good workers.

We were always served ample meals. We went to bed early and got up early. On the first day, the old man woke us at four in the morning. We washed our faces, had our breakfast, and went to his fields. We started weeding a cornfield and the old man, accompanied by his daughter, went mowing. Soon we were accustomed to our work and apparently worked well. Their attitude was sweet and kind.

In August of 1914, Austrian prisoners started to arrive to work in the Don stanitsas. Once the owner's daughter and one of the prisoners went mowing. He probably decided to take liberties with her. I could see his legs shoot up in the air, and the next moment he was lying in the haystack. The women in the Don Region were very strong.

School began again in the autumn. Everything seemed the same, but one could feel the impact of the war. The teachers were more indulgent towards us, and we became more serious and forgot about our old tricks.

The Emperor's abdication in 1917 was met with grief in the Don Region. Life as we knew it deteriorated abruptly. Bandits could be seen in the streets. We, the pupils of the gymnasium, were allowed to be out until curfew (first to second grades to six in the evening; third to fourth grades to seven in the evening; fifth to sixth grades to eight in the evening; and seventh to eighth grades to nine in the evening). As far as I remember, the system operated in that manner. Once I happened to go to Peschanaya street where my friend lived and was confronted by a group of teenage hooligans. They forced me to take off my clothes, climb on a fence and crow like a rooster for five minutes. They did not cause me any physical harm, but I keenly felt a loss of self-esteem for a long time after that event.

Once my friends and I encountered a group of hooligans near the Ataman's headquarters. Guards had been posted at this building, but they could not leave their post and help us. A scuffle started; the hooligans used their knives, and my friend Venya was wounded in his back, while my friend Shura received a cut on his hand. We were able to obtain some help as the guards had reported the incident to their commander who arrived on the scene with some Cossacks. The majority of the hooligans ran away; however, a few were arrested. These had been on the receiving end of my friend Venya's fists; they had been unable to get up from the ground, for Venya had "iron" fists.

Venya and Shura stayed in the hospital for some time, but their wounds were not serious and soon they returned to the gymnasium. But our life had become more dangerous. Army discipline increasingly became a thing of the past as a result of the orders of the Provisional Government, and the corrupting influence of Bolshevik propaganda was ever more distinct.

We heard a new name—Lenin. A decree issued by Kerensky gave the soldiers the right to create committees in military units. These committees had the right to decide whether the troops would participate in a battle or not, whether they would fulfill an officer's order or not. This decree greatly assisted the Bolsheviks who constantly stressed the propaganda theme of resisting the lawful orders given by the Army's commanders and subordinate officers. Bolshevik propaganda further advocated that the soldiers turn their weapons against their commanders, setting Russians to fight against Russians. Willingly or not, Kerensky went a long way toward helping the Bolsheviks to destroy Russia. Truly he was Lenin's accomplice.

The discipline in the Army became worse. Deserters came to the Don Region, and decay of morals and manners, as well as acts of hooliganism, increased with every passing day. There were few police, and constraints were placed on their conduct. As I remember, I saw only one policeman in Novocherkassk and one gendarme on the Novocherkassk railway station platform. That gendarme was strutting with an air of self-importance; he was surrounded by children, and gave them candies. But the Cossacks tried to keep order by all possible means, though I might add that Bolshevik propaganda had corrupted some Cossacks.

The election for the position of State Ataman was announced. General A. M. Kaledin was nominated as a candidate. He was one of the most prominent heroes of the Great War. General A. P. Bogaevsky was nominated as his assistant. However, both of them were monarchists; that's why their candidacies were sharply criticized by the leftist faction of the Cossack Assembly. These leftists were headed by such demagogues as Kharlamoff, Melnikoff, Ulanoff, Elatintseff and

Epifanoff. Under the pretext of avoiding a confrontation with Kerensky's government, they managed to cancel Bogaevsky's nomination, and, in his place, nominated his brother, Mitrophan Petrovich Bogaevsky, a teacher of history at the gymnasium named after Platoff in Novocherkassk. Mitrophan Petrovich was well acquainted with the socialists when he studied at the university, and he also belonged to the circle of "Progressives." But he was also a Cossack who understood the difference between the independence of a Cossack with his sense of discipline and the destructive anarchy advocated by the socialists. He was elected as the Ataman's assistant and, to his honor, did not bring shame on his name while holding that position; later he was martyred by the Bolsheviks.

The Emperor's abdication in favor of the Grand Duke Mikhail Alexandrovich and the renunciation of power by the latter led to the formation of a government headed by Prince Lvov and an attorney named Kerensky. Kerensky was a member of the Cadet Party, a socialist and member of a Masonic lodge. In addition to all his "virtues," he possessed a personality that could only be described as hysterical; whether he was addressing a group of soldiers or the Duma (national parliament), he liked to rant and rave. He consistently favored radical reforms and enjoyed promoting himself as the leader who would carry them out. As the Minister of Defense, he immediately signed the "Declaration of Soldiers' Rights" which led to the rapid decline of discipline in the Russian Army, especially at the Front.

These events took place swiftly. We boys could barely comprehend their significance. Besides, our main task was to focus on our studies, not politics. But our academic environment was not the same. All of us, the adults as well as the children, were swept by feelings of uncertainty about our future. Everybody was depressed, gloomy, and silent.

The presence of hooligans and the impact of leftist propaganda were increasingly affecting our lives. It was dangerous to walk on the streets of Novocherkassk even early in the evening. It would happen that a passerby would be stopped at the Novocherkassk railway station where he would be offered the "opportunity" to buy a cost.

"Hey, uncle", a boy who had appeared out of nowhere would whine as he stood in front of a gentleman, "buy a coat."

"Which coat? I already have one; it's on me."

"So, you should buy that coat now."

By this time a gang of lanky toughs would be blocking his way. If he refused to give them money, he was beaten, and his coat and other belongings were taken away. There were almost no Cossacks in Novocherkassk, only a dozen elderly cripples in the guard *sotnia* (Cossack squadron). At the same time, more and more undisciplined soldiers from the Front appeared.

When General Kaledin was elected, Don traitors who had joined with the Bolsheviks appeared on the scene. Officer Goluboff, Cossack Senior Sergeant Podtelkov, doctor's assistant Lagutin, and Cossack Cavalry Sergeant Major Smirnoff were especially active. Podtelkof headed the military-revolutionary committee of the Don Soviet Republic of the Russian Socialist Federation. I hate to even mention two other prominent traitors—Voroshiloff and Budenny—"famous" for their efforts in accomplishing the destruction of Russia.

We, the teenagers, grow up with a belief in the virtues of faith, devotion and honesty. We became indignant when we witnessed the behavior of renegade Cossacks who betrayed their elected Ataman and the Government. Goluboff was openly defiant, and he was arrested for being a hindrance to the legitimate exercise of power by the authorities. Goluboff had proclaimed himself the Ataman of the Don Region since the first days of the Revolution. He sought that goal with a fanatical spirit without regard to any obstacle. When Goluboff was arrested, the left wing of the Don State Assembly, headed by Kharlamof, Elatentseff and others, made all possible efforts to secure his release. They managed to make M. P. Bogaevsky, Ataman Kaledin's assistant, vouch for Goluboff. Kaledin ordered the release of Goluboff, who later showed his "appreciation" by actively supporting Bolshevik activities.

Podtelkoff, too, moved in a surreptitious manner toward the goal of obtaining a position of power. He joined the Bolsheviks in 1917 and had a great influence with the Soviets in South Russia. During the time of absolute chaos, Goluboff and Podtelkoff united their group of cronies who separated themselves from the true Cossacks. When Ataman P. H. Popoff left Novocherkassk, Goluboff's gang rushed there. His first act was to dismiss the State Assembly. Having appeared at the assembly hall, Goluboff ordered everybody to stand. Everyone obeyed except for Ataman Nazaroff. The following dialog took place: "Stand up? Who are you?" "I am an elected ataman, and who are you?" "I am a revolutionary ataman and my name is comrade Goluboff," and Goluboff ordered his henchmen to arrest Nazaroff and take him to the guardroom. A period of real insanity, characterized by robbery, hard drinking and executions began the next day in the city. It became known that Ataman Nazaroff, other famous Don generals, more than a hundred officers, and several hundred partisans had been shot on the morning of February 18, 1918. The Russian people ought to know how an honest soldier, who never broke his oath, died. The killers ordered Nazaroff to turn his back to them, but he said, "A soldier meets his death not with his back but with his face." He crossed himself, folded his arms and ordered, "Listen to my command: one, two, three."

Medvedeff, a former prisoner who had been convicted of murder by the Tsarist authorities, was the head of the administration of Novocherkassk. He headed the council of deputies together with Frankel and Zisserman.

Podtelkoff headed the military-revolutionary committee of the Don Soviet Republic. Smirnoff commanded the revolutionary army. All of them strived to seize absolute power in the Don region. Goluboff as a revolutionary ataman formulated his plan. First, he located Ataman Kaledin's former assistant, M. P. Bogaevsky, and brought him to Novocherkassk, hoping that he would collaborate with the Bolsheviks and help to strengthen their power. However, the speech delivered by Mitrophan Petrovich (Bogaevsky) before the assembled Cossacks was not approved by the Revolutionary Committee. A punitive expedition came to Novocherkassk from Rostov. Bogaevsky was arrested and shot on the road to Rostov in the Balabanovskaya grove, near Nakhichevan. Thus died one of the best historians of the Don region who had taught history at the gymnasium named after Count Platoff.

There was no unity among the Bolsheviks. Antonoff was afraid of Goluboff and tried to frustrate him by all possible means. Finally, Goluboff lost the "respect" of the Bolsheviks and went to stanitsa Zaplavskaya. He was recognized and shot by one of the Cossacks there.

Podtelkoff, too, was captured by the Cossacks, court-martialed and sentenced to death. His collaborators shared the same fate. The fathers of the Cossacks who had turned traitor asked for permission to carry out the order of the court and received permission to do so. It happened as it did in Gogol's novel when Taras Bulba told his son, "I gave birth to you, and I'll kill you."

Unfortunately, Ataman Kaledin's order to partisan detachments not to fight with Cossacks caused the tragic death of Colonel Vasily Tchernetsov, one of the heroes of the Don Army. His detachment confronted Podtelkoff's gang but did not take countermeasures quickly enough and was captured. Later Podtelkoff slashed Tchernetsov to death. There are several versions of the way he met his death, but now it is impossible to determine the real one; however, one thing is clear he was killed by the traitor Podtelkoff. (Even Podtelkoff's relatives denounced his actions and would have nothing to do with him.) Members of the Army Circle of L. I. Ushakoff and other trustworthy people told me, during the Zaplavsky siege, about those Cossacks who had joined the Bolsheviks and had become traitors to their people.

The Bolsheviks cared nothing for traditional Russian values. They had no morals and completely lacked the concept of law or justice. Instead, they consistently indulged in murder and rape. They spared neither the young nor the old. At the beginning of 1918, they burned to the ground more than 40 khutors and stanitsas. Now the narration of those truly monstrous deeds would hardly cause surprise, but at that time it was not easy to believe in the extent of the degradation of human beings operating under the influence of the evil premises of Communist philosophy. Many people asked the question: "How could it happen in Russia?"

In the case of the Don Region, the Bolsheviks made bold demands, and our local government seemed incapable of resisting them; instead, they made concessions to their demands and seemed to follow the line of least resistance. That's no wonder because the socialists headed the Don Cossack administration in 1917. While Kerensky's yes-men were discussing what form of socialism was best, the evil force of Bolshevism was gnawing deeper and deeper into the flesh of the Don Region. One thought made me anxious: What would happen to Cossacks of military age? Due to the traditions that were developed in Czarist times, a Cossack served for three years and then returned home. His place was occupied by younger selectees. It had been very important to reinforce the army during World War I. When Ataman Kaledin headed the Don Cossack administration, more than ten thousand young Cossacks had been trained as replacements for the casualties. Why were they not sent to fight against the

Bolsheviks? It is a mystery to me even now: Where did tens of thousands of strong man disappear? As I have mentioned, General Kaledin could mobilize up to thirty thousand young men (the population of the Don Region consisted of four and a half million people).

I think the answer to that poignant question lies in the fact that a strong faction in the Cossack Assembly did not allow General Kaledin to use young men called for military service as replacements. Kerensky was sure that the Don Cossacks would attack Moscow, and with his hysterical imagination he dictated orders prohibiting the military activities of the Cossacks. At the same time, the Bolsheviks expanded their bloody havoc.

The disruption and collapse of the Front against the German Army was in full swing. Kerensky promoted the creation of soldiers' committees which led to a breakdown in discipline among Russian combat units, increased desertion, and even resulted in the murder of officers. These events cleared the way for Lenin and his gang.

Ataman Kaledin visited stanitsas to meet with Cossacks. Kerensky immediately declared that Kaledin was a rebel who was recruiting an army to attack Moscow. It took several weeks to convince the government that Kaledin had no such intentions. A government commission with prosecutorial power came to the Don Region. After a long investigation it found that "Kaledin's Rebellion" was nothing more than a phantom of Kerensky's feverish imagination.

Two infantry regiments, the 272nd and the 273rd, were located in Novocherkassk. They were strongly infected with Bolshevik ideas. Nobody knew what "exploits" sixteen thousand armed soldiers would commit. In order to protect the peaceful population from possible excesses, the Don Government issued orders to "disarm" these regiments. The answer came back from these units: "We don't want to." The Government sent an artillery unit to Khotunka, but it refused to disarm the soldiers. Then the yunkers (officer candidates) from the Don Military School were sent there. With the assistance of a few Russian officers who managed to get to the Don area, they disarmed the unruly soldiers. This marked the beginning of the organization known as the Volunteer Army. Journeys to the Don Region were very dangerous; the railroads and the steamships were crammed with deserters hostile towards authority in general and officers in particular. Lenin's propaganda was the cause of that. Mob "justice" was a common event.

Kaledin wanted to mobilize young Cossacks. That could help to reinforce the Don Army with thirty thousand men. But the leftist faction in the Assembly talked him out of doing that. When Kharlamoff and his companions could not persuade Kaledin directly, they accomplished their goals by means of their friend M. P. Bogaevsky. Kaledin postponed mobilization and later came to regret that decision.

Due to the disarmament of the infantry regiments, the residents of Novosherkassk learned about the existence of a new force, one that was strong enough to oppose the corrupting influence of the Revolution. It had been the first test of strength for the Volunteer Army, headed by General M. V. Alekseev. But the Don Government, especially Kharlamoff, Melnikoff, Ulanoff, Elatintseff and others did not allow Generals Alekseev and Korniloff to announce openly the formation of the Volunteer Army, and prevented him from mobilizing Russian officers who came to the Don region from all districts of Russia.

The situation became even more critical when the military frigate *Kolkhida* came to Rostov. Its sailors, together with the local Bolsheviks, launched an uprising. Kaledin sent yunkers to quell it, and they were assisted by old Cossacks. The uprising was suppressed, but the volunteers suffered their first considerable casualties. I remember how they delivered wounded men to the hospital in Novocherkassk.

Cossack Captain (*Esaul*) Vasily Tchernetsoff started to form a regiment. He had been a commander of a partisan regiment of 1,500 men during the war with Germany and inflicted considerable   losses on the Kaiser's forces. *Esaul* Popoff (an artillery specialist who was commander of the 2nd battery in Tchernetsoff's army and who had served in the same regiment with Tchernetsoff during World War I) told me that the German command had promised to give a reward of half a million marks for Tchernetsoff's head.

A   new   disaster   became   evident   in   the   Don Region—animosity among the Cossack regiments. The regiments located in the Donets area stirred up a rebellion, joined with Red bandits and attacked Tchernetsoff's detachment. A number of regiments went home after that fratricidal encounter with their fellow Cossacks having abandoned their artillery and plundered the regimental funds. Rumors were started that in the Ust-

Kamenogorsk area some Cossacks returning from the front had united with Red Army soldiers and had completely destroyed a part of the railroad on the Tsaritsyn-Serebryakovo Section, an action which had deprived the nearby areas of food supplies.

At last, the Don Regional Government agreed to form a military unit to protect the Don area, with Kaledin personally proclaiming the order. Tchernetsoff's unit reacted without delay. It consisted mainly of the students of middle schools. Some other units appeared composed of young men, but these forces were not sufficient. Professional military men did not join the partisan units. We, the teenagers, knew that there were about three thousand officers in Novocherkassk and five thousand officers in Rostov in November of 1917. Many people paid with their lives for not wanting to get involved in "politics."

The Bolshevik evil was assuming threatening proportions. At the beginning of December 1917, I went to the Military School where the center for recruiting personnel for the partisan unit was located, to enroll in Tchernetsoff's regiment. An officer looked at me and said, "Probably, you, little boy, are not yet ten years old?" I was four feet, six inches in height, the shortest in the gymnasium. Another short boy, Vanya Sergeyev, was half an inch taller than me. Of course, I was not able to enlist. But I was persistent and came back, and I was enrolled after a while. Within an hour I was placed in a military unit and began training. An officer explained how to handle the rifles.

At noon we went to dinner. The head of the school was going to tell us something of great importance. The silence and cleanliness in the yunker's dining room was amazing. The tables were covered with white cloths, and everyone had his own place setting which included clean napkins. One could imagine that the former times characterized by peace and normal behavior had returned, that we were in an officer's dining room, not the mess hall of a military regiment. We lined up by the tables. There was a word of command, "Attention!" and the head of the military school, General Popoff, came in. His speech was short and was devoted to our behavior. He did not say a single word about calling us to arms; it was as if we were little boys invited to a holiday dinner. As for the dinner, it was really tasty and consisted of many types of food.

After the dinner we were divided into groups and sent to different places. Our group of twenty-four men was sent to the suburb of Novocherkassk known as Khotunok. We were housed in the barracks, from where pro-Bolshevik soldiers had been sent "home" the day before. The night was very dark and there was no light around the barracks. My friend and I were assigned to be sentinels with the responsibility of protecting our young men at night. About midnight we heard a suspicious noise. It stopped, and then was heard again. We thought it was caused by the breathing of the enemy hiding near the barracks. Our nerves gave way and we fired some shots "for courage." Our fellow recruits, with rifles in their hands, ran out of the barracks ready to fight. "What happened?" they asked. We explained the situation, and all of us started to look for the enemy. Soon the light of the burning torches illuminated the cause of our fears; it was a cow who was grazing peacefully nearby.

Two days later our platoon was sent to Alexandro-Grushevsk to join with an active regiment. It was necessary to be very cautious in that area and near the city of Shakhty because most of the miners were pro-Bolshevik. The Bolsheviks had no regular army; instead, the deserters, coming from the front, formed gangs which had as their slogans "expropriate from the expropriators." These gangs committed every imaginable abomination against the Russian people with special attention given to officers intellectuals, and other representatives of the educated strata of society. These gangs operated independently; they conducted themselves in a very cowardly manner, but their number multiplied at an alarming rate. The drain of the soldiers from the front continued and even loyal army units could not stem the flow of deserters. Conditions were deteriorating rapidly.

By July 1917, the deserters were stopped only by the Cossacks because the cavalry had already been demoralized by the decree of the Provisional Government which destroyed the discipline of the Army and hence almost completely eroded its ability to function. As General Denisoff reported, thirty-nine Cossack regiments removed from battle positions were in charge of that thankless task. I should mention that the situation in the Cossack regiment was very tense. Many seasoned combat officers had been killed in the battles of World War I, and their replacements were recruited from a class of men known as ensigns which included former teachers who were populists, doctors and other people who were better suited for rear area assignments. Those people, whose mentality was ill-suited to permit them to adjust to military discipline, caused an additional degree of disorganization in the army. Many of them were included on the infamous regimental committees.

The position of the Don Cossack Army was very unsteady at that time. It did not sympathize with the Bolsheviks directly, but it was ready to make compromises. Leftist elements in the government skillfully used the name of M. P. Bogaevsky, the Ataman's assistant, to promote policies that ultimately benefited the Reds. The moral degradation that was present in the army led General Kaledin to commit suicide. For example, it was the government that disrupted the mobilization of the Cossacks and officers in the Don Region, thus missing favorable opportunities to fight the Bolsheviks. But there were at least ten thousand combat officers in the area of Rostov and Novocherkassk! The reinforcement of the partisan regiment was very poor, too. They were formed in an almost secret manner, and many people did not know anything about their existence. Many officers were unaware of the formation of the Volunteer Army because the Don Regional Government, in fact, frustrated attempts to resist the Bolsheviks.

Our group faced the same situation. We spent several days in Shakhty, then moved to Rostov. We had an order to meet an officer of the Volunteer Army at the railway station. The station master in Rostov warned us not to go into the central part of the city as there was an "epidemic" of murders of officers and yunkers. We spent two days in the railway cars. I distinctly remember a mountaineer who played Oriental melodies on a sort of lute who entertained us during this period of waiting. He sang about the beauty of the Caucasian mountains, about pure and clear mountain rivers, blue skies, and transparent air through which one could see far into the distance for hundreds of miles. Often he was crying about his land—lost forever.

On the third day, a trolley with the corpses of five children from nine to eleven years old arrived. These were the corpses of the pupils of the preparatory class of the military school located in Novocherkassk. They had been home on Christmas vacation visiting their families in Bataysk. They had been mutilated brutally. Their noses, ears and private parts were cut as "noodles." Having seen the children's corpses, we increased our resolve to fight against the evil of Bolshevism.

In the morning we moved in the direction of Bataysk together with a small detachment commanded by General Markoff; we joined him at this position. Shooting had been going on for several days. The Bolsheviks were organizing in Bataysk. The situation appeared very strange as the Reds formed big crowds that moved to the bridge that spanned the Don River. From this position they screamed curses at us, then started shooting and later departed. We tried to save cartridges and fired only when we were sure of hitting a target. But one day the Bolsheviks began to cross the bridge under the cover of an armored train. We faced a heavy concentration of shells and bullets. An officer was moving among us along our line. Suddenly his head was torn off by a shell, and I saw him going in the direction of the line without his head, moving under his own momentum. Many people were wounded as there was no shelter under the steep bank of the Don. The Bolsheviks were slowly advancing. But we were lucky as a shell fired from our position hit the armored train which exploded with a deafening roar. A force of ten thousand Red soldiers dispersed at once. The Bolshevik attack was stopped.

We had heavy losses with almost everyone in our unit either wounded or shell-shocked (I was in the latter category). This battle occurred in mid-January, 1918, as far as I remember. Our victory in the battle of Rostov gave General Korniloff the opportunity to complete the process of forming the Volunteer Army and to prepare for the campaign against the Bolsheviks in this vital area of southern Russia.

At the conclusion of the battle we were lying on the ground which, uncharacteristically for this time of year, was thawing with the snow melting under us. I was shell-shocked and don't remember who took me to Novocherkassk, but I can still feel the icy breath of January and my wet heavy coat. When I regained complete consciousness, the Bolsheviks were ruling in Novocherkassk. The entire area was in their hands. My old nanny hid me, and my short stature helped me, too. When the Bolsheviks came to our house in search of partisans, my nanny, a Ukrainian, shouted at them, "What are you looking for? There's only an old man, his wife, and a sick little boy!" They did not touch either me or my father at that time.

Nanny brought us all the news. Thus we heard that Bogaevsky, Nazaroff, Voloshin and other outstanding leaders of the Don Government had been shot by the Bolsheviks who had carried out mass executions. Their evil actions did not spare our close friends, the Knyazeff family. Three Knyazeff sisters were married to three officers. On the same day their husbands returned from the front, these officers were arrested and killed. The next morning, the Revolutionary representatives came to apologize. "Excuse us. It was a little mistake. We shot them to no purpose. But, anyhow, now we'll have fewer people to shoot. It is very difficult to describe all our emotional experiences. I did not leave the house, and communicated with the world through my nanny. I remember in particular one of her descriptions of conditions in the area. The Bolsheviks had approached an old woman on the street and asked her to help them find officers and cadets. They promised her fifty kopecks for each head. She was very frightened and showed them the first house. They went there, found two men and shot them. In addition, they threw the sick and wounded out of the windows of the hospital, and finished them off on the spot. During the first days of their rule in Novocherkassk they shot five hundred officers, and hundreds of other people were shot "by mistake" besides that.

The fearful days of my confinement dragged on. Suddenly, on April 1st we heard reports from around the city that the Bolsheviks were leaving Novocherkassk. Cossacks from stanitsa Krivyanskaya occupied the city. And indeed I saw the Cossacks on Platoffsky Prospect! But our joy did not last long. The Bolsheviks moved back to Novocherkassk from Rostov and Alexandro-Grushevsk. On April 4th, at about two in the afternoon, I saw a column of men, among them the Zhdanoff brothers who were my old friends. They told me that they were going in the direction of the brick factory to fight the Bolsheviks who were coming from Rostov. I did not take long to consider the situation and joined the column. Somebody gave me a rifle. When we reached the designated assault position, I became acquainted with my new detachment. However, the enemy had been waiting for us. Near the brick factory we encountered heavy machine-gun fire from three directions. It was unexpected; we rushed about, and many were killed. The Zhdanoff brothers and I ran to the gorge near the factory. Those who could not run were surrounded by the Bolsheviks. We heard the curses, moans and cries, "Cut him to pieces with your knife."

The Zhdanoffs knew the Kurichya gorge very well. They also knew the narrow streets on the outskirts of Novocherkassk. That helped us to escape from the Bolsheviks. We reached the river Tuzlov. Fortunately, we saw a pupil from the gymnasium who was about eleven years old and who appeared to be waiting for us on the bank. He had a boat and used it to ferry the fugitives

to the opposite shore. He took us across, too. I remember that
boy with deep gratitude. What was his fate?
      We were about ten miles from the nearest stanitsa and
were surrounded by swamps. Moreover, we had no idea where
the Bolsheviks were located, so we went in the direction of
stanitsa Zaplavskaya, and it was the only right decision. All who
were saved from the Bolsheviks went there. When we arrived
there it was about three in the morning, but all the adults were in
the street. The council of the stanitsa was holding a meeting.
"What is to be done?" they asked.
      Dawn came imperceptibly. Colonel Denisoff and
Lieutenant Colonel of the General Staff Polyakoff came to the
balcony of the administration building. The sense of their speech
was simple. It was necessary to organize a counterattack
immediately. Not only the residents of stanitsa Zaplavskaya were
at the meeting, but also many Cossacks from Novocherkassk,
stanitsas Krivyanskaya, Besserchenevskaya, Razdorskaya,
Bogaevskaya, and other places were also present. The
detachments were formed quickly, the tasks and duties assigned,
and the picket detachment was established in the direction of
Khotunok.
      The "Zaplavsky siege" began. After plundering
Novocherkassk, the Bolsheviks moved to Zaplavskaya. They
were completely defeated by a successful maneuver carried out by
Generals Denisoff and Polyakoff. We captured many prisoners,
guns, automobiles, horses, and, of greatest importance, many
cartridges and shells. But we could not leave Zaplavskaya
without knowing the location of the enemy units. So we
concentrated on improving our defenses. Soon we received news
that the Field Ataman P. H. Popoff had arrived in Razdorskaya,
and he was on his way to meet us.
      Ataman Popoff and Colonel Gushchin came in two days.
They left their staff on a steamboat in Razdorskaya. Field
Ataman Popoff wanted Colonel Denisoff to be under the
command of his Chief of Staff, Colonel Sidorin. But the opposite
happened. Colonel Denisoff refused and persuaded the Ataman to
stay in Zaplavskaya because his departure could undermine the
spirit of the people in that location. Working together, Generals
Denisoff and Polyakoff began to plan the capture of
Novocherkassk. Our spontaneously formed army was fed with
the help of local residents. The Zhdanoff brothers found their
acquaintance, and we were billeted in her house. She had an old

drag net which we used for fishing. The ice on the river was thin
since it was April. I was the youngest, so I suggested that I
should cast the drag net. To do that, I had to enter the icy water.
As soon as I came out of the water, the Zhdanoff brothers
wrap;)ed me in blankets to prevent me from catching a fever. It
was easier to drag the net out in the morning, and usually it was
full of fish.

We had no ordnance, and the Zhdanoff brothers, being
combat artillerymen, were assigned to the headquarters.
S. Denisoff, assisted by I. A. Polyakoff, a former
associate on the Imperial General Staff, was the commander of the
White forces at the "Zaplavsky siege." I admired their ability to
create a good base and a good fighting force from nothing!
Cossacks, individually and in groups, came from the nearby
stanitsas such as Bessergenevskaya, Razdorskaya,
Melikhovskaya, and from Novocherkassk. In one day they were
reorganized into an orderly fighting regiment.

At that time the Bolsheviks were celebrating the capture
of Novocherkassk. The "constructors of the new world"
celebrated with heavy drinking, looting and random executions.
These conditions lasted for several days. On April 8th, the
Bolsheviks decided to attack Krivyanskaya. Their regiment was
defeated on the distant approaches to the stanitsa. About a
hundred of them were killed, including the commander. Then the
crafty Bolshevik leaders changed their tactics. They sent a
propaganda convoy under the command of a renegade Cossack
named Lagutin instead of another regiment. But the tactic failed.
The convoy of automobiles was stopped by the Cossacks, and
Lagutin was court-martialed and shot. Embittered by their
failures, the Bolsheviks assembled their troops under the
command of the renegade Cossack Antonoff and moved against
the defenders of the "Zaplavsky fortified area."

The fighting was brutal, and the Reds were defeated
again. We captured a lot of supplies such as ordnance, horses,
cartridges, shells and automobiles. The Cossack morale rose after
the victory, and our command decided to attack Novocherkassk.
The attack began on April 23rd, the second day of the Easter
holiday. The most severe fighting was in the area of Khotunok.
Trains filled with Reds and their loot were standing at this
location. Friendly Cossacks were waiting for our arrival. I
remember a woman who embraced me and said, "Christ is risen!"

Honestly, I was so amazed that I dropped my rifle. However, the raging battle returned me to reality.

We obtained a considerable amount of captured military equipment as we "inherited" the sizable store of loot plundered by the Reds. There were also many prisoners. The Reds fled in the direction of Alexandro-Grushevsk and stanitsa Aksayskaya. Novocherkassk was liberated.

However, fresh detachments of Bolsheviks came from Rostov and Alexandro-Grushevsk on April 25th. A grim fight developed. I was in a gun detachment. Our gun became red-hot and we covered it with wet mattresses. Colonel Buguraev's highly accurate fire kept the Reds near Khotunok; however, it seemed for some time that we were losing the battle. Our Command had used its last reserves; then we saw panic spread among the Reds, and their forward groups started to retreat. It turned out that our armored car *Loyal* provided as help by Colonel Drozdovsky, had attacked their area. His armored car came from Jassy, Romania, having covered a thousand miles. He appeared in Rostov at the same time as the German occupation troops. The Reds fled in panic and the machine guns of *Loyal* mowed them down.

I could go home now. I was feeling strange; my face was burning, my heart was throbbing. I tried to ignore these symptoms as I thought they were the result of nervous stress brought on by the fighting of April 23rd to the 27th. And here was a well-known wicket gate. I entered the yard of my house and heard a piercing scream as if something terrible had happened. My sister fainted when she saw me. My relatives were amazed by my arrival. When the situation calmed down, I asked my mother about my sister. "What happened to Vera? Is she sick?" "No," my mother replied, "but she is very impressionable and is distraught. She'll got well soon. You see, Kolya, your father had already buried you. Your classmate Makhonkoff saw you on April 4th going in the direction of the brick factory, but he did not see you among the fugitives. He told us that you were probably killed. Your father went to the brick factory and found you among the dead. You were buried. And now you arrive at the house."

It turned out that it was my classmate N. Apryzhkin who had been killed. He was of the same height, had the same hair color, and had a birthmark on his left shoulder. In fact, he could have been my twin. My father still had doubts that I had been killed. After the liberation of Novocherkassk he went to the railway station to find me among the Cossacks. I remember our joy and the warm embraces when we met at last. But our joy was incomplete; we knew nothing about the fate of my brother Peter.

I fell sick while I was at home, developing a case of pneumonia, and I spent several weeks in this grave condition. At that time my friends were clearing the Don Region from the Red menace. Cossack stanitsas rose up in arms everywhere. But when I wanted to join my detachment, the elected Ataman Pyotr Nikolayevich Krasnoff ordered all the students to leave their military units and return to school. The schools were closed in summer so the students formed groups to help the Cossacks with field work. I spent all the summer working with my friends at the khutor household.

I want to explain the tactical situation at that time. The participants, under the command of General S. Denisoff who had withstood the enemy attacks during the "Zaplavsky siege," were called the South Group to distinguish them from the North Group. The North Group consisted of the steppe Cossacks under the command of Field Ataman General P. H. Popoff. After the retreat from Novocherkassk, he went to the steppes with his Cossacks on February 12, 1918, and on April 1st he dismissed them. Some of them returned to their homes; however, the greater part of them, together with General Popoff came to stanitsa Konstantinovskaya which was free of Bolsheviks. They took a steamboat and came down to stanitsa Razdorskaya, where they founded the North Group of the Don Army headed by Colonel Sidorin. Their goal was to take Alexandro-Grushevsk. But the "Northerners" were not lucky.

I always seemed five years younger than my real age because of my short stature, but this condition gave me some advantages. For example, at the time of the "Zaplavsky siege" I often visited the headquarters, and nobody paid attention to me. However, I had the opportunity to watch everybody who was connected with the headquarters of the South Group which was under the command of Colonel Denisoff. I liked his style of command very much; he was always laconic, knew how to convince his opponents, and only spoke about the business at hand. I did not see him idle even for a minute. I met him for the first time on April 4, 1918, in the morning; later that day, he came to Zaplavskaya after leaving Novocherkassk. Entering the stanitsa, he went at once to the noisy meeting. I remember highly excited speakers who ranted that the Don Government had allowed Communism to spread and did not do anything to prevent it.

Suddenly a sonorous voice was heard amidst the noise: "It's easy to denounce the leadership! You did not help Ataman Kaledin. You went home when you should have defended him! You should act, not engage in cheap talk. People of Novocherkassk! Who is the senior Cossack present? Count yourselves and report to me immediately. This order applies equally to Cossacks from stanitsas Bessergenevskaya, Melekhovkaya, Zaplavskaya and Bogaevskaya. Those who do not belong to stanitsas, report to me." The noise stopped at once, the crowd moved, the commands were heard, and very soon the regiments were formed. Of course, I was in the Novocherkassk regiment.

Lieutenant Colonel I. A. Polyakoff was always near Colonel Denisoff. He possessed all the qualities of a first-rate strategist. Just after their formation, the regiments were sent to positions which were chosen correctly as the following events showed. The Novocherkassk regiment established a position several miles from Zaplavskaya, in the direction of *Khotunok* Novocherkassk. The orders had to be very clear due to the fact that the men were tired physically and mentally because of the troubles occurring in their home areas. The main merit of Colonel Denisoff and Lieutenant Colonel Polyakoff was their ability to inspire people. They gave them hope and united them by clearly describing the goal of the struggle.

Nevertheless our situation was grim. We had no supplies and no arms except for rifles. We had to struggle with our bare hands. We had no way to retreat, and many of us knew already what Communist "fraternity and friendship" was like. We knew that in case of surrender we would, at best, be killed. The rumors spread by the Bolshevik agents did not help the situation; they told that Korniloff's march had failed completely, that the Volunteer Army did not exist any more, and that General Popoff's march through the steppes had failed too. It was a heroic deed to maintain a fighting spirit under those conditions, and Colonel Denisoff with Lt. Col. Polyakoff managed to do this with honor. *(Later A. I. Polyakoff was given the rank of major general and was given the position of Chief-of-Staff of the Don Army. S. Denisoff became the Commander of the Don Army.)*

Colonel Drozdovsky helped us very much. His detachment came to the Don from Romania. I remember how he arrived at the most critical moment of the battle of Novocherkassk, as I have mentioned already.

In contrast to our South Group, the commanders of the North Group had neither talent nor experience. Their commander, Colonel Sidorin, did not perform very effectively at all. He tried to take Alexandro-Grushevsk twice and lost the battles. It happened that stanitsa Malikhovskaya decided to greet the Bolsheviks with the traditional ceremony of presenting "bread and salt." But their carts laden with food were intercepted by our military-political detachment.

The arrival of Drozdovsky's detachment played the crucial role in the struggle, and the Don was cleared of the Bolsheviks. Drozdovsky's men were good not only in battle; our schoolgirls and students could not "oppose" them either, and we had many weddings in the spring of 1918. May their memory live forever. Now all of them are in their graves, many of them in foreign lands, far from their native Don. Many of their gravesites are unknown. Nobody will plant snowball trees there, and a bird will not sing a sad song. May their memory live forever; may they rest in peace, the honest warrior-patriots of the Great Christian Russian Empire.

The "Zaplavsky siege" ended with the liberation of Novocherkassk. German occupation troops came to Rostov, and the Bolsheviks fled to Alexandro-Grushevsk. The combined forces of the South and North Groups were sent against them.

A military victory parade was held in Novocherkassk on April 26, 1918. Drozdovsky's men marched in orderly lines under the enthusiastic gaze of the citizens. It was very nice to see their sunburnt, manly, and joyful faces. It was a real celebration; there were jokes, laughter, and a lot of flowers were presented to the heroes. There was a real sense of the joy of life, for only a person who has overcome a fatal disease can enjoy the sun, flowers and the air. God, it's Your will. The next day, the Cossack parade was held for the heroes of the "Zaplavsky siege" and the Northern Group.

The Don Cossack Assembly was opened on April 29, 1918. It was called the Assembly for the Salvation of the Don. It was decided to accept all the defenders of the Don as Cossacks, and that resolution was adopted by the Big Circle in 1918. According to it, all the White Army Veterans who had taken part in the anti-Bolshevik struggles during the Civil War could call themselves Don Cossacks. The Assembly of the salvation of the

Don elected General Krasnoff, a famous warrior and writer, as Ataman of the Don Regional Government on May 3, 1918. At that time, at the end of April, the Volunteer Army came to the Don area. The local population met the volunteers with joy, unlike in February. Yes, the volunteers were different now; they were part of a real army, seasoned in battle, and they knew defeat as well as the joy of victory. They had experienced the bitterness of losses that could not be replaced, and they had experienced the loss of their dear leader, General L. G. Korniloff.

The new commander, General A. I. Denikin, delivered his first speech before the volunteers at stanitsa Egorlytskaya. He said, "Big and small rivers will join in a single Russian sea; stormy and powerful, it will sweep away all the evil that has afflicted the wounded and crippled body of our Motherland."

Liberation had arrived, and new times started. The decree was passed to release all the students from military duties and mobilize all the Cossacks. Our family was very happy; my brother Peter and my cousin Vladimir came back. Peter was a *Sotnik* (lieutenant of Cossacks); later he became a Captain of Cavalry of the Drozdovsky Officers Regiment, and he participated in Korniloff's march. Cousin Vladimir had been awarded the St. George Cross during the Turkish campaign. For a short time, all the family was gathered together in our house. I was recovering in the joyful environment of family coziness.

The "Zaplavsky Siege" put an end to the sufferings of many people who had experienced the "sweetness" of Communist rule. I was still somewhat ill, but I was present at the promenade of the 26th Drozdovsky Detachment. It looked more like a parade than a promenade. It was good to see the orderly lines and the sunburnt faces of the veterans, defenders of the Russian Empire. There was no sign of fatigue in their faces, and they were smiling. I was present at the parade of the combat veterans of the "Zaplavsky Siege" on April 27th; these were the men who had taken part in the liberation on Novocherkassk.

The Assembly of the salvation of the Don was created on April 29, 1918. Ataman General Krasnoff was elected on may 2nd. At that time, I fell ill with a bout of pneumonia. Fishing in the icy water at Zaplavskaya when I had to operate the dragnet while naked had taken its toll. I was sick for about a month. When I recovered, the greater part of the Don was liberated. There were Cossack uprisings in many places. It was reported that the greater part of the Kuban and Terek regions were liberated.

Many students helped the Cossacks in their fields. With the help of the Volunteer Army and the Drozdovsky Regiment, the area of Rostov and Novocherkassk was recovered from the Communists by the middle of July, 1918. In addition, the Communists were driven from Alexandro-Grushevsk which had many Red sympathizers. Some other regions were liberated too, but by July they were not yet connected with the Novocherkassk and Rostov area. The liberation was moving ahead briskly. We knew that Siberian Cossacks and the forces in the northern part of Russia around Arkhangelsk were also fighting against the Communists. We heard about the Communist atrocities and saw the tortured Cossacks—sometimes entire families. In the northern Don area, the Reds destroyed forty khutors and several stanitsas along with all the residents who could not flee, such as children, pregnant women, and old people. These things occurred as a direct result of the activities of Trotsky and Sverdlov who wanted to take revenge on the Cossacks. They had received direct orders from Comrade Lenin to carry out these brutal actions.

Time was passing. Summer vacation was over and school started. We were diligent but could not study well. All our thoughts were on the fighting, on Russia, the Red bandits, and the "Internationalists" composed of Red Russians, Germans, Hungarians, Latvians and others who helped to destroy the Russian state both physically and morally. The foreign and Russian bandits not only killed but plundered as well; their loot included gold, silver, and even underwear. Robbery was a common phenomenon.

In some places at the Front our troops could not successfully oppose the Reds, who outnumbered them, and they retreated.

In January of 1919, the Reds broke our front. Partisan detachments started to form again. I remember how I went to Divine Service at the gymnasium on Saturday. I joined the chorus. To my surprise, half of the choir members of my class and the senior class were absent. I asked what was the matter. The answer was that they decided to have a farewell dinner at the restaurant. I should mention that we never had so-called class dinners. The only things we had were the farewell dinners for the graduates (they receive Maturity diplomas).

When I came to the restaurant, most of my classmates were already a bit tight. Our teachers were present and included Viktor Genrykhovich Granjean, Alexander Petrovich Kalabukhov, and one more whose name I don't remember. My classmates asked me with reproach, "Where have you been?" My answer was simple, "In the detachment. The Tchernetsoff Partisan regiment is being formed. Tomorrow we'll be sent to the front. I did not know that you were here; they told me about the situation while I was in church."

At that time, Vanya Sergeev gave me a big glass of wine to drink. According to Russian custom, it was the punishment for those who were late. I wanted to escape having to "pay the penalty," but when I turned towards the door I saw that two of my classmates, giant brothers known as the *shamiles*, blocked my exit. *(Shamil was an exceptionally strong Muslim leader who had opposed Czarist forces in the Caucasus Mountains during the Nineteenth Century.)* There was nothing to do but to drink the wine, and so I did. We, the young men, never drank. Only the graduates "washed" their throats at the graduation party, but even then very moderately.

I'd like to say a few words about those brothers. They were fourteen year old "herculeses." At night they worked at the railroad yard. They carried one hundred pound sacks onto the platform. Nobody knew their age; otherwise they would have been prohibited from working.

The party was going on. We shared our impressions of events and sang songs; we sang about Stenka Rasin (*From Behind the Isle, There is a Cliff on the Volga, There is not a Thundering Sea*, and others.) We always started with *God Save the Tsar*, then *Many Years to the Don Army*, and other Cossack songs, as well as Ukrainian and other folk songs. We even included classical romances.

It was after midnight and we had to go home. Somebody proposed "one for the road." We drank, said goodbye, and went home. I noticed that Viktor Genrykhovich was drunk. Ilysha M. and I decided to bring him home as it was on our way. Ilysha was living not far from V. G., so we decided to do it. As I have mentioned, I was a "sturdy lad," and Ilysha helped me to lay V. G. over my shoulders. We walked slowly. It was a moonlit night, and a myriad of stars decorated the sky. We could see the falling stars, and thought about someone who had passed away and about someone who was to be born in his turn. It was strange to think that the city was sleeping as if nothing had happened, though the guns were firing not far away.

We brought V. G. home. His wife, a Frenchwoman, was very frightened. We calmed her down and put V. G. on his bed. We apologized and went to Ilysha's house. His father met us kindly, smiled and said, "Yogurt is a good medicine." He brought us a big bowl of yogurt. We rendered homage to the yogurt, and became sober. Honestly, we were not drunk, just merry. The situation at the front was serious, and in the city morale was low; we were in a state of depression. That's why the wine could not "get" to us. I went home. I was amazed by the silence. The city was sleeping without waking.

At home I did not tell my family that I had enlisted in the partisan detachment. Instead I said I was going to the gymnasium.

On Monday the detachment gathered in the yard of the beer factory named after Bazener. We were divided according to type of weapon we could use. I was placed in the artillery battery. We had several elderly men in this unit. I remember one of them well. He was an official in the Government Alcohol Control Department (I hope I named it correctly). We stayed several days at Bazenerovskoye. We were familiarized with some military techniques such as the use of guns and weapons.

They gave us tea and bread. I noticed that the official did not drink tea. His breakfast consisted of a bottle of vodka and a loaf of bread which he salted diligently. I asked him what he was going to do at the front, as there would be no vodka there. He answered, "There will be no tea either. We'll have only air to eat." He was killed in a battle. It was a pity, for he was a nice man and a good warrior.

Soon we were sent to our position. At that time, the Reds broke the front line, crossed the Don and were going to Novocherkassk. Our guards and other regiments stopped the Reds and drove them across the Don after a severe battle. Part of our battery, consisting of two heavy guns, took a stand in khutor Yassenevsky; another half of the battery, two guns, was positioned two miles farther away. Stanitsa Ust-Belokalitvenskaya was located ten miles on the opposite side of the river. Khutor Bogaty was to the right, with the Red headquarters located in it. We stopped at khutor Yassenevsky. The artillery fire continued for several days. The Reds fired hundreds of shells, while we fired one or two. Then they stopped firing for several hours. The fighting had been going on for some time. We had two artillery spotters in our battery—Nicholas Kazintseff and me. The Kazintseff family was well known as one of the few suppliers of horses for the cavalry. They were famous as owners of a major stud farm as were the Bezugloffs, Baienkoffs, Korolkoffs and others. Nicholas Kazintseff had a wonderful horse, a Don thoroughbred.

Once during a heavy artillery barrage, the battery commander, esaul Popoff (he had fought alongside esaul Tchernetsoff in the partisan regiment deployed against the Germans in World War I), surprised me and the others by the accuracy of his fire. He stretched out his hand, spread his fingers, and gave an order to his subordinates who were aiming the field gun. Soon the Communist battery stopped firing and fell silent. That was done with the help of two or three shells from our side. The enemy fired hundreds of shells.

Once the battery commander called me and Kazintseff and ordered Kazintseff to carry a dispatch to Novocherkassk. The only way to get to Novocherkassk was on an armored train. It arrived at our position by the railroad and stopped at stanitsa Ust-Belokalitvennaya on our side of the Donets river. In the evening it would be traveling about ten miles away to Novocherkassk. The train consisted of a locomotive and an armored platform with heavy guns.

Kazintseff had to be on the train at nine in the evening exactly. He had to climb on the train when it was leaving, go to Novocherkassk and bring the dispatch to the Headquarters of the Don Army. I had to take his horse and come back to the battery.

It was about ten miles from khutor Yassenevsky to the train. We went to the train. Kazintseff jumped on the train and I took his horse and tied the reins to my saddle. Our southern night revealed itself, and it was dark in a moment. I could not see anything and decided that the horse would find the way to the battery by itself. (There were a number of roads, and one could lose his way easily). But, anyhow, my horse was behaving in a strange manner; she was going down the hill. Suddenly I understood that it was moving to the Donets river where the Reds had located their gun positions. I had just considered this possibility when the bullets began flying. They had discovered me! I turned my horse around and galloped in the opposite direction. I kept up a fast pace for fifteen minutes; then suddenly Kazintseff's horse fell down. I jumped out of the saddle and approached the animal. The horse was breathing heavily, but it was not wounded. The night was beautiful. Young grass and crops covered the Don soil with a soft carpet. Soon the horse rose to its feet. I decided to give the horses a rest and let them nibble the grass.

Daylight was breaking. At first light I saw the silhouettes of the riders moving to the river, to stanitsa Belokalitvenskaya. I figured out that I was in the middle, between Kalitva and Yassenevskaya. The riders were Red soldiers but they could not see me, and nobody paid much attention to horses in the steppe. Beside that, they were in a hurry and tried to get out of our territory. After dawn I went between the horses hoping that they would not see me. Soon I found the road. A Cossack woman was riding on a cart with yoked oxen. I asked her, "Where is khutor Yassenevsky?" She answered, "I am going there. I live there." We went together. Soon we came to the khutor. My fellow soldiers were amazed. They thought I had been captured by the Reds. At night the Reds attacked Yassenevsky and there was shooting. One of the Reds was killed, and one of our men was wounded. I heard the shooting at night but did not pay attention to it because the Reds often fired just to maintain their morale. I thanked God that the Reds did not pay attention to me at dawn; they were more interested in fleeing after having carried out the night attack.

Having pushed the Reds across the Don, our command could take care of our troops by distributing the supplies, forming new detachments, and preparing for future attacks. We had little food during this period of rest, only "what God sent us." And He could not send us much; it was spring, the Cossack's stocks were almost exhausted, and most of the households had been plundered by the Reds.

Esaul (Captain) Popoff decided to reconnoiter Khutor Bogaty on the Reds' side. As he could find out all the details of their disposition, he took the chance. I joined "Popoff's adventure." The Communist headquarters was located in a big house at Khutor Bogaty. The estate was huge. A poultry yard with ducks and chickens was located some distance from the main house. That poultry yard was the source of meat for the commissar's table. We decided to cross the Donets river on horseback, hide the horses a mile from the poultry yard, take some poultry with us and return to our lines. We were sure that we had considered every aspect of the operation. Esaul Popoff and I got into the yard. The sleepy chickens did not make noise. We put them in a sack one after another. (Unfortunately, we had to behead them before we could place them in the sack). But the rooster spoiled everything. He was very old, stringy and strong. When the esaul pulled his head, the old bird did not resign itself to its fate and crowed instead. Chickens cackled, geese made a fuss, and light lit up the house. We had to run away at once. They did not follow us. Thanks be to God, we came back safe and sound. The Reds probably concluded that their own soldiers visited the poultry yard.

Then our offensive began and we crossed the Donets. Khutor Bogaty was in our hands. We visited the familiar poultry yard, but it was already empty. The commissars had good appetites.

The Reds were near in stanitsa Ust-Belokalitvennaya. We noticed that they did not like to move away from the railroad. The trains were their best means of transportation when they had to run away from us.

At the time of the battle of Ust-Belokalitvennaya one of our guns was in a desperate situation; the Reds had ranged in on it, and nobody could approach it under the machine-gun fire. It was impossible to drive a cart to us, and we had to drag the gun to a safer place under extremely adverse conditions. Our team was rewarded with St. George Crosses for that action. My horse "Little" was killed in that battle. She had been trained by me. When she heard a shot she would stand on her hind legs. When I stroked her on the shoulders she "bowed."

The new horse was too tall for me. It was not easy to mount this mare. But an interesting thing happened when I stroked her belly by chance; the horse lay down, and I could mount her without difficulty. Her former owner was probably short and had developed that technique.

Ust-Belaya Kalitva was liberated after a severe battle. We met the Chinese who were fighting for the Reds during that battle. We assaulted them from the rear, and this terrified group of "Internationalists" dropped their weapons, fell to their knees, and hung their heads in preparation for execution. I don't know what happened to them.

After the battle, our battery was transferred to Shakhty for rearmament. We received new English guns.

Kazintseff and I, being artillery spotters, were billeted with the commander. Our hostess was a woman of about fifty-five years of age. She was plump and healthy. Her daughter, about thirty years old, was also very healthy. They had many buildings in the yard such as chicken coops, cow barns and horse stables. One could understand that they had lived very well in peaceful times. We had a dugout to house us, but the hostess could not feed us.

She said, "I have nothing." In the morning, mother and daughter went to the field; it was the height of the spring season. At first we managed to buy something in the village. The next day, when our hostesses went to the field, I started to examine the poultry yard. There were many chickens. They were hatching their eggs in the grass, and I found fresh eggs. Without hesitating, I took an egg from each nest and obtained a dozen eggs. Now we had to find a frying pan or something like that. We checked the house. With the help of an old trick (i.e., removing the door from the hinges) we were able to enter the house. In the attic we found two barrels filled with bacon and pork. We took a piece of bacon to help in frying the eggs. Then we reached the cellar using the same trick. There we found stocks of potatoes, beans, and onions, as well as jars of cream by the sides of the stairway. Our hostesses must have been hiding their cows somewhere. It's a pity we did not stay there for a long time. On the last day, our hostesses decided to treat us voluntarily. The women complained during the dinner that the tomcat had developed the habit of sneaking into the cellar and eating the cream. She said she would rather give it to us. We said goodbye to each other very warmly, as we were transferred to khutor Zlodeysky. We had to stay there for three weeks to obtain our weapons. I decided to apply for leave and go home to Novocherkassk for several days.

Our battery was staying at Zlodeyskoe. That village was full of Communists. I was accommodated in the house owned by an old Cossack who lived with his wife and a daughter who was twenty-five years old. It was spring, the flowers started to bloom, and the trees and bushes were covered with small green leaves. I remember one nice evening in particular. I was standing by the "living fence" formed by the bushes. (I also remember the wonderful odor of the young foliage.) The old man and his wife were sitting on a bench in the yard. They could not see me behind the high bushes of the "living fence." Their daughter approached me. I asked her, "What are you doing?" She said, "My parents know that I want to have a baby, a Russian baby. I don't like my husband who is a Communist." "But you don't know me," I tried to dissuade her. "Yes, you are right," she replied, "but you are better than my Communist husband and his Communist friends." Her passionate patriotism persuaded me.

In two days I was allowed to go on leave and traveled by rail. But my commander made a small mistake; he did not write in my permission form the direction I could move. I decided to take advantage of this situation. I went to Rostov instead of Novocherkassk, and then I traveled to Nezhin. The 2nd Cavalry Regiment named after Colonel (later general) Drozdovsky was in that location. Its active duty roster contained individuals of many different ethnic groups and nationalities. For example, there was a Polish squadron, a Finnish squadron as well as units composed of various other ethnic groups. My brother was in the 4th Cossack Squadron under the command of Colonel Silkin. *(As a general, Silkin was delivered to the Soviets by the British authorities in 1945.)* My brother had the rank of esaul (captain), and was the commander of the squadron. The train arrived in Nezhin early in the morning.

I came out from the railway carriage and heard gunfire and shouts of "Hurrah!" I hid between the tracks. Luckily it was a short fight, and when I rose I saw an officer of the Drozdovsky detachment. I was dressed in a student coat and raised my hands to be on the safe side. I had a St. George rosette on my left sleeve which had been given as a reward to Tchernetsoff's men for valor in battle.
"Who are you, and where are You from?," asked the officer. "I am from Tchernetsoff's detachment," I replied. "I came to see my brother esaul P. F. and my cousin Lieutenant V. C." He did not believe me, and did not lower his rifle. Then he led me to the house where my brother stayed. He was away and returned in the evening. They told him that a "lad" had introduced himself as his brother. He was amazed when he saw me. "How did you get here? Why?" he remonstrated with me after a minute of embarrassment. "You may scold me or not, but I want to see you and your famous regiment," I replied. My brother asked the hostess to make up a bed for me, and promised that the next morning he would introduce me to a friend of his who was a teacher, and would then send me home in a couple of days. I met my cousin Volodya. He was an interesting man. I was not allowed to enter his room when he lived in Novocherkassk. But one day, childish curiosity prevailed and I entered the hidden room. All the walls were covered with ladies' panties. Black

panties of incredible size appeared in the middle. These were his
military "trophies." However, it should be noted that Volodya had
been awarded with the St. George Cross for bravery during the
Turkish campaign of World War I.

The next day, Peter, Volodya and I went to meet the
teacher. She was a woman approximately fifty years old and had
a kindly attitude when she met us. Her appearance was striking
despite her age. She was short, with gray hair and eyes as blue as
a sky. I was introduced to her and her daughter. But the girl was
very sad, with tears in her eyes. "What happened?" Peter asked.
Her mother answered that she had been telling her daughter's
fortune using cards and had predicted that something terrible had
already happened to her daughter's husband. He was a
Communist and had taken part in the battle that occurred the
previous day.

Then the teacher suggested telling our fortunes. Peter
agreed. The cards showed that he would be wounded in the groin,
a very cruel wound, within a month. She predicted that Volodya
would be wounded in the knee within a few days. I refused to
listen to my future as predicted by the teacher. We laughed at her
predictions and had our breakfast which had been prepared by her
daughter.

The next day a group of men from the 4th squadron was sent on a
reconnaissance mission. Volodya accompanied them. When they
returned they were carrying Volodya who had been wounded in
the knee and who required an operation to repair his kneecap.
The doctor insisted that he be sent to Rostov for this medical
procedure, and I was his escort. We embarked in a boxcar
designed to transport both men and horses; some thoughtful
Cossacks had lined it with hay. In the evening, after saying
goodbye to Peter, the train departed for Rostov. The teacher had
provided us with a bag filled with tasty meat pies. In any case,
we had enough food as the Ukrainian women were selling
meat-filled pastries, roast chicken, bacon, fish, and other items at
every station.

We were stopped during the journey. I don't remember
the exact location, but I believe it was somewhere between
Kharkov and Poltava. The reason for the delay was that our front
had been penetrated by the Reds. The train halted and it was
suggested that we move away in carts for the sake of security.
We had to wait for several days in the steppes until the Reds were
driven back from the rail line. Men from Shkuro's detachment

defended us.[1] At last we moved again, occupying the same place in the boxcar where we had been located on the earlier part of our journey.

I brought Volodya to the hospital in Rostov and went to join my battery. I was lucky to return at this time, because our battery was sent to the front a few days later. However, due to the fact that I had spent ten days on vacation instead of three, the commander of the battery made a decision to put me in the guardhouse. Then he had to forget about his order because our battery was dispatched to the front.

It was the middle of summer. Several newly trained Cossacks arrived, and their arrival was followed by the order to release the students from their military duties. At this point I realized that the reinforcements had arrived.

Having completed the formalities, I was processed out and allowed to return home. I wanted to study and sat down to concentrate on my books. My brain missed the stimulation of formal education. I looked forward with anticipation to the upcoming lessons at the gymnasium.

The situation in Novocherkassk was very bad. There were many bandits in the area, and we constantly heard reports of robberies. It was risky to walk in the streets alone. My elder sister Shura was teaching in Khutor D. On one occasion, my mother decided to visit her and I had to accompany her. We took a rooster and a hen as a gift for Shura, and I proudly carried them in a net. We got to Rostov without any problems, went to the pier from the railway station and boarded a ship. A gentleman entered our cabin and sat under the berth where the rooster and hen had been placed. He took off his hat, opened the newspaper and started reading. At that moment our rooster became nervous and the "results" of his nervousness leaked down on the gentleman's head. We had to leave and pretended that the birds did not belong to us. We thus came to Shura without a gift.

As I have mentioned, I came to my battery the day before it was sent to the front, and then I was sent home. Summer passed quickly. When the classes started, I passed my exams as fast as I could—these were for the subjects that I had missed for the previous year and a half. But very soon I lost interest in my studies and increasingly thought about returning to the front. What was going on there? We listened to the news about

---

[1] Note: I joined Shkuro's detachment.

uprisings taking place throughout Russia. (At that time, 344 uprisings had occurred in 1918, and 245 during the first seven months of 1919. Between 142 and 270 counter-revolutionary organizations had been established.) The news from the front was not very comforting.

The worst happened on Christmas Eve; the Bolsheviks approached the Don and our troops were in retreat all along the front. Once, before Christmas, I was going to the gymnasium with my books under my arm. I met my friend Venya S. several steps from the gymnasium. He rushed out with his hair in disarray. "Why are you heading to the Gymnasium?" he asked as we faced each other. "The Bolsheviks are several miles from Novocherkassk. They will be here by tomorrow. I am going to the Maryinskaya Gymnasium. Our battalion is gathering there. We must retreat to Aksayskaya." I didn't even ask him how he had learned all that. I put my books on the steps of the gymnasium, thus showing respect for our Alma Mater, and rushed off with Venya. I never saw my school again..

The whole yard in the Maryinskaya Gymnasium was full of students and was buzzing like a troubled beehive. People were arriving like us. A student-officer directed the process of enlisting. Venya and I reported to him. I was appointed commander of the first platoon, and Venya was given command of the second platoon; we were "veterans", and had been awarded St. George Crosses. I obtained the personnel roster and collected my men quickly, among them my teachers—a Frenchman, Victor Genrykhovich Granjean, Alexander Petrovich "Salustry" *(I don't remember his last name. "Salustry" was his nickname because he was teaching a class in Latin.)*, and the history teacher Kotlyarevsky *(unfortunately he had an unenviable nickname, too*—Tchoushka, *because he had a nose like that of a pig. On the whole, students and schoolboys did not spare their teachers.)* I told them to go home. "You are elderly men. They need you at school. The Communists won't touch you; you never have been in partisan detachments, and you have never fought with arms in your hands against the Reds. Go Home!" They left the detachment.

Many years later, having arrived in America, I met a Cossack who told me that he had graduated from the gymnasium in Novocherkassk and had known our teachers. They were still alive, but if they had taken part in our march they would not have survived. I often remember "Salustry"; he had a waistcoat (all our teachers had waistcoats) with two pockets. In one he kept a gold watch, while he placed a university badge in the other. We used to sing, "a golden chain on that belly." He was a very stout man, with a big belly, but he was a very kind person.

Having started the march, we soon came to Stanitsa Aksayskaya. The weather was terrible. A heavy snow had fallen and it was more than a foot deep. We were moving very slowly. Many students were wearing their school boots. I was smart enough to wear my high boots, and this decision proved to be the correct one. It was windy and my coat hardly kept me warm. I had three of my friends in my platoon, the sons of three owners of stud farms. One came from Provalsky, the second from Orel, and the third from Voronezh. They were cadets and close friends. They were tall, handsome, healthy, and strong. They treated me like a younger brother in spite of the fact that I was their commander.

We entered Aksayskaya late at night, being one of the first units to arrive. As a result of military tradition, the detachment which was the first to enter a stanitsa was in a privileged position, and its commander became the commandant. So our battalion commander became the commandant of Aksayskaya. We looked for the ataman of the stanitsa to help us accommodate and feed the people, as well as to determine what buildings we had to guard. The stanitsa was quickly filled with retreating troops. Our commander and the ataman settled those questions.

Stanitsa Aksayskaya had large warehouses for the storage of wine. My platoon was accommodated in the house of the owner of the warehouses. I had to post sentinels at these locations and change them every two hours. It was cold and my men were not dressed properly. The winemaker had a big house with adjacent buildings. We settled in the house and in the buildings. When everyone was settled in, the three sons of the stud farm owners disappeared. They returned in approximately thirty minutes and invited me to dinner. The employees of the winery lived in one of the buildings. They cooked ham, geese and other delicacies for Christmas. In addition to the food, excellent wine was on the table. There were five hosts. Our dinner was long, and we started to say goodbye in the morning. The heavy meal did not prevent us from taking care of the sentinels and relieving them from their posts at the appointed time. All the sentinels had their meals.

The Kuban Regiment entered the stanitsa in the morning. Colonel Kubantseff came to the winemaker's house and settled there. His Cossacks found the warehouses and wanted to take some wine, but our sentinels did not allow them to do that. This was reported to the Colonel, and he sent a platoon to arrest the sentinels. At the same time he ordered them to arrest us. I remember his question: "Who is in command?" I answered. He said, "Arrest and shoot everyone!" "Colonel! What crime are we guilty of?" "We'll determine that later," he answered. They led us into the street. A dozen Kuban Cossacks led us beyond the outskirts of the stanitsa. I saw my friend Venya and told him to find our commander and tell him that Kuban Cossacks were leading us away to execute us. Our commander reacted quickly, spoke to the Colonel, and we were released. *(Such an incident only could have occurred because of the chaos of the Civil War. The Colonel was not a typical representative of either the Russian Imperial Army or the White Forces.)*

We were ordered to move to Olginskaya immediately. In a moment we started on our difficult journey. The winter was very mild that year. There was snow and muddy slush in which we sunk up to our knees. I felt pity for the guys who were wearing shoes; my boots saved me.

We passed Olginskaya and Mechetenskaya. We spent several days in Egorlykskaya where we stayed in the house of an elderly woman who lived with her daughter and grandson. Her son-in-law had been killed in the war. We asked her to sell us some food, but there was no food in the house. My friends, the sons of the stud farm owners, went around the stanitsa and purchased the food.

Then we moved in the direction of stanitsa Novo-Pashkovskaya. We halted several times. On one of the halts my friends treated me to excellent, big sandwiches. I asked, "Where did you obtain this luxury?" "Our hostess had a pantry hidden behind the house. We found it, and there we saw two dozen plucked geese (two of them had already been roasted). We took them and left two rubles for the hostess. We also took a big piece of bacon and some ham." And I had been wondering why their bags had become so big!

Time seemed to move at a slow pace. We were frequently stuck in the mud but kept moving on. We came to Novo-Pashkovskaya late at night. The Commander informed us that we would stay there for several days to rest and clean ourselves. My friends and I were accommodated in the house of an old Cossack and his kind wife.

I had diarrhea and suffered a great deal. The old woman took some dried pears and made a thick uzvar. I drank two cups and felt better. My boots, trousers and other clothes were very dirty. The woman washed and ironed them. Everything was ready in only five hours. I had an interesting conversation with the old Cossack. He said, "You are so short, your carbine is bigger than you are. You probably can't shoot at all." I should mention that the old man had a big orchard. "Hey boy, let's go to the yard. You take your rifle, and I'll take mine", he suggested. We went to the orchard. He stopped by the tree and asked me to wave my hands. I waved, and he approached a tree and took an owl from a branch. "Do you know how to catch owls?", he asked. "Yes," I said. I noticed another owl on a tree, and caught hold of it successfully.

An owl is a very interesting bird. It cannot see well during the day, but it likes to take in the sights. It takes such a great interest in what is going on before its eyes that it forgets about the danger. "I can see you can catch owls," the old man said, "but how is your skill at shooting?" There were many ravens in that garden. The old man saw a raven and killed it with an accurate shot. "Now, boy, you shoot." I shot and killed a flying raven. Believe me, it was mere luck. But the old man felt respect for "the boy" and shook my hand. We spent several days in that stanitsa. We made a fire in the evening and our platoon sat around it. The nights were not all that cold.

There was a student in our platoon, the son of the philosophy professor named Sokoloff. He told us our future by reading our palms by the light of the fire. He told my friend that he would experience serious trouble. Indeed, this individual soon fell ill with dysentery and typhus, and subsequently died. I showed him my palm. He predicted that I would travel a lot, that several times I would be close to death, and then I would go far away across big waters and return to Russia when I was very old.

In a couple of days, the order came to send all the students to the military school. My friends, the sons of the stud farm owners, decided to join the Sumskoy regiment. They knew in advance that I would join them at the nearest stanitsa. So we came together again in the Sumskoy regiment. We received horses and became cavalry men. There were not many people in the unit, no more than half a hundred, but they were very skillful and brave warriors. The regiment experienced heavy losses, and it was not easy to get reinforcements; the regiment was moving, with Budenny's Red cavalry on its "tail".

We had a battle at stanitsa Tunelnaya. How did it end? Who gained the victory? Where were my friends? I don't know. I came to myself in Novorossisk, in a house, under a table. A bowl of soup with dumplings had been placed by my side. The kitchen of the house and the yard were full of retreating Cossacks. I did not pay attention to anybody and ate my meal. I became even more hungry. I must have been unconscious for several days and had eaten nothing. An excited crowd was in the yard; somebody shouted that the hostess had poisoned a Cossack and that she should be shot. In order to calm down the crowd, I shouted that the Cossack had died of typhus and that the hostess had saved me and had given me food. Everybody quieted down.

Everybody said that we should go to the shore of the Black Sea. I was accustomed to the situation and put myself in order. I decided to go to the shore, though I was very weak and hungry. There was a crowd of people, carts, and horses. I saw a heap of rye bread. Nobody paid attention to it. Everybody had decided what to do. There were no steamships to the Crimea. Could we go up into the mountains? Hunger prompted me to take a loaf of bread and I bit into it. I could understand the conversations around me. General Morozoff and Colonel Eliseeff wanted to surrender and were negotiating with the Reds. There were rumors that Eliseeff had already surrendered. Some people wanted to go to the mountains. There were tens of thousands of people in the port and no ships. Some people were in despair. I saw how a Cossack made the sign of the cross over his wife, kissed her and shot her; then he kissed and shot his horse, and fired the last bullet into his forehead.

There was an overcrowded ship at the Novorossisk pier. I remember a man who looked like a mountaineer who went up the gangplank, only to be stopped by six men from the ship patrol. After a short exchange of angry words, he returned to the shore. The ship was overcrowded.

I was at a loss. I had lost my detachment and my friends. I was alone. I don't remember how it happened; I mounted a horse and urged it to swim to the nearest barge which was standing out in the roadstead, a half mile from shore. Somebody dragged me onto the barge, and I fell asleep. As a result of the shell-shock, I was very weak. Then somebody pushed me and I awoke. I found that I was sleeping near the winch and it started working, pulling the anchor. The winch pushed me; the barge was stuffed with people. But I wanted to sleep—it was my only concern. I managed to find a place for myself, and woke up in Feodosia.

My clothes dried and when I went ashore I looked like the other men. I was the only Cossack, but there were all kinds of military men there. The square was full of the banners of different units; the caps of men from many detachments could be seen. These included units commanded by Drozdovsky, Alexeyev *(former Chief of the Imperial General Staff)*, Kornilov, and Markov. I decided to join Drozdovsky's men because I had spent three or four days with that regiment while visiting my brother. We were led to the suburbs and accommodated in the houses in that area. They gave us cigarettes and food, and it seemed that a new life had started.

I was dressed in a broadcloth gymnasium uniform and had my brother's wristwatch. He had purchased it in 1914 with his first paycheck. The watch was excellent, made of blue steel, with a black cover and real hands. I received an allowance for bread, canned food and cigarettes. All of us were divided into regiments. All "the colored" (i.e., the officers of special regiments of the Volunteer Army such as Alexeyev's, Markov's, Kornilov's, etc.) were sent to their detachments to join the Volunteer Army in Crimea. As I have mentioned, I joined with Drozdovsky's men. I was lucky; thanks to my short stature everybody considered me to be underage and treated me like a child.

A rumor was spread in our barracks that the steamship *Don* was coming to Feodosia. The next day it was supposed to go to Evpatoria, then to Sebastopol. I talked to the sentinel who was standing on guard in the yard of our house. He complained that he wanted to smoke but had no cigarettes. I offered him my pack of cigarettes, but it was forbidden to smoke on duty. I suggested that I stand in his place to relieve him for a while. He agreed. After two minutes, I left the gate and went to the port to have a look at the ship *Don*.

It was a real oceangoing steamship. It could carry as many as two thousand people with comfort. When I came there, they were taking the gangplank away, and the ship was ready to leave. Suddenly, (oh what a miracle) I heard a call: "Nicholas! What are you doing here?" I looked up and saw my brother's good friend, Boris Kunitsin, on deck. They used to participate in sports and play music together. Boris was an excellent flutist. They used to sing, too. My brother was a baritone, Boris a tenor.

I was lucky again. They threw me a rope from the upper deck. I tied it to myself and was pulled onto the deck. I enlisted in the Guards Ataman Convoy and had a hot meal for the first time in a long while. Boris knew that I used to play cornet in the gymnasium. When he saw me standing on the shore wearing my gymnasium uniform, he talked to the Aide of the Convoy about enrolling me in the orchestra. They had an urgent need for a cornetist at that time. He agreed, and that's why I got the rope. I was the smallest guardsman in the orchestra.

I often remember the stories told by the old Cossacks. It did not matter in what detachment they were serving; all of them spoke proudly about their commanders and their regiments, but the guardsmen were especially proud. I remember a story concerning a controversy which took place during a meeting in a stanitsa, convened to reallocate the land strips. As always, the old men occupied the places of honor. The oldest and most famous Cossacks occupied the front seats, "the ragged" were seated behind them. This does not mean that "the ragged" were the poorest, but they were less prominent in social life and military operations. So "the ragged" protested at the meeting when the best allotments were given to "the eminent." They said it was unfair.

Then a guardsman rose from his place in the front row. He was a tall, slender old man who stroked his beard and said in a stentorian voice, "Hush, honest inhabitants of the stanitsa. An active member of a Cossack military unit wants to speak. Why are you arguing?" he asked of one of the most vocal of the protesters who was seated on the last row. "Why are you speaking such nonsense? What do you want? I have two sons. Both of them are guardsmen, and you only have a daughter-in-law who has loose morals in addition to that." The old man stopped speaking. The man in the last row was ashamed and kept silent. Order was restored, and land was reallocated in an orderly manner. I was proud that I had become a guardsman.

We arrived at Evpatoria to take additional passengers on board. I was as yet unaware that a large group of Cossacks had traveled to Feodosia and Evpatoria, and that the *Don* had stopped in these ports with the specific mission of transporting these men to Sebastopol where Cossack regiments were being formed. Boris told me about that. He asked if I knew anything about my brother Peter. I thought Peter was in Nezhin, and that the men of the Drozhdovsky Cavalry Regiment were in Poland. It seemed to me that we would retreat in that direction, but I knew nothing about Peter.

We disembarked in Sebastopol at the Korabelnaya side of the inlet. I put myself in order. I had a Caucasian saber, and a "Bulldog" revolver, but I don't remember how I obtained it. I had my brother's watch and his picture which I kept with care in the pocket of my shirt. That was my inheritance.

We were idle while living at the Korabelnaya side of Sebastopol. We ate smoked *khamsa* (small fish). We gulped down large numbers of them along with bread. Our orchestra often played at funerals. The monotonous life was not interesting for me. I found out that a landing on the coast controlled by the Bolsheviks was being prepared. I wanted to take part in it, for there were persistent rumors that the population of the Don region had risen against the Reds again.

I handed my application to the Commander of the Ataman Special Escort Detachment. I wanted to be transferred to a partisan regiment, but General Khripunoff wrote a brief comment on my application: "Rejected." Then I addressed the duty officer with a request to let me go for a walk in the center of Sebastopol. He approved it and I went directly to the office of the Don Ataman. I believe it was located on Nakhimoff Prospect, in a big mansion on the embankment. I asked the duty officer to report to the head of the office that a student, N. V. Feodoroff, wanted to see him in connection with a very important affair. To my surprise, the head of the Ataman's office received me.

I said that I was enlisted in the Ataman's Escort and had given my application to the Escort Commander requesting that he send me to a partisan unit, but the Escort Commander had rejected it. For that reason I asked for the Ataman's help. General Alexeyev (*not related to the General Alexeyev who had been Chief of the Imperial General Staff*) was the head of the office of the Don Ataman. He asked me to give my last name, as well as my first and middle names, and asked me about my father. I was very nervous. After a short conversation he let me go and said, "Everything will be done. I wish you success." I thanked him and returned to Korabelnaya.

Two of the Escort Commander's men were waiting for me; they led me to a small shack and locked me in there. I understood that I had been placed in a guardhouse. Two men had been confined there, but now three of us were located in that facility. I spent more than a week there. When I was released, the duty officer told me that I had been placed in the guardhouse because of my self-willed attitude in trying to obtain a decision from the Head of the Ataman's Office. Why did this occur? The explanation was quite simple. The Head of the Office had a purpose in asking me the identity of my father. He was acquainted with my father and saved my life by placing me under temporary arrest. Nazaroff's partisan detachment was completely destroyed by the Reds. Only Nazaroff himself remained alive.

Now I understand why the General acted in the way he did, and I am grateful to him for saving my life. But at the time I was seriously offended, and decided to leave the band any way I could. An artillery battalion was being formed at Sebastopol at that time. It consisted of two batteries. I had experience serving in an artillery unit and decided to enroll in the battery. At this time, my application was accepted by the commander and I became an active member in the battalion which included the third and fourth batteries. I was enlisted in the third.

After completing brief organizational activities, our battery was sent to the village of Ivanovka (not far from Simferopol). I was settled in the house of a Tatar. He had a fourteen-year-old daughter and a son who was ten or eleven years old. The boy had the habit of hanging around me all the time and liked to stroke my saber. He put his head near the saber and whispered something to himself. The girl also spent much time in our presence.

We spent about a month in that village. Very often we chased the "green bandits" *(the "greens" were bandits who were associated with neither the Red or White forces, and who took advantage of the troubled conditions of the Civil War to commit robberies)* who hid in the nearby mountains and assaulted us. We went swimming often. I had new friends; one of them was a student from a private gymnasium in Novocherkassk, and the other two were from the Cadet Corps Military School. Usually when I entered the sea, I took off my watch and put it in the pocket of my field shirt. Once I went into the water with my shirt on. I felt it was too deep and decided to take it off. I forgot that the watch was in the pocket, and the watch fell into the water. We repeatedly dove in an attempt to locate it but could not find it.

Our common friend, Boris Sevrugov (a schoolboy from a private Novocherkassk Gymnasium), was swimming at that location on the following day and found my watch. At first he thought it was a seashell, for we collected shells. Full of joy, I rushed to a watchmaker with my watch. My brother's watch was fixed, and I again had it my possession.

Often we had short skirmishes with the "Greens." Fortunately, none of us were killed. Then our commanders decided to relocate us to North Tavria. When I said goodbye to the Tatar family, the Tatar said, "Don't leave. Stay here, for my house is your house. You are a nice person. Marry my daughter. You'll live quietly." I said that my detachment was going to be deployed in battle. If we beat the Reds, I would return and marry his daughter, but now was the wrong time.

General Popoff was the Commander of the artillery battalion. He was a tall, thin man with the eyes of a hawk. His aide was Lt. Colonel V. V. Shlyakhtin, a man of average height, but strong, with a narrow forehead and prominent cheek bones. Our battalion reached Tokmak successfully because the road to Melitopol had been cleared of the Reds. The front line was already in Tokmak, a German colony. I was on duty at the battery when bad news arrived all of a sudden; the Reds had broken through and were moving to Tokmak. This occurred in June of 1920. I mounted a horse and rushed to the battalion commander. When I arrived at the house I saw a strange scene; Aide Shlyakhtin was rising from his chair with a stern look and a grasped fist at if he wanted to strike the General who was standing behind him with a fly-swatter in his hand. It turned out later that the General was killing the flies which were abundant there. A fly sat oh his Aide's head. The General could not resist the temptation.

I made a report and informed him about the order to move the battery deeper to the rear and to be ready to repel a blow from the enemy. The Commander, in turn, ordered me to "fly" to the aviation detachment and inform the pilots about the oncoming danger. The airplanes were located two miles from us. The aviators were sleeping peacefully when I rushed there and woke them. The engines roared. I, too, sat in the cockpit, and we flew fifty kilometers (thirty miles) away from the front. General Popoff allowed me to fly away with the aviators because it was too dangerous to return. Besides that, our detachment was marching, and it was impossible for me to locate its route.

The next day, a severe battle with the Reds led by Zhloba took place. As is known from historical sources, the Reds were defeated. We captured many prisoners and weapons. I won't describe all the details as they are well known from the writings of military historians. I watched the battle from the air. *(The Commander of the aviation detachment took me with him, and we were flying above the battlefield, throwing bombs on the Reds.)* The next day, the aviators returned to their airfield, and I joined my detachment which returned to Tokmak. Then our battery took part in many fights with the Reds. But the general situation, in spite of Zhloba's defeat, was not in our favor.

The victories raised our spirits for a short time only. We had no reinforcements, and our ranks grew thinner. The Crimea is a small territory, and it could not supply our army with the necessary reinforcements or resources. Russia, with its arms factories and immense population, was in the hands of the Bolsheviks. In addition, Poland signed a peace treaty with the Soviets, and the Reds transferred their forces to the Crimea from the Polish Front. The White Army began to retreat inexorably. Enormous enemy forces pressed against us; even as we retreated, we launched counterattacks, holding back the onslaught of the Reds and preparing new positions. A planned retreat gave us the possibility to carry out the Crimean evacuation without panic.

The main even took place on a narrow, unfriendly strip of land, connecting the Crimea with the Continent. It was buffeted by winds and we froze to the marrow. Hunger and cold were our major torment. But our youth was in our favor; we did not lose heart and cheered each other on by singing. We found a smoldering fire on one of the halts. I stirred the ashes and found a baked potato. I have never eaten anything better; we ate it with my friend Boris Sevrugoff. We were so hungry that I ignored the fact that the potato was very hot and burned my larynx.

The Commander's Aide, Lieutenant Parchevsky, was in our battery. It seemed to me that I had seen him before, maybe in Rostov, Novocherkassk or Nezhin. But I could talk to him only on the way to Kerch, where we retreated. We found out that we had common relatives; one of them was Vasily Stepanovich Bogaevsky, Army Lieutenant-Colonel retired. Bogaevsky was my great uncle, and his wife was Parshevsky's grandmother. Lieutenant Parshevsky had four brothers. Two of them had been killed in World War I. The third had emigrated to France. Nothing was known about the fourth. Finally the lieutenant came to New Zealand where he worked as a veterinarian; he had graduated from the Institute of Veterinary Science in Russia.

After a long march, we came to Kerch and were accommodated in a big warehouse by the pier. We stayed there for several days, waiting for embarkation. Once a man on duty called me. He said a boy and a girl were waiting for me. I was very surprised because I had no acquaintances in Kerch. When I came out, I was amazed even more for the two little Tatars, in whose house I had stayed before, were waiting for me. "How did you find out that I would be in Kerch? How did you manage to get to Kerch from Simferopol?" I was very glad to see them. We talked and began saying goodbye. They said they would be back in a moment. And, indeed, soon they delivered me two bags of apples which they had transported by donkey!

On November 3, 1920, our battery embarked on the *Alkiviadis*, a small vessel which carried coal from Rostov to the stanitsas in the lower reaches of the Don in the area of Azov. There were more than forty men, but the ship could not take all of us. We stuffed as many as possible into the ship; the rest embarked on another ship with the Cossacks. We left our native land on that frail ship which belonged to a Greek Jew from Rostov. We were sure that we would come back. We went into the unknown, but we were not afraid of that unknown because we believed that the truth was with us, that we were high spirited, and that Russia was with us. We trusted our leader, and he was with us, tall, slender, with the look of an eagle—Baron General Wrangel. He was an excellent strategist, a true son of Russia, and an outstanding warrior.

But there were tears, too. We were crying, saying goodbye to our Motherland. We believed that we would return, but we knew that it would not be easy. Our true friends, the horses, remained on the shore. Soon the horses, the city, and the Crimea disappeared. Constantinople lay ahead.

Chapter 3
ON THE WAY TO THE UNKNOWN

The Commander-in-Chief ordered all the ships to stand on a roadstead, and then, at a certain hour, we moved into the unknown. It was November 4, 1920. Our *Alkiviadis* was towed by a big transportation ship.

The Black Sea is very stormy, resembling the North Sea. Its waves are short, high and abrupt. A ship often hangs in the air above the waves; this is dangerous because excessive strain is placed on the hull of the ship and may be the cause of a shipwreck. On the other hand, ocean waves are long and not abrupt. All parts of a ship are supported by such a wave.

Autumn and spring are the most dangerous navigation seasons on the Black Sea. When we sailed out, the Black Sea was raging. The rope which connected our vessel with the transportation ship broke soon after we were under way, and we were left by ourselves, with our hopes set on God Almighty. The wind tossed our ship about the sea for five days. It was not until the sixth day that we saw the Turkish shore. The patrol ship led the *Alkiviadis* to Constantinople. At the port we were surrounded by two or three Turkish boats which brought bread, figs and khalva *(a confection)* for sale. Of course, we were hungry and thirsty.

I saw an example of "nobleness," displayed by a Turk. When one of our soldiers offered him a golden ring with a ruby to pay for bread because he could not pay with anything else, the Turk gave him one loaf of bread, taking the expensive ring in exchange. I don't know why and how (probably hunger was the motivation), but I took a lance and maneuvered it in the Turk's boat and skewered several loaves of bread on it. The owner of the boat started spitting and shouting, and all the boats pushed off from the *Alkiviadis*.

We had a small boat which, to our surprise, had not been swept off during the storm. We took the risk of lowering it, and (with the consent of the Division Aide Shlyakhtin) Boris Sevrugoff and I rowed to a commissary ship standing nearby. It was a French ship and they welcomed us. Fortunately, Boris was fluent in French. They gave us excellent food, including bread and sausages, and, most important, informed us that soon they would start to supply us with food regularly. We came back to the *Alkiviadis* in a very happy mood.

A few days passed before we were allowed to go ashore. I should say that my skill in playing the cornet turned out to be very useful for me at that time. I had my cornet-a-piston with me. The American Red Cross was located not far from us. They distributed hot cocoa and donuts. I allowed a young American to play my cornet, and we received a package of donuts in return.

The district of Galata in Constantinople was infamous for its women of easy virtue. Many apartment houses were set up to facilitate rendezvous. The sailors, missing warmth and care, could knock at a glass door and see if the hostess was busy or not. One of those women began to harass us in Russian, but we did not pay attention to her. Then she ran out of her dwelling, grabbed my friend's cap from his head, and ran away laughing. What was he supposed to do? He had to go and retrieve his cap, and I had to wait for him for a long time.

I heard a stevedore in Galata speaking abusive language in such pure Russian that I approached him and started to talk to him but he did not answer. I discovered that the only Russian words he knew were curses. Probably Russian curses are the best for expressing the feelings of a man of any nationality.

The Cossacks who had arrived at Constantinople were taken to the camps in Chilingir, Kademkoy, and other places. The barracks and sheep sheds were built there. We were ordered to wait for the train to Chilingir. Grisha Snesareff, a former student of the gymnasium named after Ataman Platoff, was among the artillerymen. He was a student from the same gymnasium but was older and taller than I. So the three of us—Boris Sevrugoff, Grisha and I—decided to play a trick. There was a food warehouse belonging to the French Commissary located along the railroad track. It was guarded by Arabs who were French sepoys. Boris was fluent in French. We convinced Grisha to walk along the railroad line and see what food was not guarded properly so we could take it and place it in the railroad cars. At that time, Boris and I had to amuse the sepoys. Sacks with grain and kerosene were the most important items for us. So this is what happened. As a result of our courteous conversation with the sepoys we took (without asking) a sack of grain and a big can of kerosene. Soon the train delivered us to Chilingir.

The proverb which states that an uninvited guest is worse than a Tatar is bitterly true. We were uninvited guests. However, we had found shelter with our ancient enemies, the Turks, while our allies, France and England, gave new meaning to the verb "ingratitude." They gave us food in return for money, ships, and so on. Thus, robbing the exiles, they thanked Russia for her effort in World War I where the Imperial Russian Army had saved Paris and ultimately England. I don't want to speak about America because increasingly it was controlled by elements hostile to Russia. The politicians and business bigwigs defamed the Emperor's government.

A sheep-shed was like a large barn, roughly constructed from planks and open on one side. A flock of sheep would be penned there during a storm to protect it from wind and snow. We found Don Cossacks living in such a sheep-shed. Some of them were squatting, some lying or standing. The sheep-shed was built to accommodate about five thousand sheep. There were even more Cossacks. Five of us, myself, Boris, Grisha, a cadet whose name I don't remember, and a Cossack about fifty years old, decided to sleep under a fence in the yard. The fence was made of cobblestones about one and a half or two feet thick. Thus we had our own "apartment." We went to sleep about three or four in the afternoon, and got up at ten in the morning. After waking, we cleared away the snow that had drifted in during the night. Having spent another night in that condition, we decided to make a dugout. We made a big dugout, with a "column" of earth in the center designed as a fireplace. We had only to make the roof—but how? There were some ties near the railroad which protected it from snowdrifts. We took three ties and put them on the dugout and covered them with branches and brush. Our dwelling was ready. We cut out benches along the walls of the dugout to serve as beds and chairs. I should say that we were much better off than our fellows in the sheep shed. We added the millet from Grisha's sack to our rations. We used the can of kerosene to provide us with light. Kerosene was good currency, too. We could trade a cup of kerosene for a dozen eggs at a local village, and so we did.

I believe that our acquisition of the dugout saved us from death. Cholera broke out at the sheep shed, and we buried our fellow Cossacks every day. The song sung at burials, *Eternal Memory*, could be heard constantly. I think that several thousand men died during that winter. Chilingir became known as "the death camp."

The sun warmed the air by noon, and the Cossacks came out from the sheepfold to stretch their limbs and fight lice. Hopelessly they inspected their shirts which were filled with lice and muttered, "The guilty ran away, and the innocent is sitting here." That saying meant, by the way, that the fleas had run away and the lice remained. Our elderly Cossack was somehow odd. He used to drink about six cans of tea. We received less than twenty grams of sugar per day. He put his sugar in a can with a one liter capacity, drank it, and said that it was too sweet and he should add some hot water. He added water several times. At night he would run away "to look at the moon."

Our rations were very scarce, even with additions from Grisha's sack. Because of our hunger, we frequently gazed at the flocks of sheep grazing at a distance. Once, having observed their movements, we dug out two traps masked with branches. The next day, we found two sheep in the hole. Our rations had become much better.

Once we went to the nearest village to sell a tablecloth saved by Boris. We wanted to obtain some bread. The first man we met was an old Turk who was smoking a pipe, sitting at the gate, and looking at us with hostility. We showed him the tablecloth and said, *"Calif" (Turkish for gentleman)*. The Turk rose silently, went to his yard and unleashed the dogs which were well-fed German shepherds. We were lucky that there were many stones nearby, for this enabled us to drive off the infuriated dogs. We went farther.

Going along the boundary wall, we heard women's voices. We called them and Boris displayed the tablecloth. Boris began to negotiate, showing "ten" with the help of his fingers, but one of the women stretched her hand across the fence and stroked his cheek tenderly. Oh, that weak heart of a man! He exchanged the tablecloth for only six loaves of bread.

There was a rumor that all the Don Cossacks were to be transferred to a new camp on the island of Lemnos. Once it had belonged to the Ottoman Empire; however, later it had been transferred to the Greeks. The Turks had sent their convicts to that island. According to rumor, the conditions on Lemnos were terrible, there being no water, no food, no residents. Many Cossacks left Chilingir and went to Bulgaria. The rest decided to go to Lemnos. Many filled up their mess-tins with water in order to have a final, small supply of the precious liquid. Then the order came to embark on the trains which took us from Chilingir to the pier in Galata.

We spent our Christmas at Chilingir, but were eager to leave the place as soon as possible; we were prepared to get out of that "death camp" and go anywhere we could travel. Even the gloomy Lemnos did not frighten us. It turned out that there were settlements on the island including a small town of Moodros. Our fellow Cossacks greeted us at the pier. They had come to Lemnos directly from the Crimea. It turned out that supplies of food and water were plentiful on the island. We were attached to General Tatarkin's detachment. General F. F. Abramoff was the Commander of the Corps of Don Cossacks. When we went to set up our tents on a hill to the left of the pier, it suddenly started to rain heavily. Of course there were not enough tents, and our group, as was the case with many other Cossacks, had to spend the night in the rain. However, it was warm, we were young and were not upset with our new position.

I should mention that the island of Lemnos was under *de facto* French control. Its commandant was a French colonel, and we were surrounded by French soldiers and sepoys. We were told not to go to the town without permission; otherwise, we would be arrested by the French.

Military men usually do everything very quickly. The next day, our part of the island was covered with tents provided from the stores in the French warehouse. During World War I, Lemnos had been the supply base for the French and British armies fighting the Turks and Bulgarians. There was no lack of either tents or food supplies.

General Tatarkin liked to sing and dance very much. The young officer Sergey Zharoff was under his command, and Zharoff was the aide of the general who conducted the chorus of Lemnos. But, in fact, it was Zharoff who conducted the musical group. I joined the chorus and started to sing. The members of

the chorus received additional food. Besides the three of us, Boris
(cornet), Grisha (trumpet), and me (cornet-a-piston), there was
Vasya Ananyevsky (baritone horn), as well as two horn players
and a drummer. Later we were joined by French horn, clarinet
and bass players from the French forces, and two additional
musicians from among the Cossack ranks. Thus, a nice orchestra
was formed. General Tatarkin was very glad, but General
Abramoff gave the order to attach us to the Ataman's school. The
school was located to the left of the pier. The infirmary was
located nearby in a large tent.
        General Maksimoff was the head of the Ataman's Military
School. He had only one son who was partially crippled
(something was wrong with his leg). General Dymsky was one of
the officers. He was a serious music-lover. He helped us to write
the score for the anthems, *God Save the Tsar, March of the
Preobrazhensky* Regiment, and a small piece by Ippolitoff-Ivanoff
(I don't remember its name). Dymsky sang the tunes of the
anthems and marches, and I chose the music that I would play on
my cornet; thus, we wrote the scores. We prepared to play before
an audience consisting of the sick and wounded at the hospital,
and we constantly tried to expand our repertoire. We learned to
play all the pieces by ear because, naturally, we had no sheet
music.
        But food was our main concern. The rations were not
sufficient, and we tried to find additional food. For some time I
solved that problem as a Stone Age hunter would. A pile of
stones, a favorite haunt of octopuses, was located in the water
near the shore not far from us. Every day I speared an octopus
with my lance. I brought those sea creatures to a Greek tavern by
the pier. The owner of the tavern paid me twenty-five Greek
drachmas for each octopus. A loaf of bread weighing one
kilogram or a bottle of Greek cognac cost twenty-five drachmas
exactly. Usually I took turns; one day I bought bread, the next
day cognac. Every day my friends from the Ataman's School
were looking forward to my return from the morning hunt. Once,
having become better acquainted with the owner, I suggested to
him that our orchestra could play at the dances held in the tavern.
My suggestion involved a certain risk because officially we were
prohibited from leaving the territory without receiving permission
both from our commandant and the French commander. The
French checked the passes at the camp exit. But the idea of
earning some money at the dances, and perhaps just a strong

eagerness to plunge into civilian life and its joys for even an hour were very tempting to our young hearts.

The Greek agreed to my proposal. He said that a loaded vessel came from Greece every Saturday. Its captain liked to drink and dance. So we passed the French posts successfully, without permission, and came to the tavern on Saturday. The captain was already waiting for us and asked us to play. Necessity is the mother of invention; we, in fact, had no repertoire, and we played the same tune as a march, waltz, and polka, and even imitated the mournful Greek melodies. The captain was very pleased, and he was very generous when he gave us drachmas. He threw us more than two hundred drachmas. Three of us played, including Boris, Vasya, and me.

This situation lasted for several Saturdays, and we got used to our new "job." Not only the captain but some other Greeks came to listen to us, though the tavern owner closed the doors of the tavern while we were playing for fear of the French patrol. Once, on Saturday, when the merriment was in full swing, somebody knocked at the door. The tavern owner opened it and, to our great horror, we saw the Commander of the Don Cossack Corps, General F. F. Abramoff. "Who is in charge?", he asked us coldly." "I am, Your Excellency," I answered in confusion. "Return to the camp immediately."

F. F. Abramoff turned around abruptly and left the tavern. We collected our money and sneaked back to the camp. Thanks to the general, there were no "repercussions." Moreover, we continued to go to the tavern on Saturday, learned a number of Greek melodies, and became a famous tavern orchestra on Lemnos. There was a positive aspect to this activity because we bought cigarettes for the Russian Military School with our money. Maybe, due to that fact, our commandant "did not notice" that we had violated the rules of the camp.

There was a store in the town of Moodros, about two miles from our camp. The owner was an elderly Greek. His granddaughter, eighteen to twenty years old, helped him. Usually I went shopping there, a pleasant experience since the owners were kind to me. A young, pretty Greek woman, a teacher, also went shopping there. The aide of the Ataman's School, Vasya Markoff, and my patron, General Dymsky, already had been introduced to her. Once I told the teacher that it would be nice if the mayor invited the head of the Ataman's School and all the yunkers to the city festival. Our orchestra would have played there, the yunkers could have demonstrated their valor at the parade, and we could enjoy consuming the modest refreshments. According to Greek custom, local residents cook the food, and then those present can treat themselves. The teacher liked my idea. Soon the mayor sent invitations to our command and to the yunkers to take part in a church holiday. A parade was held after Divine Service. The impression made was highly favorable. We tried hard, and it was very nice to march under the enraptured gazes of young Greek women. We were playing with enthusiasm.

The teacher treated Vasya Markoff and General Dymsky very kindly. Young, stately, tall, and broad-shouldered, Vasya was courting the teacher. However, the fifty-year-old General Dymsky did not look like a decrepit old man and was not indifferent to a pretty teacher. Sometimes he took me with him when he visited her. According to the old custom, it was indecorous for a young woman to invite one man alone. That's why we took turns. One day Vasya and the general visited her, and the next day the general and I would come by for a visit. Of course the general preferred to take me instead of Vasya. Once we were sitting with the teacher, and suddenly the general spoke about the beauty of ladies' legs, about nice shoes, about famous shoemakers, and then knelt before the teacher and touched her feet. At first I thought he had gone mad. The teacher felt awkward too. We sat for a while, had a cup of coffee, and returned to camp after witnessing that strange event. The next day, I noticed that the general was squaring a piece of wood, but he tried to conceal from me what he was doing.

So the teacher celebrated her birthday. Vasya obtained a bottle of perfume, and the general carried a package. I took a box of candies, and the three of us went to pay a visit. The teacher was very glad to see us. Vasya solemnly kissed her hand and gave her the perfume. She was delighted and kissed his cheek. The general kissed her hand in an elegant manner and handed her his package. She opened it, and, oh, it was a miracle! In front of her was a pair of ladies' shoes, perfectly fashioned. She could not believe her eyes, for at that time shoes were a rare commodity in Lemnos. She took off her shabby footwear and put on the new shoes. They fit perfectly. The teacher kissed the general's forehead and lips. Then I understood why he had knelt before her and touched her foot.

Once a Greek from Moodros came to our camp and asked my friends and I to play at his daughter's wedding, but I did not want to take such a large risk. It was one thing to play in a tavern on Saturday with the doors closed, and it was quite another thing to play at a noisy, open Greek wedding. I had to get permission. Of course, the Greek could not obtain permission from the French authorities, but he suggested that we get civilian clothes so that we could look like ordinary Greeks. So we did.

Everybody was happy including the Greeks whom we entertained all night, and because we gave away all the money received for playing at the wedding to the school's store which supplied their needs for items such as tobacco, etc.

"Appetite comes with eating." I started to look for a job for our small orchestra. I found out that a church holiday was going to be celebrated in a village about twelve kilometers (approximately seven miles) from our camp. On Sunday a Cossack horn player and I went to the celebration. After praying in the church, we settled in the square for the performance. As soon as we started to play a Greek melody, a group of very old women (they looked to be a hundred and fifty years old) began to dance briskly. The public was delighted; the young people joined them, and soon everyone in the square was dancing. In fact, I was playing alone, for my friend was busy collecting the money given freely to us from all sides. Besides that, they treated us well by providing us with Greek delicacies. We played until evening. then the mayor invited us to have supper at his house and to spend the night there. For the first time in four years we were sleeping on real mattresses, covered with sheets, provided with pillows, and we were under blankets, a forgotten comfort. The bedding retained the smell of the sun and the sea. Its fresh, charming smell reminded me of my house, and I fell asleep thinking about my native city, parents, brother and sisters.

We got up late. The kind host made us a nice breakfast. Having eaten well, we wanted to go, but he asked us to visit his friend, a store owner, and play a Russian march for him. The owner was a Russian Greek. We went there and I played the *March of the Preobrazhensky Regiment* and something else.

We said goodbye as if we were very good friends and went to the camp. The night was wonderful with nice quiet weather and a full moon. One could read in its light. About halfway back to the camp, I suggested to my friend that we rest by the shore. Although I was surrounded by divine silence, I was still very hungry. When I had played the night before, I had not eaten anything. Suddenly, my friend took some sausage, *khalva* and bread out of his alto horn bell. His pockets were stuffed with food which the Russian Greek had given him. He had some wine with him as well. It was one of the unforgettable picnics of my life.

Coming back to the camp, we fell asleep. In the morning I went to Moodros and bought bread, *khalva* and figs for five hundred drachmas *(I earned two hundred and fifty drachmas, and the owner of the store lent me an additional two hundred and fifty drachmas).* I loaded the food on a donkey, which the owner kindly lent me, and brought it to the yunkers. They surrounded my "store," and their delight was unlimited. I went to sleep, and in the afternoon was awakened by a yunker who brought me my share of bread, khalva and figs. All the treasure was divided equally.

I thanked him, got up and decided to bring the donkey back to the store owner. After several days, having earned a few dollars at the tavern, I repaid the money too.

I remember an interesting episode. The French wanted to send us back to the Soviet Union. Like Communists, they promised us a "bright future" in the U.S.S.R. The French commandant even arranged with our commandant that we would be gathered together to listen to his inspired speech about happiness in the Soviet Republic. The propaganda was delivered in a blunt and forceful manner, and some of us were taken in by the fraud. The French exerted economic pressure, in particular reducing our rations and limiting our freedom of movement on the island. So all the yunkers gathered not far from the hospital to listen to a Frenchman who made a long-winded speech. He came and spoke through an interpreter about freedom, equality and happiness in the Soviet homeland. He spoke for a long time, and with such words as: "Enlist, a ship will come soon and take you to the wonderful country of the hammer and sickle." I could not stand to listen to such nonsense and shouted, "Don't trust him! He is a liar! Have you forgotten the actions of the Reds?" The commandant and his sepoy guard became very nervous and wanted to arrest the "agitator." But my friends closely surrounded me and made it impossible for the French to find the "agitator."

Easter was approaching. There was a horn player in our camp who was married. His wife was in a refugee camp. She was baking Easter cakes and kindly invited me to celebrate Easter with them. Easter night was special—warm, clear and quiet. Our priest celebrated the Easter service. The church was set up in a tent and there was not enough room for all the people. I was standing outside along with many Cossacks. A Cossack of about twenty-four years of age was standing by my side. He passionately told me about his stanitsa and cried. "Why are you crying?" I asked him. "All of us are far away from our native homes. I'm illiterate," he answered, "and I really want to write a letter to my wife. We had just married, and on the first night I had to run away from the Reds." I decided to teach him to read and write. I drew letters on a paper and told him to copy them. Then I showed him how words are formed. In an hour he could produce words, though, of course, without confidence. But when the liturgy ended, he could write a few words to his wife. His name was Titoff. It was a bitter, sad Easter in a foreign land.

The liturgy was over and we congratulated and kissed each other according to the Orthodox custom. We went to our tents with uneasy thoughts; what was going on in our Motherland? The Easter parade was held at eleven in the morning. Our orchestra was playing, and the Don Cossacks marched to the sounds of the *March of the Preobrazhensky Regiment*. After the parade when I could leave the orchestra, I went to the refugee camp to join Mrs. Shashina for Easter dinner. Poor Natasha met me crying; not a crumb remained of her wonderful Easter cake. I tried to calm her down and asked, "What did you use to bake the cake?" "I baked it in a 'general,'" she said. I should explain that in former times they called a chamber pot a "general" and placed it under the beds in all the hotels. "But I cleaned it with sand and boiled it in sea water," Natasha said to justify herself. "The cake was so nice, so tasty. But you came too late." However, there were good snacks and wine at the table. We enjoyed the food, and said goodbye, having given each other the traditional Orthodox Easter congratulations.

I should say that life on the island was very monotonous. Once the governor of the Greek islands visited us, and we greeted him with a musical salute—our orchestra played the Greek Royal anthem. He liked our orchestra very much and invited us to visit the island where his headquarters was located. Boris and I agreed, and a small steamship arrived for us. It delivered food to Lemnos and took us away. On the island of Metelena, the governor suggested that we work for him as his orchestra. He offered us a good salary and nice living conditions but on one condition—we had to accompany him on his visits to the island and play the Greek Royal anthem when he came down the gangway.

But we firmly told him, "We left Russia together with our fellow veterans. They are completely without a source of entertainment. We cannot leave and deprive them of such a little pleasure as our orchestra." After that, we wished the governor all the best and returned to Lemnos.

Soon it became known that Bulgaria was going to accept us. Our doctors vaccinated all the Cossacks against typhus before we departed the island. Unfortunately, there was a lack of syringes and facilities for their sterilization. I had my shot and soon my arm was badly swollen. I had excruciating pain all over my body. Having examined me, the doctor said that I had a big abscess under my left armpit and would need an operation. The doctor tried to cut my skin with a dull scalpel (it would have been better to have used a razor) and without anesthesia. A nurse was holding me. At last he managed to pierce my skin and extracted a clot of pus as thick as a finger. They poured alcohol on my wound and applied a bandage. After the vaccination, the Ataman's school and, it seems to me, the Alekseyevskoye Kubanskoye Military School embarked on a ship and sailed to Bulgaria. Crossing the Sea of Marmora we met a ship with our Commander-in-chief, Baron General Wrangel, on board. We joyfully saluted him. It turned out that he had been waiting for our transport to make sure that everything was all right with us.

We were transferred from the place traditionally known as the island of criminals. At Lemnos we saw a number of elderly people missing a hand or fingers. We already knew what that meant. Looking back at our path we often thought we were lucky; we successfully crossed the Black Sea, came through the death camp of Chilingir, left behind Lemnos which was also known as the island of criminals, and now were moving gradually in the direction of Russia.

I will never forget the attitude of the French. It could not be called friendly. They wanted to get rid of us by employing primitive propaganda which spread lies about life in the Soviet Union with the aim of returning us to that totalitarian dictatorship. But when the Cossacks did not respond to their lies and refused to return to the U.S.S.R. voluntarily, the French resorted to economic pressure by reducing the rations (which were scanty already). Soon the propaganda theme of "going home" was coupled with starvation rations. In addition, any sepoy could humiliate a Russian officer, not to mention a common Russian soldier or a Cossack. The sepoys guarded us as if we were prisoners, and we could leave the camp only with the permission of the French authorities—and they had been our allies who had been saved by the Imperial Russian Army many times during World War I. Russian attacks distracted the Germans, forcing them to transfer their troops from the area of Paris to the Eastern Front. Now they "thanked" us by doing all that was in their power to deliver us to the Red killers who would gladly tear us to pieces when we set foot in the Soviet Union. Yes, now they did not need us; we were just excess baggage. They were ready at this point to strike a deal with the Communists. Honor and praise be given to our Commander-in-Chief, General Wrangel; he managed to achieve his goal of having us admitted to Bulgaria and Serbia. Again I say honor and praise to him.

Our ship docked at a pier in the Bulgarian city of Burgas. I do not remember if we were transferred to Yambol immediately or spent some time in Burgas, but I remember my first impression of Bulgaria; they gave us a very tasty soup. It was a rich broth with greens which are abundant in Bulgaria, and beans with a big piece of pork. For the first time we could have a second helping and eat as much as we wanted.

We were settled in the barracks of the Tenth Gendarme Regiment at Yambol. Musicians of the Ataman's Military School occupied one of the stables which was next to a big room with plank beds. There were only twelve of us and we settled in comfortably. The rations were generous and nourishing. On Saturdays we played at the officer's club of the Tenth Regiment. It was very good to see how, after the humiliations suffered under the French, the Russian officers were admitted to the officers club on an equal basis with their Bulgarian counterparts.

I consider it necessary to explain the situation facing the Bulgarian Army in 1918-1923. The Allied Forces (USA, Great Britain, and France) ordered defeated Bulgaria to reduce the size of its army to forty thousand men, ten thousand of whom were gendarmes who were under the absolute control of Stamboliysky who gathered his support from the Agrarian Party. The infantry, thirty thousand men, were under the command of Tsar Boris and served as frontier guards.

The Christmas of 1921 and the New Year of 1922 approached. We had to play at the Officers' Club on New Year's Eve. I remember that the Bulgarians arranged a lottery. The animals were among the prizes. I won two rabbits, took them to the barracks and put them in a cage under the plank bed. At that point I had to consider how I would care for them. This problem was solved when my neighbor provided me with cabbage leaves.

The new year brought many changes. The Stamboliysky government informed us that the White Russian Army would have to feed itself. Winter was not the best time for implementing such a decision. The ground was covered with snow, and no jobs were available. Some of us cut firewood in the forest or cleared brush lying on the ground in parks and forests. The White Russian veterans carried these products to the city and sold them for pennies. Others took up fishing, but fish were scarce in the mountain river. Everyone was concentrating on new methods for obtaining food until Easter arrived.

On the night before Easter, one of our friends George, a Don cadet, disappeared. Usually we gathered at the barracks at night and shared our experiences, miserable as they might be. The midnight hour had arrived but George was still missing. After midnight, he rushed in, somewhat merry, with two big sacks in his possession. He carefully put them down and invited us to break our Lenten fast. The big sack was full of decorated eggs, while the smaller one contained Easter cakes. We ate the food with pleasure and later asked him where he had found these items. His answer was simple, "At the cemetery...."

Bulgarians, as is the case with Russians, follow the custom of visiting their relatives and close friends' graves on Easter. They place bottles of wine, eggs and Easter cakes at the grave sites. George had "cleaned" the graves of the food which was doomed to be wasted. Inspired by his initial foray, George went back to the cemetery, again returning with full sacks. The Americans were known for producing big and durable sacks.

We ate eggs for more than a week, supplementing them with products purchased with our irregular income derived from temporary work. But we had to develop a more regular source of income. So, five of us (Boris Sevrugoff, two Don cadets, our elderly Cossack and I) went to the villages looking for employment. We reached the village of Ivanovka, near Burgas. Later we found out that they had an epidemic of malaria in that village and in the surrounding territory. Local residents met us with kindness, and we agreed that in summer we would work on their farms for a minimum wage but that they would have to feed us very well. Before the season started, they were to give us on a daily basis one kilogram of bread, a rope of garlic, a bunch of dried peppers and a hundred grams of *brynza (sheep milk cheese)*. We had no better offers and so we agreed to these terms.

At that time the prime minister of Bulgaria, Stamboliysky, declared that Russians were prohibited from relocating; they had to remain where they were from the moment the order was issued. For that reason we could not move to another village, though we heard that they needed farm hands at that village's location. We settled in a tent on the outskirts of the village. We mostly ate garlic, ten heads a day, and modified its pungent, burning attributes with a bit of brynza. Its taste, in addition to the relief it provided from the burning sensation of the garlic, was unique.

So we survived through the month of April and the first half of May. In the middle of May, we started working in the fields. The villagers fed us well. When the spring planting at that location was finished, we went to work for another employer, but for normal pay. The Turks were also hired to provide seasonal agricultural labor there. We were paid at a piece rate, while the Turks were paid by the hour. The five of us produced more bales of hay than thirty Turks.

I should mention that the Allies allowed Bulgaria to have as many as three hundred thousand people assigned to labor brigades (*trudovatsy*). Young men received some military training in these brigades while performing socially useful labor. For example, a railway line to Haskovo was under construction. In addition to members of the brigades, local residents living along the route of the future railroad were ordered to take part in the construction. Everyone had to dig out six cubic meters of earth. However, if a resident did not want to work himself, he could hire a substitute worker. As a result, they needed our labor. We signed contracts, worked well, and received good pay. Thus we had steady employment until winter.

If my memory does not fail me, the Ataman of the Don State Army, General Afrikan Petrovich Bogaevsky, visited us in September of 1922. At that time, our school was located in Yambol. The adjutant ordered me to go to the nearby villages and gather the yunkers and Cossacks who worked there on the farms. I saddled a horse and rode away. There are many vineyards in Bulgaria, and the road was located between the vineyards. Women were working in the rows of grapevines, their kerchiefs adding color to the vines, and you could hear their songs.

I managed to carry out the order and passed the information on to every White Russian I could find. An amazing event happened during my trip. Passing by the women who worked in the vineyards—they were bending while working—my horse (it *was the only horse, a Don pedigree, taken by us from the Crimea)* suddenly stepped to one side and changed its pace to a gallop. I told the adjutant about this phenomena. "Nothing strange here," he answered. "That horse was wounded by a machine gun, and she saw the man who had wounded her in a bent position. Since then, she has been frightened by any person who is in a bent position."

Autumn came. The agricultural tasks were completed. My friends dispersed in different directions. In the middle of November, I received a letter from the Zhdanoff brothers in Stara Zagora. They were on the staff of the Don Army located in this city. The letter said that the bandmaster of the Twelfth Starozagorskaya Balkanskaya *Druzhina*, Captain Kovacheff, was looking for a cornet player. He was very interested in me. In a couple of days I received a letter with an invitation from Captain Kovacheff to join the military orchestra. At that time, I was out of money and even lacked the funds to pay my transportation fee. I needed more time to earn money so that I could get to Stara Zagora. At last I arrived at Captain Kovacheff's office. He treated me kindly and I showed him the invitation. He looked at it and said, "But that was issued two weeks ago. Now I have a cornet player. You did not respond at once, and I could not wait. I am very sorry, but I have no vacancies."

I had only one *stotinka* in my pocket. What was I to do? My friends, the Zhdanoff brothers, went to Sofia to work at a railway depot. I had no more friends in this location. I slowly turned around and went out. "Wait a minute," I heard the captain's voice. "I need a trumpet player." (In Bulgaria, a trumpet resembles a bugle [cornet].) He called a pupil from the orchestra and told him to bring a trumpet. So I was standing in front of the captain with a trumpet in my hands. He opened a book containing the notes of a popular overture with a trumpet solo, and asked me to play. But how was I do it? The silence lasted too long.

He called the pupil again and told him to bring a cornet. "I want to know how well you can play a cornet," he said. The bandmaster opened the book to the notes of a popular Bulgarian dance, and I played it easily. He admired my skill, and told me of his decision. "You stay here. But I need a trumpet player. I will give you a week to learn. You'll sleep here and take your meals at the noncommissioned officers club. Mehmed!" he called the pupil again, "you'll take care of that subofficer (petty officer). His quarters will be behind the classroom. Provide him with a bed, take him to the dining room, and make sure that he gets a meal." Then he addressed me, "If you learn to play a trumpet in a week, I'll give you the salary of a non-commissioned officer with the pay period to begin as of today; then you'll teach Mehmed how to play the instrument."

I was happy. I had been on the edge of disaster, without money or friends, and now I had the prospect of living in a comfortable room and eating decent food. I thanked God for that miraculous gift. I thanked the bandmaster, too. I took the trumpet and went to my room. But it was Saturday, and band members were not allowed to practice on that day.

I would like to amuse my reader with a story of how I learned to play a popular Bulgarian dance tune on a cornet. Our small orchestra, Boris, Vasya, George and I, played several times at a Bulgarian tavern. One of the regulars at the tavern used to sing Bulgarian popular melodies. Vasya Ananyevsky was a very gifted man; he could grasp the essentials of any melody and play it on a baritone horn. Moreover, he could pick up any instrument such as a violin or a clarinet and, miraculously, quickly learn to play it with proficiency. One day there were many people at the tavern. Bulgarians, as well as Turks, like to sit with a cup of fragrant coffee set before them accompanied by a glass of *mastika* (*anis liqueur*).

That night everybody was anxious because the bandit named "Hasko" was reported to be nearby; he attacked markets, grabbed money from the merchants, and then gave it away to the poor. The police had been unable to track him down. Suddenly the tavern became silent—a tall, slender Bulgarian with a kind face arrived, accompanied by five men. He asked us to play Bulgarian music. We played the only piece of music we had in our Bulgarian repertoire, which happened to be called *paidushka*. The guy ordered two portions of *mastika* for us and his friends. Then he suggested that we go to his house to play there. We agreed and left the tavern.

There was a light frost (it was November of 1921), and light snow covered the dark ground. We went through a forest for a long period of time, traveling along an inconspicuous path, and then we reached a large clearing with a house located on it. Here we understood that we were in the hands of the bandit Hasko. He knocked at the door four times and a beautiful, young Bulgarian woman opened the door. Crying, she showed Hasko a deep wound on her neck bleeding through a bandage. Hasko stroked and kissed her. Then he brought out a pail of anis liqueur, and invited us to help ourselves. Next he asked us to play and then he left.

He soon returned, but had something with him; he had a dead tomcat in his hands. He explained to us that the black tomcat had attacked his girlfriend and had left serious wounds on her neck. Hasko killed the cat in revenge. Everyone kept on drinking and singing Bulgarian songs. Sometimes we played the Russian music with which we were familiar. Having drunk a great deal, Hasko decided to bury the tomcat. He went out with a group of his friends and went to a hidden place. Hasko himself dug a pit, put the cat there, and, sitting in a manner that suggested he was bidding someone farewell, he asked us to play Bulgarian melodies. While we were playing, he covered the corpse of the cat with earth and was in a state of deep sorrow. Then he asked us to return to the house and celebrate the cat's memory with another pail of anis liqueur.

At two in the morning, we shyly began to ask Hasko to let us depart. He did not detain us and said, "You are alone and persecuted as we are." His guards led us to the outskirts of the city and we said goodbye, walking swiftly to our barracks. Now when I hear Bulgarian melodies, I am reminded of that memorable night spent with Hasko.

I was looking for a job and finally I found one with a man who sold wine and vodka. The old owner had a granddaughter; all his other relatives had died. In a week he told me that if I performed my work well, he would permit me to marry his granddaughter at which point he would leave his business to us. I should mention that his business was prosperous. Usually the buyers from the nearby Villages came on Thursdays and Fridays, and I had to run to the cellar all the time to bring the next portion. *(The old man kept his goods in the cellar which had a tiny window through which a dim grey light could barely penetrate even on a sunny day).* The owner conducted a wholesale trade; the buyers brought barrels, jars and so on. By the end of the day, I felt intoxicated because I had inhaled the alcohol fumes. Having worked at that location for two week, I said goodbye to the old man and his granddaughter.

So let's return to my musical career developing in Stara Zagora. I decided not to loss my chance and worked daily on *lose* developing a good embouchure for my trumpet. This involved training my lips, as musicians say. On Monday the orchestra arrived. I saw a tuba player, a well-built man of about forty with a light mustache and a military bearing. I asked him in Bulgarian how to play the scale. He kindly demonstrated this skill for me. I grasped all the necessary techniques and played a scale on my trumpet, but a trumpet differs from a cornet. It's difficult to play the note C flat on a trumpet. Communicating with the bass player, I discovered that he was a Russian, a colonel of the Border Service of Imperial Russia. He was a kindly man and an excellent storyteller. I got acquainted with another Russian who held the position of first chair trumpet and who had joined the orchestra three or four months before me. He was a Don Cossack by origin. His name was Misha Polykhin.

I blew in the trumpet for four days and nights. I developed my embouchure and was able to make clear, distinct sounds. The rehearsal was held on Friday. The bandmaster wanted us to learn to play a potpourri of Bulgarian music for the Christmas performance at the Officers Club. I thought that if Misha was the first trumpet player, it would be much easier for me to play behind the cover of his back until I got accustomed to the new instrument. I entered the rehearsal room and suddenly heard the bandmaster's voice, "Why did you come?" I was embarrassed by his question. "But you gave me a week to learn to play. The time is up, and so I came." "Sit down!" he ordered. I sat behind Misha. But Misha took the score for the second trumpet part and gave me the score for the first trumpet—I had no time to argue with him.

The orchestra started playing, and I tried to concentrate on my part but could not produce the correct sounds on every occasion. Besides that, I was embarrassed by the situation that had been created around me. For the first time, I found myself with four clarinets next to me, cornets on the other side, horns croaking in my ear, an oboe squeaking under my nose, tubas roaring to the back of my head, and the tender sound of the baritone horn (mellophone), combined with the celestial sounds of French horns which held their own through all of that chorus. Then I saw an inscription on the score which read solo first trumpet. How did I manage to play and what did I play? I don't remember, but my heart throbbed with joy when the bandmaster stopped the rehearsal and told an elderly musician, "You have tried to play a trumpet for many years and have failed, and he had only a week to learn the skills necessary to play the instrument in a professional manner, and he has succeeded. We could not play that potpourri before because we lacked a competent trumpet player, and now we can perform the music."

The bandmaster told me after the rehearsal, "I admit you to the orchestra. Your salary will be that of a non-commissioned officer of the Bulgarian Army. You are enrolled as of the day of your arrival. You will be able to keep your room and dine at the noncommissioned officers club. Mehmed will be your pupil; he wants to be a musician. He will clean your room, wash your clothes and so on." I could not believe what I was hearing. I obtained not only a good salary, but an orderly.

Good times began. I played my trumpet all day long. Now I could make the most difficult note—C flat. We had many rehearsals and I became so skilled that the bandmaster sent me with other musicians to play in the orchestra of the city gymnasium (secondary school) to make it sound better. The gymnasium paid for that service.

The bandmaster, Captain Kovacheff, had a daughter of seventeen or eighteen years of age. I don't know the reason, but he invited me for dinner a couple of times. His daughter was very kind and an also excellent hostess. She was also an excellent cook. According to an old Bulgarian custom, a man could not meet with a woman on the street. Only a relative could speak to a woman while she was walking outside of the house. Men who were not very good friends of the family could visit with and speak with the woman only in the house of her relatives or close family friends. That's why I could not meet Miss Kovacheff outside her house.

My new life began at Stara Zagora and I could hold up my head like a normal human being. I could hardly remember my half-starved existence in Yambol when I wandered around the barracks in late autumn and dreamed about a piece of bread. Once a little dog, a mongrel, came up to me. I stroked it and gave it a piece of sugar from my pocket; I felt that the dog and I were in the same situation. The dog ate the sugar, and I went to sleep in the stable. Late at night I thought I heard someone coming to the stable, but it was the dog. I stroked it and fell asleep. The next day, the dog was fidgeting around me. At night it ran away. I woke up when it pushed me with its paw.

I opened my eyes and saw that the dog had put down a mutton leg. I remember our evening meal. I washed and boiled the leg, ate it and treated my unexpected benefactor. But I was anxious; according to Bulgarian custom—if a dog stole something, its owner was held to be guilty of the crime and could be vulnerable to mob law and killed. Now, being in the orchestra, I was well off, but deep in my soul I was alone like that dog.

I had to play at many performances arranged by the gymnasium and private organizations. Thus I was able to earn supplementary income. I was fortunate to meet another Russian at Stara Zagora. He worked at a liquor factory and was entitled to receive three bottles of alcoholic beverages in addition to his salary. On a couple of occasions, he brought bottles of alcohol to exchange for food. I received a large amount of food; I ate at the noncommissioned officers club and received my food ration in addition to that.

On the whole, however, the situation for the White Russians was bad. Under pressure from the Soviet Union, Stamboliysky imposed new restrictions on us. These restrictions did not apply to those Russians who were in military service, including me. I remember how we managed to help a Russian captain who could play a clarinet. During the war he had been wounded and captured by the Germans. He had to suffer numerous difficulties, as did all Russian veterans living in exile. I told Captain Kovacheff about him, and he was enrolled in the orchestra. I was already rich by that time and had rented an apartment. I invited my new friend to stay with me.

My apartment included a big room furnished with a couch and bed. As I remember, we went to a restaurant, had a good dinner with a couple of drinks, and went home. I offered him the use of the couch and went to bed. In the morning I was surprised by two things; first, there was a strong smell of anise-flavored vodka in the room, and some vodka had been spilled on the floor. I also noticed that my friend had only one eye. "Don't be surprised," he said, "My eye is here, in the glass of water. I lost it in a battle, and they made me an artificial eye." I should tell you that the eye was made perfectly and looked like a natural one.

The secret of the spilled vodka was simple, too; our friend from the liquor factory came to the apartment before we returned and had brought me three bottles of anise vodka, placing them under the couch. My new friend, not knowing about that, threw his heavy army boots under the couch and broke two bottles. The smell of *mastika* lingered in the apartment for an entire week.

My situation regarding my correspondence with the Zhdanoff brothers can serve as an example of the pressure exerted on us by the Stamboliysky government. Usually a letter from Stara Zagora arrived in Sofia in two days, but my letter was delayed for three weeks; moreover, it had a Moscow postmark on it. So my letter had been forwarded to Moscow and someone had written on the envelope a notation to send it back to Sofia. This was not an exceptional event, and other White Russians noted that their mail had been tampered with. The Bulgarian authorities willingly sent white Russian officers' letters to Moscow. In addition, General Abramoff, General Koutepoff and others were deported. Moreover, police and members of paramilitary units (gendarmes) attacked White Army veterans who were serving in the Bulgarian army which was under the command of Tsar Boris.

It was obvious that Stamboliysky's government was opposed to the monarchy. As I was a petty officer in the Bulgarian army, I never walked alone at night. We always traveled in groups. Once my friend, a Bulgarian officer, and I walked down a street and heard somebody shouting in a lane. We rushed to that location just in time; a friend of ours, who was a musician, had been beaten by two policemen. Having seen us, they left their victim and ran away.

The Bulgarian press published false information about the White Russians. For instance, they published false documents, supposedly signed by General Wrangel, declaring that the white Army would come from Gallipoli to "conquer" Bulgaria, making it a base for launching an invasion of the Soviet Union. The signatures of General Wrangel and General Shatiloff were faked in a highly professional manner. But, as they say, be sure your sins will be found out. The authors of the forged document overlooked one thing; neither General Wrangel nor General Shatiloff had been present at the placed where the "order" supposedly had been signed. The forgery was exposed at a later date but, before the lie was refuted, we felt a strong current of hostility from the Bulgarians whose anger had been aroused by the false document.

On the other hand, Cossacks and White Russian officers were being enticed to return to the U.S.S.R. with the temptation of generous promises. Some could not resist these blandishments and yielded. Their fate was truly tragic. The promises resembled those spread by French propaganda on Lemnos which had extolled the benefits that would come from returning to the Soviet "paradise." The French even employed the ruse of false employment; they announced that they were recruiting workers who were to be employed in Greece. Approximately two thousand men enrolled in this program. However, General Abramoff warned us that there was no lack of workers in Greece and that there was something strange about the recruitment effort.

If someone wanted to leave our camp and "go to Greece," he could move to the refugee camp. From there the French filled the steamship *Rashid-Pasha* with White Russians and departed. Only then was it declared that the ship was sailing to the Soviet Union. Many people jumped into the water and swam back. Of those who returned to the Soviet Union, five hundred were immediately shot when they landed at the port, and the others were sent to concentration camps.

For that reason, the White Russians on Lemnos were reluctant to enroll in schemes that promised work abroad. Many of us already knew the eventual outcome. I might add that, after deportation from Bulgaria, Generals Abramoff, Koutepoff and many others found asylum in friendly Serbia (by this time known as the Kingdom of Yugoslavia).

Stamboliysky's government increased its attack on the Russians and on the Bulgarian infantry controlled by Tsar Boris. I don't want to mention those people who defected to the Bolshevik's from the White camp. They were few in number but caused a lot of harm. They penetrated the organizations of the White Russian veterans and tried to demoralize them by means of deception and provocation, playing off one faction against another. However, the Communist uprisings were suppressed by Bulgarian patriots in 1922 and 1923. Stamboliysky was killed and his assistants escaped to various countries. Life in Bulgaria began to return to normal, though the Reds continued to send their agents, supplied with large sums of money, to undermine the legal governments in the Balkan region.

In the summer, our orchestra, which was part of the Twelfth Balkan Regiment, gave performances in the city parks during the day. After a short intermission (the performance had two parts), the musicians mixed with the public. An elderly Bulgarian approached me a couple of times and asked me how I had managed to enter Bulgaria. I evaded giving an answer, like a diplomat, and tried to ask him innocuous questions in order steer clear of this sensitive issue. I would ask questions such as, "Where is the Valley of the Roses located? How is rose oil made? How do you distinguish between genuine rose oil and the false product?" That man was obviously concealing something. I felt his curiosity differed from that of the ordinary man in the street.

Time was passing. I became a real trumpet player. Probably I played well, because I received a couple of invitations to play in other orchestras accompanied with good pay offers; I was supposed to play at the main rehearsal and performances, and I would have a better salary. But I refused because I had become accustomed to playing in my orchestra. In addition to that, I had made friends with a Russian colonel and Misha Polykhin. The headquarters of the Don Cossack Army was located near Misha's house, and the Cossacks lived in the barracks there. In short, I felt at home in that place.

Once I was coming back after a nourishing dinner at my friend's quarters, a Cossack who made his living selling clothes. He bought comparatively cheap American or English trousers, jackets and underwear, and sold them at a profit. Suddenly I met a Bulgarian who had already approached me in the city garden during our performance. He said he was very interested in Russia and the U.S.S.R. and invited me to visit him. I thanked him but refused to go, saying that I was too busy because of the rehearsal scheduled for later that night.

I arrived at the barracks at seven in the evening. This occurred in the second half of September. Captain Kovacheff and the orchestra's first violinist were already in the barracks occupied with a task. Seeing me, they asked if I wanted "to have a look" at a rifle. I agreed and received a rifle. After that the captain informed us that a Communist uprising was going to begin. "It's better if you would remain here", he told me. Everyone stayed at the barracks. The lights were turned off so as not to make us targets.

At eleven in the evening, the captain suggested that we go to a barracks which was located about half a mile from the musicians' quarters. There was a forest located just behind these buildings. The trees were also between the barracks and the musicians' quarters. The night was not clear as the moon was hiding behind the clouds. We moved cautiously in single file. We saw a shadow, and moved to surround the form. We captured two Bulgarians, dressed in peasant's clothing, and led them to the regimental prison. Then we went to the barracks where the White Russians were living. In one of the barracks the Russians were very excited. At ten in the evening, they had been attacked with rifle fire. A bullet had stuck in a pillar where an icon hung, but none of them had suffered any wounds because the lights were turned off.

The arrested "peasants" had about a quarter million dollars in Greek, Yugoslav, Turkish and Bulgarian currency on their persons. We departed in order to return to our quarters, but the battalion commander stopped us about half-way, ordering us to move to the battalion area and to be ready for anything. We did not sleep. Rifle fire began early in the morning. But nothing special occurred in Stara Zagora, and our detachment was sent to Kazanlyk. There was a fight in progress at that location. After several hours we defeated the Reds and moved on to Nova Zagora.

There we saw that a group of Russian invalids were surrounded by the Communists. The Reds, seeing the approach of a unit from the Bulgarian army, surrendered. We went farther to Plovdiv. The Communists were located in a nearby village which possessed a brewery. The Reds resisted, but the fight was short and they surrendered. We were informed that Plovdiv had been cleared of the Communists as well as the capital, Sofia. We stayed two days in Plovdiv and then returned to our barracks. Heavy fighting had taken place on the banks of the Danube. The anti-Communist forces, both Bulgarian and White Russian, had fought with valor, and Tsar Boris' position was restored.

It was reported that the Danube turned red from the blood of the slain Communists. Everywhere White Russians joined the small Bulgarian army to help crush the common Communist foe. The decisive role the White Russians played in defeating the Communists in Bulgaria entitled them to request that Tsar Boris' government investigate the forgery of General Wrangel's and Shatiloff's signatures and the presence of the underground network of Communists who aimed at subverting the legitimate governments in the Balkans.

Peace was restored, and the attitude of the Bulgarian population and authorities toward the White Russian community improved considerably. On one occasion a captain who played a clarinet, a colonel who played a tuba, and I decided to visit our friends in the city of Pernik where the barracks of Korniloff's men were located. We wanted to entertain them. We traveled to

Pernik on a train, hoping to depart at four in the morning, as indicated on the schedule. A parade was going to be held at ten in the morning, so we wanted to be in place at the barracks at that time. A real celebration took place there, with plenty of food and drink provided. So we played, ate, drank, and missed our train. The distance between Pernik and Stara Zagora was about fifteen kilometers. There was nothing to be done, so we departed on foot.

Soon there was not a trace of our previous joy. "Don't lag behind," the tuba player told me, "or the wolves will eat you." All kidding aside, my puttees continually slipped down and hampered me, and I constantly had to stop and adjust them. I dropped behind my friends, and I don't remember how I ended up in a large shack which had a big stove in the middle of it. I awoke and saw an old man placing firewood in the stove. I could not do anything better than to ask him, "Where is Stara Zagora?" He did not reply. My watch had stopped and I got up and went outside; where was I? What was the time? The barracks were on a hill and I saw city lights about two kilometers away. In some places, the city was illuminated with street lamps. So as it was dark, I knew I had missed the parade and would have many problems.

When I arrived at our barracks, my pupil brought dinner to my former room (sometimes I stayed for the night in the barracks, and my pupil was always ready to serve me). Having eaten, I fell into a deep sleep. I awoke when the orchestra started playing in an adjacent room. When the rehearsal was over, I went to the office to explain the reason for my absence. Captain Kovacheff said that he had to punish me to maintain discipline so that the others would not get the idea that he treated me better than the rest. I had to stay in my room in the barracks for a week and was not allowed to leave my quarters. My pupil was to bring me food from the noncommissioned officers club. I was under house arrest.

Soon our detachment went on maneuvers in the mountains, linking up at that location with other units of the Bulgarian army. In the city of Stanimaka, a big building with a restaurant and a cinema was being built by a tobacco company known as *Asenova Krepost*. The directors of the corporation decided to organize a symphony orchestra of twenty-five to thirty men. Asen Stoyanov, a young Bulgarian who had graduated from the Berlin conservatory and who had been a professional musician for more than ten years, performing both as a flutist and a conductor, was to head the orchestra. He was recruiting musicians, and I received an invitation from him to be a cornet player. I agreed, but in order to leave Stanimaka, I had to be officially dismissed from the Twelfth Regiment. Though I was a civilian musician, I was also a noncommissioned officer and was obliged to observe established military procedures for discharging personnel.

I informed Captain Kovacheff about my invitation to join the symphonic orchestra and asked him to release me from my military obligations. Of course he was against the proposal. We had a long, unpleasant conversation. Finally we decided that I should wait for a week until he found someone to replace me. I spoke to him in a frank manner and he agreed to wait. A week passed, but a substitute had not been found. I told Captain Kovacheff that I would leave in three days. "You may arrest me, it is your right, but you cannot prohibit me from playing in the symphonic orchestra." Kovacheff agreed, and a new trumpet player arrived on the third day.

I put on civilian clothes. It was a warm day, and I waited for the end of the rehearsal to say farewell to everybody. The orchestra was playing in the yard. I again heard the familiar overture with the famous solo for the trumpet. Now I listened for the trumpet solo that started with the infamous C-flat, and the new trumpet player could not play it. The band director was angry, halted the rehearsal, and rushed to the office saying, "I cannot let you go." I replied, "You may arrest me, but I am still leaving. I kept my word. You are an officer, and you must keep yours. I am grateful to you that you admitted me, but there is a time for everything, and now I am leaving." And I left. I thought that he would send soldiers to detain me, but that did not happen. I went to Stanimaka and joined the symphonic orchestra.

Stanimaka was a small town, inhabited mostly by Greeks, situated fifteen to twenty kilometers from Plovdiv. I rented a room in the house of a Greek. The house was constructed in such a way that I could get to the roof of the first floor from my room on the second floor. The flat roof served as a balcony.

I found the conductor, Stoyanov, and asked him about the details of my new employment. The orchestra had just started to be formed and they only had half of the required musicians at that time, but they planned to start functioning as an orchestra in two weeks. The schedule gave us a free day on Monday, while from Tuesday until Friday we had rehearsals from nine to eleven in the

morning. We had to perform at the restaurant from five to seven
in the evening every day. The work was not demanding, and we
had plenty of spare time which I used to work in my landlady's
vineyard and garden. The old woman kept everything in
order—the vegetable garden had been planted, and the vines were
properly trimmed. She worked her land every day with my
assistance. Having noticed my diligence, she suggested that I join
her in a project to breed silkworms and cultivate tobacco. I
agreed, and the terms stipulated that all profits be shared equally.
We also kept chickens in a small coop. Our days were occupied
with numerous chores.

When the Balkans had been occupied by the Turks, the
Bulgarian Tsar Asen escaped to the Volga River and was saved
from capture; however, his sister was captured and placed in a
Turkish harem. The story goes on to relate that she could
correspond with her brother by writing short notes and sending
them tied to a dove's wing. He, in turn, wrote a note and sent it
back using the same dove. Before the Turkish invasion, Tsar
Asen had built a fortress near the Arda river (I hope the name is
correct). The fortress is still there. In memory of the Tsar's
correspondence with his sister, the Bulgarians have a custom of
sending letters in March with small ribbons designed to look like
the national colors, inserted in the envelopes. These ribbons are
known as *martovitsy*. The directors of the tobacco cooperative
called itself The Cooperative Tobacco Society of Asen in memory
of Tsar Asen.

Time passed, and March was approaching. A hint of
spring could be felt. The old woman said that soon we should
start breeding silkworms. It was time to purchase their eggs.
"And how shall we breed the worms from the eggs?" I asked her.

"Very simple," she replied. "I'll wrap the eggs into a
small bundle and then keep it next to my breast. The worms will
soon appear. Then I'll place them on mulberry leaves and they'll
start to feed. After eating, they will fall asleep; then they will
awake and start eating again. Later we'll have to give them large
mulberry branches. During the final stage they become big and
transparent. Falling asleep they wrap themselves into a cocoon."

It was hard work, but it promised to return a good profit.
We bought the eggs, and the old woman wrapped them in a towel
and kept them next to her breast for more than a week. At the end
of the week we unwrapped the towel and saw millions of almost
invisible worms. The leaves of the mulberry trees had appeared

by that time. We gathered young leaves and put them on plank beds together with the worms. They started to grow. During the last stage, we cut off whole branches with leaves and gave them to the gluttonous three-inch worms. They ate with an audible sound, but suddenly it became very quiet; the worms had started to wrap themselves into cocoons.

Our first attempt gave us up to five hundred pounds of silk. It was a silver silk of excellent quality, and we had several pounds of golden silk. We earned some money. The next spring we planted tobacco seeds. When we planted seedlings, our farm occupied an acre. We planted a vegetable garden as well. Generally we worked from dawn until dusk. The work was interesting and not too hard. For example, when the tobacco matured we had to work at night and tear off the first big leaves because this task could only be performed during the cool temperatures of the night. It is difficult to tear off a leaf during the day because it sticks to one's fingers. Besides that, the dew can spoil a leaf. Turkish varieties of tobacco produce very tender leaves. Next we strung the leaves and hung them in the shade. This phase of the operation required us to hire additional labor. We had to work day and night assisted by three or four women. This occurred several times during the tobacco harvest.

Greek houses in Bulgaria use an ancient architectural design and are mainly two-story buildings. Upper floors overhang the ground floor, and over the city streets the upper floors of the opposite houses stand close to each other; sometimes you can stretch out your hand and shake your neighbor's hand. My contacts with the local residents were limited. We exchanged our views only during intermissions at the restaurant. As in other countries, in Bulgaria they have a good custom for greeting the musicians. Once a waiter brought me a glass of wine during a break. He said that some "patrons" had sent me the wine from the table that he indicated. I took it, waved in the direction of that table and took a few sips.

When we finished playing, my "patrons" were still at the restaurant. They included a husband, his wife, and her sister who was a schoolgirl in a grade equivalent to a senior in a United States high school. I spoke to them for a while and left as I had to leave to play at the cinema. One day they invited me to their home. They had prepared an excellent dinner. After that we met several times. Shortly thereafter we developed a friendship that lasted for many years. The schoolgirl, Tsvetana, was very kind to me, but I could only meet her in her house or on the street when she was accompanied by her relatives.

I remember autumn. The ground was covered with a thin layer of snow. Sometimes the snow was mixed with rain. A cold wind was blowing. The actors from the Russian Art Theater came to Plovdiv. They had a dress rehearsal on Monday which, at the same time, was a matinee for the students. My friend, Motya Voznesensky, a clarinet player in the symphonic orchestra, and I decided to go there. We left Stanimaka early in the morning, walked more than fifteen kilometers and arrived in Plovdiv. The performance was over at six in the evening, and we, being very tired, could not return again by foot. We managed to convince the theater director to let us spend the night in the theater, so that we could depart early in the morning. We asked, in advance, to be excused from the rehearsal which was scheduled for Tuesday. The director not only agreed but said he would be glad to listen to a performance of our orchestra.

Motya's brother was a famous doctor from Kiev who had been killed by the Reds at the beginning of the Revolution. Motya, himself, had been an officer in the Imperial Army. During a battle, a bullet pierced his mouth, knocked out his teeth, and stuck in his throat. In that condition he was captured by the Germans. They could not extract the bullet, but made dentures for him.

Once Motya became "a bit tight." The next day we had to play at the Sunday parade. Motya woke and could not find his dentures—he had left them somewhere. It is impossible to play a clarinet without one's teeth, but it was impossible to locate his dentures, and it was difficult to find a dentist. I made a little wooden "saddle" for his lower jaw, so he could produce the embouchure for the clarinet. He played with tears in his eyes. Maybe the thought of his lost dentures made his pain worse. Later a dentist helped Motya.

Our business with the old woman was going well. We sold tobacco, as well as silkworms, but in two years the tobacco market suffered a serious decline and many people quit the business. When I was leaving Bulgaria, there was plenty of unsold tobacco at our warehouse. Ultimately, it had to be written off as a total loss.

While staying in Bulgaria, I tried to find my brother, Peter, and cousin Voloyda. I wrote to the League of Nations (they had a department for tracing lost personnel) and to Russian newspapers in Paris and Czechoslovakia. But there was no news. Once, while walking in the park in Stanimaka, I saw a familiar silhouette. I couldn't believe my eyes; the director of the Platovskaya Gymnasium, Feodor Karpovich Froloff, was standing in front of me. We talked to each other. His son Misha was my brother's friend. At last, we mentioned Misha in our conversation. Where was he? Fortunately, he was alive, thanks be to God, and was living in Poland. But I forgot to say that I was looking for my brother, and did not ask him how he was doing. Then I did not meet Mr. Froloff for several months.

There was a small restaurant in Stanimaka, owned by Colonel Leplinsky. I often went there for dinner. When I came for the first time, all the seats were occupied except one where an elderly man with a stern appearance was seated. The owner told me that he had been a famous professor at the universities of Kiev and Kharkov, Boris N. Bibikoff, and he would go and ask the professor if I might sit down at his table. Boris Nikolayevich agreed, and I sat down. We got into a conversation. I told him about myself, and he told me that he was a chemist and had been a professor of organic chemistry in Russia. On the Christmas and Easter holidays he went to inspect liquor factories. We met several times after that dinner.

Stanimaka is a small town. Once he invited me to his laboratory. He was teaching at the local gymnasium. The laboratory was in a small room on the first floor of the gymnasium. The walls were covered with shelves which held bottles containing liquids and other items such as seeds, blades of grass, etc. "Would you like to taste a chemical?" he asked me. Then he took one of the bottles, two glasses and poured the liquid. "Try it!" I took a sip; it was *pertsovka (pepper vodka)*. Boris Nikolayevich said that there was vodka in all the bottles containing different roots and plants. He was tireless in his experiments. "This is just for us. And that is for the students," he said as he pointed to a number of bottles containing acids.

I made friends with Boris Nikolayevich. Because of my short stature he called me *shpingalet* (bolt) or *karandash* (pencil).

The tobacco business was in decline in Bulgaria, and the tobacco corporation was ruined. The restaurant was closed, as well as the cinema, the orchestra was dissolved. I decided to go to Sofia to be with my friends. I met F. K. Froloff before my departure and promised to send him my new address so that he could mail it to his son in Poland who, in turn, could contact my relatives.

Here I will say a few words about my adventures in the Stanimaka area. They were typical of all cities that I had visited. The Ottoman Empire had stretched far to the north and west, but its territory shrank constantly as a result of wars. The last war in 1877 was especially hard for the Turks who had settled in the Balkan states. The rapid approach of Slavic troops, the capture of Turkish fortresses, and the hasty Ottoman retreat forced the residents to hide their valuables in secret places in the hope that they would eventually return. I, as was the case with many others, tried to find those treasures. Two places were especially promising—big stone troughs which served as watering places for sheep and a huge tree with a hollow which could hide a man. Also, a tunnel in the fortress of Asen, leading to the Arda River, attracted my attention. I got into the hollow tree on many occasions; there was a thick moss buildup to a depth of three or four feet inside.

The police watched all the likely places where treasure could be located; that's why I could not conduct my search openly. I could not throw away the moss because that would have attracted attention; however, I could not reach the bottom of the hollow tree in any other manner. There was also a problem with the tunnel in the fortress of Asen. Many years after I had left Bulgaria I read in a Bulgarian newspaper that in 1970 a shepherd was standing near that prominent tree when, suddenly, a lightning bolt struck and splintered the tree. The shepherd saw golden coins, estimated to be worth two million dollars in today's currency as they were pure gold. The government took ninety percent of the hoard and shepherd was allowed to keep ten percent of their value. And that find was not the only one. There are many such treasure hoards located in Bulgaria, Serbia, Macedonia and Greece. These buried treasure sites are evidence of the tragedies which rapidly overtook many people.

I informed my friends Kostya and Vanya Zhdanoff that I was going to Sofia. My work in Stanimaka was over, the symphonic orchestra had been dismissed, and I accepted, with pleasure, an invitation from the First Regiment in Sofia to join its orchestra. My parting with my old landlady in Stanimaka was very touching. She wanted me to marry her granddaughter, and I should mention that her granddaughter was a very attractive girl, and very diligent and serious besides that. The grandmother had prepared a dowry for her and gave her a donkey as a gift. But I thought that one donkey for her was enough, and she did not need another one. I then said goodbye.

Donkeys are very interesting animals. When I worked in the fields, especially during my first months, I often asked the old woman what time it was. She said, "I don't know; wait until noon." And indeed, exactly at noon all the donkeys in town raised their tails and brayed, always at the same time, in spite of the weather. Their braying is unpleasant, but at least you don't need a watch.

I went to my friends as soon as I came to Sofia. They lived at Krklysayskaya Street, not far from the railway depot. Kostya Zhdanoff was an engineer, while Vanya was a technician. They lived in an excellent apartment owned by the widow of the former mayor of Sofia who had been killed during Stamboliysky's rule. My friends were happy to give me shelter, and I did not worry about food and lodging for some time.

I could easily find a job. They needed musicians, not only in the First Regiment, but also in the Police orchestra *(in many European countries the military orchestra could be configured with or without strings as the occasion demanded).* That's why I did not rush to the Regiment but first went to the office of the Police orchestra.

Conductor Pipko received me well and offered me the position of a trumpet player. I noticed during the audition that he liked me and started to bargain. I said that I could play only on certain days, depending on the schedule of the First and Sixth Regiments which had already offered me a job. He agreed to my conditions, and I became a solo trumpet player giving concerts. Conductor Pipko was a tall, slim old man who resembled our mountaineers. He was eighty years old but appeared very hearty. He told me the story of his life.

In his youth, he led a wild life; he drank, smoked and entertained young women. When he was twenty, he fell ill, was unable to sleep, lost his appetite, and was losing weight and so forth. The doctor examined him and said that if he didn't stop drinking, smoking and "having a good time," he probably would not live for more than six months. Having heard that advice, Pipko went away from the doctor and sat down by a fence, his head swimming with thoughts. He reasoned that if he was doomed to die in a short period of time, he might as well continue to smoke, drink and "entertain" at an even faster pace. "And so I am eighty years old now, and the doctor who did not drink or smoke died many years ago. His son died, too, and I am still alive," he said.

So, I was employed by three different orchestras. Each Sunday, one of the orchestras played at the park. Each Sunday another orchestra played at the officers club. I received from each orchestra the salary of a noncommissioned officer.

Soon I moved to an apartment, which was located in a very convenient location not far from the First Regiment and the police barracks. I attended rehearsals once a week and had plenty of time. Sometimes I joined the chorus of the former Russian Embassy church. I wanted to enter medical school at the University, but I had no certificate from the gymnasium, and here, Feodor Karpovich Froloff, director of the gymnasium named after Count Platoff, came to my aid. I sent him a letter asking him to give me a gymnasium graduation certificate, and also reminded him to write to his son in Poland who might have some news of my brother.

Feodor Karpovich was teaching Greek and Latin in the local gymnasium. I received my certificate in two weeks along with a note that he had written to his son asking him to help me find my brother.

I sent my application to the medical faculty, and was enrolled. The university administration was probably impressed by my rank of *podkhorynzhy (noncommissioned officer of a Bulgarian regiment)*, but it turned out later that I could not stand the sight of cadavers. I fainted during one of the laboratory sessions. It was strange because I had seen hundreds of corpses on the battlefield, but here, on a table in a laboratory, I had some trouble. I withdrew from the medical school and entered the school of business administration at Svobodny University.

Once, coming home from the university, I met my landlady waiting for me at the door. She asked me, "Why did you not tell me that you have relatives?" She was a sweet, elderly lady. She felt genuine sympathy for Russians and hated the Communists. Where did she discover that I had relatives? I did not discuss my personal problems with strangers. "Your relative is worrying about you," she continued. Seeing my surprise, she added, "I am a fortune teller. The cards say that you'll get a letter from him soon." I smiled and soon forgot about our conversation.

More than a month passed. I found new friends and "lost" Kostya Zhdanoff; he went to study in Czechoslovakia to obtain an engineering diploma. He had no visa, but Vanya and I supplied him with money and he crossed the border successfully. After graduation from the Polytechnic Institute in Brno, Kostya moved to France and began to work for the Renault company. While he was studying, Vanya and I sent him money to pay for food and lodging. As soon as he settled in Paris, he invited Vanya to come and join him; the brothers always were inseparable.

I received food rations from the regiments and brought food home. My friends dropped in, took what they liked, and carried it away. At that time, many Bulgarians as well as myself did not know anything about locked doors, nor did we worry about burglars. One day my landlady met me at the door with a big envelope in her hands. She said joyfully, "Oh, I told you! Who wrote you this letter?" I took the letter; it was from my brother. She gave me a letter from Feodor Karpovich, too. It informed me that his son Misha had given my address to my brother. My brother was safe and sound. He was employed as a manager of the estate of Prince Radsivill. I was deeply touched by those letters. My brother wrote about many good things. Honestly, I hoped that I would be able to find him. I had a feeling deep in my soul that he was alive, but I did not hope to meet with Volodya. Indeed, in the second letter from my brother which arrived two days later, he told me about Volodya's death; Volodya had been bayoneted by the Reds.

Peter came to Poland in the following way. The Second Cavalry (Drozdovsky) Regiment was retreating, being a part of the Army of General Bredoff. In Poland, my brother met colonel Mikhail Feodorovich Froloff, his former friend at the gymnasium. The Reds exerted heavy pressure on Poland. Colonel Froloff and my brother organized a Cossack regiment of nine hundred sabers. Then the position of the Reds in the Crimea deteriorated, and the Soviet government hastily signed a peace treaty with Poland which was "advantageous" for Poland. After that the Red forces were transferred from Poland to North Tavria to fight against the troops of General Wrangel.

Poland, in its turn, disarmed the Russian detachments, including the Cossack regiment. My brother received the highest award of the Polish Army, the order of the White Eagle, for his part in fighting against the Reds. But he did not accept the award, because by accepting it he would have to become a citizen of Poland. The fact that he had been considered for the award, however, helped him to make useful acquaintances and contacts such as Prince Radsivill who offered him the position of manager of his estate after the Cossack regiment had been dismissed. My brother wrote me that he wanted to quit, however, and move to Czechoslovakia.

Our correspondence continued during 1924. Then my brother suddenly became silent. In half a year I received a letter posted in Paris as he was working in Alsace-Lorraine with his friends the Panoff brothers. He described the terrible working conditions, such as a lack of safety measures in the mines, life in the barracks without hot water, and the lack of ventilation in the mines where you could smell the pungent fumes after the charges had been detonated. His next letter was from Belgium. He wrote that he had quit the mines, along with many other Russians, and had settled in Brussels where he was allowed to engage in commercial activities. But what would he sell?

Joining with some Russian friends they pooled their money and bought a pig which they fed for eventual sale. They wanted to butcher it and sell it, and even made arrangements with the buyers. Then it came time to kill it. But who would be brave enough to do the deed? They cast lots, and one of the Panoff brothers had to do it. He tied the pig to a tree, took an ax, and struck the head of the poor animal. However, the pig turned its head to one side, and Panoff cut the rope along with a part of the head. The squealing pig rushed down the street before the eyes of a large crowd. The local population was shocked to see a bloody pig and a man with an ax running after it. The police arrested Panoff and confiscated the pig. After this commercial failure, Peter went to Antwerp, hoping to obtain work as a sailor on a ship traveling to Romania. He asked me to help him leave the ship in Burgas and to send him money as well.

I started waiting for the ship from Antwerp. Two months passed, but there was no ship. I managed to settle the question of legally taking Peter from the ship; the Chief of Police of Sofia arranged that. Besides that, I sent money to Peter. The year was 1927, and I was in a sad mood because I knew nothing about my brother's fate. Then my landlady told me my fortune. "The cards show that your brother is in a locked room, but it's not a prison. He worries about you and wants to inform you about himself. You'll get his letter soon." And indeed, soon I received his letter from New Jersey, U.S.A. It was a short note that said, "I am alive and healthy. Soon I'll send you a more detailed letter."

The next letter arrived, and it turned out that the ship did not go to Romania, but had first sailed to London, departed for a voyage to the Belgian Congo, and later sailed for a destination in the United States. My brother wrote about his good impressions of America and about his wish to take me there. He told me that the best way to enter the country was as a student enrolled at a university. For a number of years I had considered going to Munich in Germany, because I had sent my documents to a technical school there, and they informed me that I had been enrolled in their institution. Then I applied for a visa from the German Embassy in Sofia, but the Embassy official had demanded that I would have to deposit thirty thousand German marks, or an equal sum of money in Bulgarian levs, in a bank as a guarantee that I would have the ability to pay for my studies in Germany. I could not come up with such a large sum of money and my plans to study in Germany were thwarted.

My life in Sofia was interesting enough—I liked the customs of the Bulgarian people. I was walking down a street at twilight and suddenly heard a woman's scream coming from a nearby lane. I ran there and saw a girl with a hobo standing near her. The dim light of a street lamp illuminated my police style shoulder straps, and the hobo ran away. I asked the girl where she lived and accompanied her to her house. It was located on the outskirts of Sofia, and we had to walk in the mud until we arrived there. Her mother, brother and sister thanked me and invited me to spend the night at their home saying, "You are always welcome. Our house is your house." A similar thing occurred when I saved a teenager, about sixteen years old, from attack. His tormentors ran away when they saw my uniform. Probably they thought I was armed. The teenager's father treated me kindly and showed me a room. "This is your room. It will always belong to you." This custom of showing gratitude was common with the Cossacks, too. Usually a Cossack had a bungalow and a house in his yard. There was a bench and a table with food in one of the rooms of the house. Anyone could enter it, eat, rest, and depart on his way.

I learned about another interesting Bulgarian custom that takes place on Christmas Eve. Before the first star appears in the sky, the head of the house would go to a place where he could find a homeless person; he would take him to his home and feed him. Then the homeless individual was allowed to sleep in one of the best beds. Of course, these customs existed in Bulgaria before the Bolshevik regime was established.

When I went on maneuvers with my regiment, we passed through Bulgarian villages. There I saw German propaganda posters which depicted a naked Cossack on horseback with a tiger skin draped on his shoulder, holding a wounded baby whose blood was gushing on the Cossack's face. But the local residents, who kept those posters, only laughed at the Germans who were ignorant of the fact the Cossacks had liberated the Bulgarians from Ottoman oppression, that many Cossacks had married Bulgarian women, and that the Cossacks certainly were not man-eaters.

I experienced two earthquakes while I was living in Bulgaria. One of them occurred while I was living in Stanimaka. I was sleeping in my bed and the earthquake happened at night. Part of the house was damaged, but the wall and part of the floor which supported my bed remained untouched. I was alive. The strongest earthquake in Bulgaria occurred in 1927. I lived on the first floor of a two-story house on the outskirts of Sofia, across from the park of Tsar Boris. This took place in spring, as I remember. I awoke, and then I went to the window and opened it. Then I started washing my face and felt that the ceiling was in motion. I jumped out of the window and ran to the road near the garden. At first I acted on intuition, without realizing what was going on. My house sank to one side, and the earth was shaking. Soon everything calmed down. The house was not destroyed because it was a new concrete building.

However, in my memoirs I somehow deviated from the theme of my profession. My professional skills improved and I was invited to play at the Bulgarian opera orchestra because their trumpet player was ill. I remember they rehearsed the opera *Aida* with A. I. Ziloti conducting. Later I found out that he was Russian, a relative of Admiral Ziloti who was once a key staff officer of Imperial Russia's Baltic Fleet.

Once I was greatly surprised. I heard someone knocking at the door, opened it and almost fainted. N. Tsvetana was standing in the doorway. "What happened," I asked. "Nothing," she said, "I want to live with you." She came in, and I explained to her that marriage is not a simple affair, and that she must first get her parents' consent. Besides that, I was not going to get married because, according to Stamboliysky's law, foreigners (including Russians) could not obtain a government job if they married a Bulgarian, and a Bulgarian woman who married a foreigner lost her citizenship. I told her, "You can't stay here; you should go home. You are young and pure; you'll find a good husband. As for me, I am searching for my brother and will join him sooner or later." Tsvetana cried a little, then common sense prevailed, and she went home.

Time passed and I received an application form from Columbia University in the United states, completed it, and sent it back. In two months I received notification about my enrollment. But I was enrolled as a student above the quota. That meant that I had no right to work but only to study. I was informed that a ticket to America would be sent to me, and that the American Consul in Bulgaria must approve my visa.

When the consul found out that I was a professional musician, he gave me my entry visa without further delay, but I had to sign a statement that I would not play for money in any American orchestra. I signed the document, and started preparing to go to America.

Now, reflecting on the past, I remember the friendly, kind relations that existed among the White Army veterans, which united us as one family of fellow exiles. We had one major goal—the renaissance of Russia, its salvation from anarchy and from the destructive forces of Communism. That goal made our hearts beat with one rhythm, directed our thoughts with one aspiration towards our Motherland, and united us with a brothers' love.

In our youth, we retained our hopes for a better future. Those hopes sustained us during the most difficult times. Neither storms on the Black Sea when we were leaving the last inch of our native land, nor "the death camp" at Chilingir, nor the humiliations and ingratitude of our Allies, especially the French who would have sent us back to die in the U.S.S.R. and who first tried to destroy our morale and then tried to destroy the White Russian Army, nor the humiliation heaped on us by our "brother" Stamboliysky, nor the mines and the heavy road work involving tasks such as crushing stones in winter weather, nor hunger and cold—nothing could break the morale of the White Army veterans. On the contrary, our misfortunes made us stronger. We were alive and continued to support the cause of defending Russia, and placing our hopes on its forthcoming renaissance. We trusted our leaders, above all our Commander-in-Chief, General Baron Wrangel, and our faith united us around the pure and sacred White Idea.

I want to say something in the manner of the Russian writer Ivan Bunin and reaffirm his words, "Though the clothes of a White warrior were not always like a mountain snow, may his memory be sacred forever."

Chapter 4
AMERICA

I was in correspondence again with my brother who remained in America as an injured sailor. He helped me to get a place as a foreign student above the quota which restricted the entry of foreigners into the United States. I should mention that Columbia University is one of the few in the United States which admits foreign students in a ratio up to ten percent of its student body. I enclosed with my application my certificate showing that I was a student of Svobodny University in Bulgaria and my certificate of graduation from the Count Platov Gymnasium. Soon I received notification of my enrollment. In a few days I had a ticket on a Greek ship. One question remained unsolved; how was I to obtain the means to sustain myself? I mentioned my brother. After a long hesitation, the Consul gave me a statement to sign that I would not play in a professional orchestra in the United States, and I received my visa in two days. It was easy to obtain Yugoslav and Greek transit visas (I had to go to Athens and embark there).

My packing was quickly accomplished. I practically had nothing. I earned a considerable amount of money by Bulgarian standards, but I spent all my money on friends and on those in need. I gave my cornet and trumpet to my Bulgarian friend. I did not have much in the way of underwear. It was very expensive then, and a worker had to starve for a week in order to buy a pair of socks.

I crossed the Bulgarian border on April 10, 1929. I obtained a room in a hotel in Athens where I became acquainted with a Greek Colonel. He was an educated, well-bred officer. I don't remember what language we used—I think French—but we understood each other well. He hated the Communists as I did. I spent two days in Athens, and on April 13th the ship left Greece.

The ship was not large and had the capacity to carry approximately four hundred passengers. My room could accommodate four people, but there was no bathroom. The food was good, and they even served wine. We stopped in Naples. Somebody, I don't remember who, said, "See Naples and die." I saw it and did not die. Of course, I was in such condition that I could not appreciate the beauty of Naples and its surroundings our next stop was in Portugal where we stayed half a day. In quiet, fresh weather we sailed out into the Atlantic Ocean.

I asked a sailor to prepare a bath for me. He said he could prepare it upstairs on the captain's bridge. Soon the bath was ready, and I went upstairs. I took the bath with great pleasure, but soon the storm began and tossed the ship about. I got out of the bath, put on my clothes, and went downstairs. The waves swept over the dock. A strong storm was approaching, and the captain made a decision to put in at a port. We stayed in port for two days, and moved on to the New World when the storm had passed. We were supposed to arrive at New York, but we docked in Providence, Rhode Island, instead.

I was feeling well, despite the storm, but all the other passengers were seasick. I was the only one who was sitting in the dining room and eating as if nothing had happened. I had been sailing since childhood in a small boat, a *doushegoubka*, in both quiet and stormy weather, and I had become acclimated to movements of a boat. I did not suffer from the pitching and the rolling of the ocean-going vessel.

The Immigration Service had to examine us before we could move without restriction in the United States. Some Romanian Jews who were students were traveling with me. They could not speak English, but the Immigration Service personnel approved their entry. The individuals on the immigration Service panel consisted of four Jews and an elderly woman of English extraction. I learned English on the ship but could not speak it yet. One of the members of the panel asked me if I received a "wire." Probably he meant a "telegram," but then I could not understand what kind of wire he was talking about. I could not answer. They asked me from what part of Russia I originated. I replied, "From the Don." An uproar began. I could not understand anything, but I felt that they wanted to send me back. The American of English extraction spoke to me. She said, "Good, well," and I was led to a "lockup" where those "under question" were held. They provided me with an interpreter, and I managed to send a telegram to my brother informing him that I had been detained and had been sent to the Boston Immigration Center. I had to wait there for two days until my brother obtained my release, through the influence of Columbia University, and I was allowed to stay in the United States. The official reason for my detention was that I could not speak English. Columbia University countered that argument by stating that they had a special department which provided intensive language training and that they were waiting for me at the university. Having received all the papers, I embraced my brother within five hours. So on April 29, 1929, I arrived in the United States.

My brother told me, "Nicholas, you should take off your student cap. Put on a hat. Soon we'll go to the university. You'll have an interpreter, but you need to study English seriously. You'll spend the summer at Bar Harbor, Maine. My friend is looking for a hotel there. You'll help her. You can't officially work and receive a salary, for then you would be deported back to Bulgaria, but you can receive gifts. You figure out the rest—you have gone through the school of hard knocks three years of war, revolution, and wandering around the Balkans."

In two days I went to Columbia University and enrolled for the fall semester in an English language course. I spent two weeks with my brother and went to Maine in the middle of May. But while spending time with my brother, I did not see him much because he was very busy with Cossack affairs, in addition to his work. He was the Ataman of the First All-Cossack Stanitsa, named after General Krasnoff, with headquarters in New York. Once on a Sunday, we went to Long Beach, a resort not far from New York. As we were enjoying the white sand and sharing our impressions and concerns, we did not notice how time was passing by. I wanted to know how Peter came to America.

A Catholic cardinal helped him and his friends *(the Panoff brothers, Sergey Karlash, Nemkin—all of them had been officers in the Drozdovsky Cavalry Regiment)* get on a ship in Antwerp. The ship belonged to a British company. The captain asked Peter if he was a sailor. Peter replied that he was from the

Black Sea. The captain liked his answer very much, for sailors from the Black Sea had a very good reputation. Peter was assigned to be a pilot. He had to stand by the helm and guide the ship. Peter was fluent in many languages—German, French, Polish. He could speak English well enough. The ship went to London instead of Constanta, and then proceeded to sail for the Belgian Congo in Africa. But his service as a pilot ended very soon, just after the ship departed Antwerp. When the captain gave a command, the pilot had to repeat it. And then Peter's poor command of English surfaced.

The captain commanded, "Ten degrees northeast," but Peter thought he said, "ten degrees northwest," so he repeated the erroneous information. Of course, the next words were addressed directly to Peter, "What the hell?" But Peter repeated these words for all the crew to hear. The boatswain and a sailor appeared immediately, led Peter to a separate room, and locked him up there. In an hour, the boatswain led him to the captain, having said that Peter had insulted the captain and must be court-martialed. "But why?" Peter asked. "I only repeated the command; I did not insult anybody."

When the boatswain told the captain about that, he laughed and ordered Peter demoted from the rank of a sailor first class to the lowest rank a seaman could hold. He gave Peter a month to learn how to guide the ship; after that, he could be reinstated. They went to the Congo from London, returned to London, then traveled to Jersey City in the United States. When they were leaving the United States, there was an explosion on board the ship. Several sailors were killed, and Peter was injured. He spent more than a year in the hospital. I remembered a Bulgarian fortune-teller who told me that my brother was in a closed room, but not in a prison, and that he could not write to me.

When my brother finished his story, a short girl approached us and addressed us in Russian. "Excuse me, my mother and I heard you speaking in Russian. May we talk with you?" "Of course," we replied, "invite your mother." An elderly woman approached us. We introduced ourselves. The ladies were from Rostov. Their last name was Lent. "Lent?" asked my brother, "I am very familiar with the Lent ship company in Rostov." "Yes," the elderly woman replied, "that was our family." We told her that we were from North Tavria. "I thought you were from Novocherkassk. I don't like Cossacks," Mrs. Lent said. "Why?" Peter asked. "Your ships carried mostly Cossacks along the Don."

"That is correct, but during the Revolution of 1905 I was standing by the gate of our house one day. A Cossack was passing by. He ordered me to close the gate and stay inside, because it was dangerous to go out. I obeyed, but as soon as he disappeared, I went out; it was very interesting to watch what was going on. I was so carried away by the drama of the events that I did not notice that the Cossack who inspected the block had returned. He ordered me to get out of the way again. That happened several times. Then a skirmish started nearby. I went out to watch it. The Cossack came up, shouted at me, and lashed me with a whip. I went home and did not appear after that."

"So you hate Cossacks because one of them saved your life," Peter said, "and what about a stray bullet which could have killed you?" "Yes, but he had no right to strike me." It was senseless to continue that conversation; many people did not learn anything from their life experiences.

In a couple of days I went to Maine. I became acquainted with two Swedish girls who were swimmers, at the hotel where my brother found a job for me as a helper. I used to swim with them from one island to another. It was very interesting. I collected gifts worth about five hundred dollars. I had to do all kinds of work such as washing dishes, mopping floors, carrying luggage, covering and cleaning tables, and so on. The clients were rich and generous. When I returned to New York, my brother recommended that I deposit my money in a bank. Then I went to the university.

I was enrolled in an introductory course in the English language. I promised the administrator that I would bring the money on Monday (I had spoken to him Friday as I recall). But when I came to the bank on Monday, I saw a raging crowd in front of it. The bank had gone bankrupt, and I was left penniless. It was a surprise to me that banks in the U.S. were private and not state-owned. My brother did not know about that either. That year was full of reports of financial disasters in the U.S. With great difficulty, I managed to come up with enough money with the help of my brother's friends, sufficient to pay for half of the course. But how could I pay in the future? How could I pay off my debts? It was practically impossible to find a job. The millionaires of yesterday had become paupers. What could I do?

I received a special card from the administration, ordering me to meet with a special advisor and to report to him about my progress. I received my class schedule as well.

On the scheduled hour, I came to the classroom. The door was closed. I waited for fifteen minutes and knocked on the door. When it opened, I saw an auditorium full of people. The female professor was already sitting behind the table. I gave her my registration card. She invited me to sit down, but I did not understand her. Then she stood up, pointed to herself and said slowly, "Mrs. Troop. Sit down," and she sat down. I repeated her words as if I were a parrot, "Missy Feodoroff, sit down," and I sat down too. The entire audience was observing this performance with interest.

The lecture lasted for two hours, until nine at night. A woman approached me after the lecture and started to speak to me in English. Then, noting that I could not understand a single word of her conversation, she addressed me in German. I had forgotten the German I had learned as a student in the gymnasium, but I still managed to understand the ideas she was trying to convey; she was offering to help me learn English.

I was enrolled in a remedial English course designed to help those students who already knew English and just needed to improve their pronunciation and their skills in forming sentences. Miss Hilda Geshilda, for that was the name of my tutor, arrived at the lecture hall at six in the evening, an hour before the beginning of class, to help me improve my English language skills. By the end of the second week, we both determined from what part of Europe we had originated, and Miss Geshilda was very surprised that I was a Cossack.

"It's terrible!," she exclaimed. I could not understand what she was talking about. In two or three weeks she explained the situation when she told me, "You are not a Cossack. You are a cultured and intelligent gentleman; that's why you can't be a Cossack." Her opinion about Cossacks was formed in Germany where she had been influenced by propaganda posters similar to those I had seen in Bulgaria which portrayed a naked Cossack on horseback, eating a baby. I enthusiastically presented her with a favorable description of the Cossacks, and soon we understood each other.

However, I was not able to speak English fluently, despite my studies. I had no opportunity to practice conversational English, for seventy-five percent of my course work was devoted

A COSSACK GALLOPED FAR AWAY   113

to learning the rules of grammar, with the remaining course time
devoted to suggestions for improving pronunciation. But I could
not understand spoken English, and listening to the rules of
grammar was a waste of time for me. Besides that, I was listening
to English speech for only six hours a week; the rest of the time I
was immersed in Russian speech.

Then I decided to go to nearby churches where I listened
to the well-delivered sermons of the priests and ministers. But
this did not help me improve my spoken English either. In any
case, I managed to complete two semesters with difficulty. The
summer of 1931 arrived. The administration asked me which
subjects I wished to study. I wanted to study engineering, but I
was sent to a number of professors for consultation.

Professor Mosley, the famous historian, was the first
faculty member I consulted. I spoke to him with the aid of an
interpreter. He was satisfied with my knowledge of the history of
Europe, Russia and America. He said that if I wanted to
specialize in history, I had to select a topic approved by two
history professors and then, maybe, I could receive a Master's
Degree the following year. He wrote in the advisor's report that I
had interesting life experiences which I should write about at a
later date.

I next met with a physics professor. He wrote that I had a
vague knowledge of physics, and recommended that I enroll in the
second semester of the introductory physics course.

I consulted with a professor of mathematics as well. He
gave me an algebra problem to solve. I started to consider the
relationship of a with b and c, but I had completely forgotten my
algebra. After a short conversation he recommended that I
register for algebra and trigonometry classes.

I brought all the cards with my recommendations to the
administration. The head of administration asked me which major
I wished to declare. I replied that I had chosen civil engineering.
He smiled and said, "You don't know anything about the field of
civil engineering." I argued that I wished to work at construction
sites. "But ninety-nine percent of the engineers in the United
States work in offices, and only one percent work at construction
sites," he said. I was resolutely determined to carry out my plan,
however.

I registered for classes in physics during the short summer
semester. Frank Knox, an American of Scottish origin, was
among the students. We quickly developed a friendship and, as

Frank worked as a foreman at a construction site, he recommended me to the project engineer. But I did not possess the right to officially hold a job so I received a dollar a day as a "gift." I worked three days a week. On the other days I went to my physics classes at the university. I thoroughly studied construction terminology.

Summer passed by quickly. The fall semester arrived, and I registered for analytic algebra and trigonometry classes. My English was still very limited, but already I knew a few words. Trigonometry was easy for me. The next semester in the spring, I took a topography course. It was an evening course taught by Professor William Krefeld. His speech was so rapid that it could be compared with a machine gun. I could not understand anything he said. I was sweating because I was very nervous. The lecture was completed, and all the students left, but I continued to sit in the lecture hall. Professor Krefeld approached and spoke to me. I could not understand what he was saying, but, looking into his eyes, I saw that he wanted to assist me. I could only answer "yes" or "no" without being able to be sure if my responses were appropriate or not. He wished me all the best and I went home. The English language remained my main difficulty. It was a real torture for me to read my lecture notes or textbooks, but the designs and illustrations helped me. I managed to pass that course.

In summary, I decided to take a course in conversational English. I had no money to pay for it so I went to the nearby hospital and asked for a job. I told the woman on duty, "Please call your supervisor and tell him that a Columbia University student, a Mr. Feodoroff, wants to discuss an important matter with him." The receptionist called the chief physician and he agreed to see me. I went to his office and introduced myself. I said that I had no money to pay for my classes, and I needed a job. He listened to my poor speech and shook his head. "Unfortunately, there is no job available for you at this hospital." I left with my head down. But in three days I returned and said to the woman at the reception desk that I was a Bulgarian student and would like to see the administrator and that I had an important matter to discuss with him.

Once again I asked for employment, and once again he rejected my request. In a week I returned and introduced myself as a Russian student. The chief physician received me, probably out of curiosity. He said, "You say that you are a student at

Columbia University, that you are a Bulgarian, and now you say that you are a Russian student." I replied, "Yes. I am enrolled at Columbia University, I was formerly a student at a Bulgarian university, and I am a Russian." The physician said, "Well, wait a minute." He called the head of food service for the hospital.

A tall, slender woman, dressed in a dark skirt, appeared. She reminded me of a typical teacher at the Mariinsky Donskoy Institute. To make the resemblance even more accurate, Mrs. Lee was holding a lorgnette in her hand, bringing it to her eyes from time to time. The physician told her that Mr. Feodoroff, a student at Columbia University, was looking for a job. "Oh!" she said. "We need a cook in the kitchen. It is now summer, and our cooks go on vacation one after another. We need a person who can work for twelve weeks." We went to the kitchen. The chef introduced me to the cooks and helpers and explained my duties to me. They were very polite because they thought I was a protégé of the chief physician.

My first task was to chop onions. I carried onions in a pot from one corner of the room to the other and started to chop them. Tears were streaming down my face. I had chopped about a hundred pounds; then, with my eyes full of tears and half-blind, I began to put the chopped onions into the pot, and, of course, I dropped part of them on the floor. I picked them up, put them in the pot, and returned to the chef. He said that I would be the "head cook" on the serving line in the cafeteria where the hospital employees ate. I would have two helpers, and we'd have to distribute two thousand portions. I had to cook pancakes for the first breakfast that I prepared. The dough was already prepared, but we had to cook the pancakes ourselves on the cafeteria serving line.

On my first day I became acquainted with the system of "self-help" which existed in the kitchen. When the work was finished, I received a big bag of food from the chef. I understood that the food was taken from the kitchen "unofficially." I refused the offer and said that I did not deserve to be "rewarded." The chef nodded indicating that he understood, we went outside, and he gave me a bag. I was very confused, but I knew that if I did not take it this meant that I would not be accepted as part of the chef's crew. So I took the bag thinking that no one could accuse me of stealing the hospital products if I received them in the street, not the kitchen.

The bag contained a pound of butter, two large smoked sausages, three pounds of ham, and a dozen eggs. Those items of food proved most useful, since my brother and his friends were unemployed. When my brother learned that I was a cook, he was amazed. "How can you be a cook if you don't know how to boil an egg?" I said that I was responsible for the serving line, not for cooking the food. I had to distribute pancakes next morning. To make sure that I would succeed in performing this task, I asked my brother to describe how pancakes are made.

I went to bed early. My agitation did not leave me, and I got up at five that morning to go to the hospital. I found a kitchen worker and asked him if he knew how to make pancakes, but he did not know the technique. I had to make the dough. He helped me to open the pantry where I removed eggs, flour, milk, salt and pepper. Using a mechanical mixing machine, I made sufficient dough for a thousand people. I sent it upstairs to the cafeteria where my assistants met me. They showed me a flat, cast-iron grill with holes in it, but it was impossible for me to use it to prepare the pancakes. However, my assistants, who were Puerto Ricans, said that the former cook could make excellent pancakes using that grill. There was nothing for me to do but to turn on the grill.

When it was hot I poured the dough on it in small portions. When I tried to turn the pancakes over, I found that I had been right to make my gloomy predictions they stuck to the grill. I told my assistant to go to the kitchen and obtain two thousand boiled eggs as there was no hope for cooking the pancakes in time. I threw away two barrels of unsuitable pancakes. Only four of them, more or less, looked acceptable. I solemnly put them on a plate as an example of the art of cooking. Mrs. Lee came to the kitchen, and we greeted each other politely. "Is everything all right?" she asked. "Yes. The breakfast has been served," I answered, having cast a severe glance at my assistants so they would not mention anything About the disaster I had with the pancakes. "May I taste them?" Mrs. Lee asked, seeing the dish of pancakes. I gave her a pancake, she took a bite, and made a wry face. "They are well baked, but there is something burning."

"These are Russian pancakes, Madam." I quickly came up with an additional explanation, "There is pepper in the dough, and it produces a warming effect." Mrs. Lee said that the pancakes were very original. So the ordeal of breakfast was over.

Lunch and dinner presented no difficulties for me, because I just served the cooked dishes. My working days passed uneventfully, and every day the chef gave me a bag of food. At first I opposed the practice, but my protests became weaker with each day, and soon I was waiting with anticipation for the next bag.

On the whole, I was amazed by the scale of the pilfering. When, for example, chicken was delivered, not only kitchen workers, but elevator operators, janitors, laundry workers, furnace maintenance men and other workers scurried to the kitchen to receive "gifts." Later I learned that the chef and the head of food services received twenty percent of all the food products that were purchased. But it was not actual theft as the suppliers themselves sent extra products, so their competitors would not undersell them and gain an advantage with such a lucrative customer as the hospital.

Summer brought success as I earned enough money to pay for the summer semester as well as half of the fall semester. One of the subjects I was scheduled to take during the fall semester was entitled "The Resistance of Construction Materials." It was taught, of course, by Professor William Krefeld. As a rule, the students gave their registration cards to the professor to give him an opportunity to get to know them. Having seen my name, the professor asked me to stay after the lecture had been presented. "I'm glad to see you, Mr. Feodoroff," he said. "Do you remember what I told you last year? Don't live among your own people. Attempt to communicate with Americans and speak English. How is your English now?"

My English language skills had improved. Before, when reading a book, I had to consult a dictionary to determine the meaning of each word, and now I could understand the content of a text four times faster. But I was far from having achieved perfection. I told him that I had not been able to understand anything in his lecture. "But you answered 'yes' and 'no,' and the responses were appropriate for the questions. How could you reply if you did not understand the questions?" "I could sense from the look in your eyes that you had given me good advice," I said. "My instincts told me that you wished me well." The professor once again wished me all the best and left. I should add that I successfully passed the course on "The Resistance of Construction Materials."

The economic conditions from 1929 to 1937 were terrible. Tens of thousands of people lived in poverty with the onset of the Depression in the United States. About thirty thousand lawyers lost their job in New York alone. Tenants had no money to pay their rent. Entire city blocks were uninhabited, and, at the same time, many people were forced to live on the streets, in the parks, in slums with huts made from empty barrels, cans, boxes. Hot soup was distributed in the streets, and it was the only meal for many thousands of people.

I often went to the Columbia University library. I became acquainted with a young lady and could practice my English with her. She was a professor of literature at Yale University and was a Shakespearean expert. I obtained a great deal of useful information from her. The library closed at eleven at night, and I used to stay there until the last minute. Once, on a rainy night, I crossed a street near a bar. A big man was standing on the corner. He called to me, "Give me a dollar!" I pondered the situation and offered him my books, "I have no money. Take my books and sell them." I was illuminated by a street-lamp; I had a torn shoe with a white sock protruding from it, and a crumpled hat.

The man look at me and said, "You are a poor guy, and you must be a nice one. Come to the bar with me; it's my treat." He ordered two beers and took a handful of coins out of his pocket. He tried to give me a five dollar bill and repeated that I was a nice guy, and if I was in need, I should come to him and he would give me money. I refused to take the money. I met that peculiar hobo almost every day over a period of many years, and we developed a certain degree of friendship. I might add that he was Irish.

I worked part of the summer of 1933 transporting books from the old library to the spacious, newly-constructed library building. During the rest of the summer I had to practice land surveying techniques and prepare topographic reports. My practice surveying took place at a student camp for engineers which was located in Connecticut.

The spring semester ended well thanks to the support I received from Professor Krefeld. He was the head of the construction and testing laboratories. At that time Columbia University, as was the case with many other colleges, was conducting research on and testing various types of building materials. This was being done in connection with lawsuits initiated by contractors, not only from the United States but other countries as well. Professor Krefeld needed an assistant, and he selected me, thus allowing me to earn some money to pay for my education.

The students of the civil engineering and mining faculties had benefited from having two months of practice at the summer camp. I had a four-week break before the practice session started. I spent this period working at a boardinghouse, preparing it for the vacation season. The boardinghouse was located on the shore of a bay where amateur fishermen spent their holiday. Once, early in the morning, I was still in bed when I heard a heartbreaking scream originating from the bay. I ran outside in my underwear and saw a boat which had held two men and which had capsized not far from shore. The men had swallowed a good deal of salty water at this point.

Without hesitating, I jumped into the water, grabbed one of them, and pulled him to the shore, telling the other man to hang onto the capsized boat. When I reached the shore, a crowd had already gathered. They helped me drag the man up on the shore. I was tired and happy to have an opportunity to catch my breath. People came over to me, shook my hand and spoke to me. That episode won me the favor of my neighbors at the boardinghouse.

Soon my work was finished, and I went to the student camp. It was the first summer I had spent in the company of Americans. I had to speak English exclusively, and it was my first opportunity to be immersed in a setting where only English was spoken.

The summer camp was equipped with barracks which had small rooms, each designed to accommodate two students. The rooms were equipped with two beds and possessed a large table in the middle where we could prepare the maps. The course was designed in such a way that the students were divided into several groups of four, each with its assigned task. I shared a room with Dan Lomb, the great-grandson of the inventor of large telescopes, cameras, and other optical products. He was a millionaire, and his driver delivered three trunks containing nothing but underwear.

We conversed after dinner; Dan was a quiet, calm sort of guy. He had two sisters, a mother, father and a grandmother who was about a hundred years old. He was a Bavarian German by origin. His father and grandfather were both physicists. His grandfather had graduated from a university in Germany and had come to America where he established a company "Bosch & Lomb." His partner was also a German. Dan's father had a big library containing many books on physics, and some of the books had been published in the 18th and 19th centuries. That valuable library was donated to Columbia university. We talked until it was late. At last, we decided to go to bed. I watched with interest as Dan searched his trunks for a pair of pajamas; I counted a dozen pair.

Many rich people studied at Columbia University. Columbia is a world-class educational institution, and the tuition there is four or five times greater than at an average American university. Columbia is a private university and is maintained by donations from private individuals and organizations. Each professor in the engineering or science departments has no more than ten students. The tuition fee covers only one-third of the expenses incurred by the university; however, private contributions and endowments cover the shortfall. Other universities, as a rule, operate from funds derived from student tuition payments; that is why their student/faculty ratios range from thirty-to-one to as high as fifty-to-one.

After long deliberation, Dan selected his pajamas, pushed the rest in the trunk, turned off the light, and went to bed.

You were required to be up by six in the morning, with breakfast scheduled for seven, and instruction set for eight. After that, each group was taken to a field site where they could practice what they learned in the classroom. We were provided with box lunches and could work until five in the afternoon. Then the automobiles arrived and drove us back to camp. Dinner was served at six. Classes were held every day except Sunday. In the evening, the students made their calculations, completed their drawings and prepared their reports. We worked until two or three in the morning. I was fortunate; my group was very diligent. Dan and another student, Irving Gould, had a knowledge of engineering, and we were the first to finish our daily tasks, drawings and reports.

George Osterberg, a Swede born in America, was the fourth member of our group. It was the first time that he had ever spent his summer away from his family, and he cried for the first few days. After he had overcome his homesickness, he looked back on that period of his life and laughed. I made friends with Dan and George, but it was not as easy to make friends with Irving. He liked to tease me and ask me ambivalent questions. I did not reply, and this enraged him. In the area of English vocabulary he asked me with malice, "Why don't you repeat after me, but you repeat after Dan teaches you a word?" I felt that he tried to teach me obscene words and phrases, and I did not repeat his "lessons." He was a childish boy.

George understood that I was a musician and told the dean of the faculty, professor Finch, about my talents. One day the dean asked me if I could play a trumpet, and I said that I could. "Could you play reveille on the trumpet to wake the students, and then could you play your trumpet to summon them to breakfast?" "Sure, why not?" I replied. The camp supply administrator brought a trumpet (it was a military bugle), and I played reveille, then the signal that breakfast was ready. The dean was delighted, and I became the bugler for the camp.

Fraternities are very popular in American universities. Some of them are organized just to provide recreation, but others were organized for scientific purposes. In order to be enrolled in the fraternity, one had to do errands for one of "the seniors." One day I returned after completing the experiments in the field and saw half of my bed sticking out of the window. I had to work hard to return it to its proper place. On another occasion, when I had gone to bed, the end suddenly tipped up, and the room turned into a "battlefield"; a practical joker had put a dozen Chinese firecrackers under my bed. But I had gotten use to explosions, and these Chinese firecrackers did not harm me.

On Sunday after breakfast, all of us went outside on the lawn, and Arwink started to tease me. "Irving," I said to him, "Want to wrestle?" He agreed saying, "I'll show you, Russian, how I will pin you on your back; I'll throw you." But it was he who was thrown by me in a short period of time. This infuriated him even more. But everybody liked the idea of wrestling, and soon we entertained ourselves.

Once the dean came up to me and said, "Your name is too difficult for an American to pronounce. May I call you by your first name, Nicholas or Nick?" I understood that I had been accepted as an American. Our practice session had been successfully completed, and the fall semester started in September. One of the first lectures was in the field of hydraulics. It was delivered by the dean, Professor Finch. But before the lecture started, George asked to be permitted to read aloud an interesting article from a newspaper. It dealt with my "heroic deed" in saving the drowning men near Amityville, Long Island. I knew nothing about the article, and George kept it secret from me. And now, in the presence of the students, he read it. On the one hand, I was feeling somewhat awkward; on the other hand, the Americans became even more sympathetic towards me.

I got an opportunity work as an "apprentice" on a construction site, again receiving one dollar as a "gift." Our foreman had a sister. She was studying at the Faculty of Arts at the university, waiting for her Master's Degree. She was having problems in school, especially in trigonometry, and the foreman asked me to help her. *(She was a middle school teacher. In order to be promoted, she needed, in addition to her length of service, good recommendations and an extra diploma.)* I solved problems, made clear drawings, and wrote explanations. As for her, she received excellent grades and was released from having to take the final examination due to the excellent grades she had received during the semester. One day when I arrived home, I found an envelope containing twenty dollars and a short note which said, "Thank you. My sister received her Master of Arts diploma." I had agreed to help that woman without pay, but if her brother sent money. The money proved to be of great help to both Peter and me at that time. Sometimes it occurred to me that I could receive a Masters Degree as well.

Once, at the end of November, the dean called me along with some other students to his office and said that the owner of a large estate near New York City wanted to divide his property. It would be good practice for us to do this task. We could do the land surveying work only on Sunday. I was wearing a very "light" coat, but I was not the only one shivering. Tom Quilt, the senior student, was shivering too. I convinced him to go to a barn, where some hay was stoked. He appointed another man to be in charge in his place. I covered him with my coat, and returned to continue surveying the land.

On Monday, Tom came to class. He was very pale but healthy, and thanked me for the loan of the coat and for my care of him. In two days I received a letter from Professor Quilt (his father was a professor at New York University) to come for a family dinner. I agreed with pleasure, for this would be the first occasion I had to dine in an American home. The Quilts were Scottish in origin but had lived in the United States for many generations. The dinner was truly sumptuous with excellent wine, superb steaks and marvelous appetizers. I believe that this was the first formal dinner I had attended since the events of 1917. Tom's sister was a teacher, her husband an instructor of mathematics at Manhattan College. We later became good friends. My relations with Americans were friendly. Only Irving treated me as if I were a leper. The winter semester of 1933 went smoothly, and, again, I prepared for the summer engineering camp. As I have mentioned, I arrived in the United States as the Great Depression was beginning. *Asenova Krepost*, the Bulgarian tobacco company, asked me to market their tobacco in the United States. I was interested in this offer, because I had eighty thousand pounds of tobacco grown by me and the old woman, my landlady, stored in the company warehouse. In the autumn of 1933, I went to the School of Commerce and Administration at Columbia University. At the entrance I encountered a middle-aged gentleman, and, quite unintentionally, said "hello" in Russian. He stared at me in surprise. "How do you know that I am Russian?" "Maybe by your gait," I replied, not being able to come up with a better answer. "My name is Kushnareff. Glad to meet you," he said as he introduced himself. "Kushnareff? By chance, are you related to the owners of the tobacco company of Asmoleff and Kushnareff in Rostov." "I am the son of Kushnareff, the owner of the company. I am graduating and receiving my degree soon. Why are we standing here? Let's get a cup of coffee." He noticed my embarrassment. "Don't worry, it's my treat. I am working as an accountant's assistant in a big steamship company here."

We went to the cafeteria where breakfast was being served, and he offered me a snack. He ordered Irish stew for both of us and related the following account of his life. When he left his ship in Boston, Massachusetts, he had no idea where to go or what to do. He went down the street with his head lowered. He was hungry, and he was looking for a cheap hotel. His father's accounts in Europe were frozen. He received a small sum of money from his mother which proved just sufficient to permit him to travel to America. Suddenly, someone called to him. A man ran out from a store, rushed up to him, embraced him, and pulled him into the store, repeating his name. He was surprised, but followed. It turned out that the store owner was a Jew who had worked for his father in Rostov. The Jew gave him five hundred dollars and recalled sadly how nice life had been in Rostov. Then Kushnareff asked me about myself. "I am from Novocherkassk. My godmother, Sofia Kapustianskaya, was a merchant. She sold fabrics in Rostov. She had stores at the railway stations near Rostov as well. She had no children; she and her husband had saved money to pay for my education at the university," I told him. Kushnareff returned to his problems. "I thought that my father's connections with the tobacco giant Philip Morris would help me establish myself in America and, indeed, it has helped find a job. The owner of the Philip Morris Company took me to the chemical laboratories of his enterprise. There I saw for the first time in my life that many chemicals were added to American tobacco. He disclosed another detail—about fifty percent of the contents of the cigarettes were herbs, not tobacco. This had taken place because of the difficulties in obtaining tobacco from Turkey, a place which had formerly sent much of its tobacco crop to the United States. Because of the interruption in tobacco shipments from that country, Philip Morris had to develop a formula which involved adding domestic herbs. He suggested that he would pay for my tuition until I could stand on my own feet. He gave me a good recommendation when I applied for work at a steamship company, where I am currently employed."

Then he asked me with concern, "And how are you?" I said that I was penniless, but managed to get by. "Sometimes I work at the restaurant at night. There is plenty of food, and I bring home a big sandwich which I share with my friend, a student from Armenia. But it's not so bad. Anyhow, it could be worse. Your story about tobacco has dampened my enthusiasm for searching for buyers of Bulgarian tobacco. I now understood that American companies prefer to use chemicals instead of natural tobacco."

Having abandoned my hope of marketing tobacco in America, I also lost my hope of selling silk thread *(a Bulgarian company, which bought silkworm cocoons, also asked to find potential buyers)*. I contacted an American company, but they answered that at that time they imported light silk into America, not heavy Italian silk. Unfortunately, the heavy variety of silk was grown in Bulgaria. The main suppliers of silk in the 1920s were Japan and China.

Professor Krefeld was instructed to investigate the causes of the failure of a dam at River X. Our laboratory received two pieces of concrete from the dam, each weighing about a ton. We had to examine the quality, contents, and properties of each ingredient. The professor told me that I would receive the salary of a regular student for my work. The task took several months to complete. I devoted my spare time to the project.

A student, Mr. Appelbaum from the Massachusetts Institute of Technology, had transferred to our university. He had received excellent grades, and was considered to be a very promising student. His father was the second violinist of the New York Symphony Orchestra. But he completely ran out of luck at Columbia University. He failed three subjects during the first half of the semester and was going to be expelled. Professor Krefeld asked me to talk to Appelbaum about the critical nature of his situation, and he did not want other students to know about this matter or to discuss it.

Appelbaum took my warning in the proper spirit, and said, "I can't understand how I could fail my mid-term exams. Maybe, I'll have to change my behavior." As I have mentioned, there are many organizations and fraternities at American universities which often help students cram for exams. Appelbaum had been a member of such a group in Massachusetts. Having a good memory, he could quickly comprehend the practice examination questions which had been maintained in the archives of the fraternity, and he successfully passed the examinations. Having failed as a new student to become a member of a fraternity, he did not have access to the practice exams and failed. However, after our conversation he started to systematically study and finished the semester with decent grades. He and his father invited me for dinner.

The analyses of the concrete has lasted for a long time, but by the spring of 1934 the laboratory responsible for studying the elasticity of structural materials and received a contract to analyze the poles and planks made from various kinds of wood in order to determine their suitability for use as construction materials, as well as the degree to which they could be considered fireproof. I took part in this project and, as a result, I could pay for my education. In addition, I could make better contact with my professors.

I remember an interesting job involving the testing and analyzing of soil conditions at Flushing Meadows, New York, designated as the site of the World's Fair. The soil was clay, about twenty-five meters (eighty feet) thick, and once it had been part of a swamp. The contractors had decided to compact the soil of this area. They dug a network of channels approximately two-thirds of a meter in depth, and then they started to fill in the ground between the channels. They brought in earth and dispersed it. They put truckloads of earth in heaps and wanted to spread it evenly. But the heaps of earth settled, for the particles of clay separated and absorbed those piles. The contractors lost hundreds of thousands of dollars.

Then they contacted Professor David Burmeister of the School of Engineering at Columbia University. For many months, under his direction, I analyzed the clay from that property and the professor made recommendations to the contractors as to how they could create a viable construction project at that location.

By the way, an excellent method for compacting swampy land was developed in Russia during the period when St. Petersburg was built. The famous Isaakievsky Cathedral, like many other buildings in our country, was built on piles. Of course, it was a very expensive process, and it took a long time to complete the project which employed thousands of workers.

A minor event took place in 1934. President Roosevelt recognized the U.S.S.R., and a group of Soviet engineers arrived in America to inspect our universities, including the private laboratories devoted to testing and developing construction materials. They were especially interested in obtaining studies involving the resistance of construction materials to conditions involving expansion and compression. In addition, they wanted to copy the plans of the construction machinery, having as their goal the duplication of this machinery in factories in the U.S.S.R. A Soviet group came to Columbia University, and each specialist had two "interpreters." But those "interpreters" acted in a very strange manner; they could barely speak English, and Professor Bayer asked me to translate his comments into Russian so as not to waste time by getting involved with these so-called "interpreters."

At that time, Columbia University had the largest compression machine designed to test materials. The explanations were well received. The Soviet engineers (half of them were Jews) made drafts, and each of them studied his part. Then one of them asked to be put in contact with the School of Mining and Engineering. I promised to introduce him to Professor K., and told him that he would have to talk to him using an interpreter. I made a phone call to Professor K. and asked the Soviet engineer to take the receiver. But he waved his hands saying, "Please translate my request." I answered, "You have two

interpreters or should I say 'minders.' Let them translate." The
Soviet engineer suddenly became angry. "I order you to translate.
I have the rank of a People's Scientist of the Soviet Union." "And
I am a combat veteran of the White Army," I answered calmly,
"and I am not under you command." I put the receiver on the
table and left the room. I don't know what his conversation with
Professor K. was like. But when he next saw me, "the People's
Scientist" said goodbye to me politely, and invited me to visit the
Soviet Union.

Winter was over. It was a hard time for me, because my
English was still poor. Americans have some special expressions
which are not easy to understand. I attended three to four lectures
every day, read dozens of pages of related textbooks, but I still
managed to read only half of the needed material. I got very little
sleep, reading until four or five in the morning, and sometimes I
lost my train of thought because of exhaustion. Besides that, I
was forced to take an outside job at night, working at a restaurant
several nights every month. There were times when I had no time
to return home after my night work and had to go directly to the
university. I would show up at about five in the morning; the
night guard at the university knew me well and let me go to the
classroom where I slept until eight-thirty at which time the
students arrived. It was understandable that I was looking
forward to the summer camp.

I had several weeks of vacation before the summer camp
began, and again I spent them working at Amityville. But now I
was a supervisor and had a helper who exhausted me more than
my hard routine at the university. My helper would approach a
task that would normally take two to three hours and would
managed to stretch it out for more than twelve hours. He spent
most of the day sitting idly on the steps. When I asked him what
he was doing, he would reply that he was very busy. I asked,
"What are you doing?" "I am waiting for a phone call."

That's why I went to the summer camp with great
pleasure. That period of instruction was very interesting. Initially
our group was given a task that required us knowledge of
hydrometry. We measured the depth of a lake in Connecticut and
put the depth contours on a map. Four young ladies who were
rowing a boat were interested in our work. We explained what we
were doing, and they offered to join us. Our work was very
interesting to them, and we finished the task that was supposed to
take three days by three in the afternoon of our first day. Our car

was scheduled to arrive at five. We made friends with the girls
and met later.

One of the professors told us not to give our report to the
dean because he wouldn't believe that we managed to complete
our task so quickly. That professor treated us to ice cream when
our work was done quickly and with great precision. I never have
eaten so much ice cream as I did that summer.

Once Professor Oaki invited Dan and I to a tavern. We
had some beer and watched the girls who were dancing the
"shimmy." It looked like a parody of the Arabian "belly dance."
The difference is that in the Arabian version the belly and all its
muscles are involved, while in the "shimmy" only the breasts are
shaking. I wanted to be the bugle player as I had been the year
before. Once Professor Finch asked me to play something for
him, and I understood that he appreciated good music. There was
a Swede named George in our group. Sometimes Swedes sing a
melody which resembles our song *Stenka Razin*, though the words
are absolutely different. Many people in America know the song
Otchy Tchernye (Dark Eyes), and some people know the melody
of *Hey, Ukhnem! (Hey, Let's Add!).* Without hesitating, I
suggested to George that we create a chorus. He talked to the
other students, and soon we started rehearsals. We learned four or
five songs, including *Vecherny Zvon (The Evening Chime).* Once
we approached the dean's house—he lived outside the camp—and
started our performance. He and his wife liked it very much and
invited us for tea. "This is the first time in my life that I have
heard serenades like these," he said.

I experienced an unpleasant incident. I had to climb over
a barbed wire fence while I was conducting a land survey. We
had to inform another owner that we would be working on his
land. But neither George, nor Dan, nor Irving wanted to do that.
So, I decided to go, but I caught my trousers on the barbed wire
and tore the back of them. At that moment the lady who owned
the land appeared and invited us for lunch. She asked me, "Why
are you holding your hands behind you all the time?" I blushed
and said that I had torn my pants on the barbed wire. "You are
not the first," she said. "Let's go." She offered us some wine and
a delicious lunch. Then she took my trousers and mended them
very neatly.

Summer studies were finished. We went to the mines and
helped construct a narrow-gauge railway, became acquainted with

the operation of hydraulic power plants, helped to reinforce part of the ocean shore, and so on.

The fall semester began. Time passed by quickly, and soon the spring semester was on its way. Professor Krefeld told me to conduct a test of the tensile strength of wire and a test of doors covered with a fire proof material. Those doors were supposed to be installed in hotels in New York, and they had to withstand temperatures of up to four hundred degrees centigrade.

Final examinations drew near, and I had developed a toothache. Nothing could diminish the pain, so on the eve of the exams I went to a dentist. The dentist said that she had to extract seven teeth; that was the only thing that could be done to stop the pain. I agreed. She extracted the teeth, and I choked with blood and was in great pain. My mouth was full of blood, and the dentist could not stop the bleeding. At home I put cotton, soaked in peroxide, on my wounds. This helped to stop the bleeding. My jaw ached badly when I tried to say a word, and I had an important exam the next day.

I don't know why, but I decided to visit my friend, a Spanish girl. Her family—mother, grandmother, and great grandmother—lived not far from Columbia University. She wrote verses, played guitar, and sang. They treated me kindly; the girl recited her verses, while the others were engaged in their sewing and knitting. I sat there in silence, swallowing blood from time to time. The next day I took the exam and passed it. I received my first Bachelor Science diploma, and had to pay twenty dollars for it. I borrowed the money from my friend because, at that moment, I was absolutely penniless. I should mention that in order to receive my diploma I had to prepare a thesis which had the title, "Infiltration of liquids through a porous granular media."

I made friends with Professor Charles Kayan during the spring semester of 1935. He was a specialist in thermodynamics. He felt great sympathy for me and organized a party in my honor when I received my diploma. I'll describe him later.

So I graduated from the university and had no idea what to do. There was no work available for engineers. There were no employment opportunities for ordinary workers either. I applied to the Immigration Service, asking them to change my status from that of a student to that of a political refugee, and I also requested that they give me an employment authorization.

As before, I had an opportunity to work at the boardinghouse during the summer. I was fortunate; one day I went to the university, the dean invited me to his office and said he had been looking for me. "You should enroll for one more year at the university. Then you'll receive a diploma as a civil engineer." I almost fainted. I remember a student who received his bachelor degree and wanted to continue studying, but the dean rebuked him and said that he could continue his studies, but only at another university. And suddenly—such an offer! It came as a great surprise to me; I could barely keep my balance.

During the fall and spring semesters of 1934-1935, I worked at the laboratory devoted to the study of the mechanics of earth and hydraulics. It was very interesting work.

In 1936, I received my second diploma as a civil engineer; that diploma was superior to that of the diploma of Master of Civil Engineering. Here is a short description of the civil engineering career field. There were military engineers in America prior to 1820. They were divided into different categories such as construction specialists, mechanics, ship builders, etc. In 1820, the United States Congress passed a law establishing a Civil Engineering Society. There were differences between the civil and military engineering career fields. The military engineers came under the control of the Army and were mainly responsible for constructing pontoon bridges, military roads, and fortifications. Civil engineers were employed by non-military authorities to construct offices, apartment buildings, highways, railroads, etc.

All the branches of the engineering field which were not controlled by the military were designated as "civil." Later designations such as mining, mechanical, sanitary, land surveyors, and construction were developed to meet the needs of the expanding and increasingly specialized engineering career field. When I was about to receive my second diploma, the chief engineer, who was responsible for the water supplies of the Hawaiian Islands, including the heavily populated island of Oahu, came to Columbia University. At that time, Hawaii was organized as a territory, not a state. Oahu was the principal producer of pineapples, and the capital, Honolulu, was located on this island. The chief engineer needed a specialist capable of estimating the precipitation, studying its runoff patterns and conserving it for the befit of agriculture, industry and the local population. As it was, most of the rainfall was flowing into the ocean.

My professors at Columbia University recommended that I would be a good candidate for a civil service position that required examining rainfall patterns and developing methods to collect and hold the precipitation for later use. I agreed to take the position and soon, accompanied by my friend Dan Lomb, began my journey to Hawaii. The journey was very pleasant and began with train trip to San Francisco were we boarded a ship for Oahu. The entire distance from New York to Honolulu was about six thousand miles, and it took ten days to complete the trip.

I might add that we were able to see many scenic places on the American continent such as the Grand Canyon. This depression, formed by the Colorado River in Arizona, stretches for three hundred kilometers (a hundred and eighty-six miles) in length and has a depth which varies from three hundred to two thousand meters (a thousand to six thousand, six hundred feet). Geologists from every continent come here to examine the various exposed layers of the earth's crust. By the way, there is a similar but smaller depression in Hawaii located on the island of Kauai. We also visited the redwood forest in California where we saw thousand-year-old sequoias of gigantic size. One tree in particular caught our attention because it was possible to drive a car through an opening in its trunk.

Sailing on the ship was an interesting experience. I was able to see a variety of marine life including sea horses, flying fish, various species of sea birds, and, of course, dolphins. The Pacific Ocean proved to be quiet indeed. No storms appeared during the trip which lasted for five or six days. The waves were long and not high when compared with the waves I had witnessed on the Atlantic. On that ocean the waves were short and reached the height of thirteen to fifteen meters (forty-three to fifty feet).

I can still recall the beauty of the morning when we arrived at the port of Honolulu. There was not a cloud in the sky, and there was a crowd on the shore waiting for the arrival of the ship. In those days, when a ship entered the port of Honolulu, the population treated the event as if it were a holiday. Each passenger received a lei, a beautiful garland of flowers, which was placed around their necks. A pretty lady presented Dan and me with one of these lovely garlands. She was the wife of the chief engineer of the island. All the shops were open, but even the owners and the customers crowded along the shore to greet the ship. At that time, the residents of Hawaii were not acquainted with the problems of crime such as burglary, robbery or murder.

Unlike the continental United States, it was very difficult to escape being apprehended and punished on this small, and at that time, thinly populated island.

I settled into an apartment located not far from the city hall. An elderly teacher was renting an apartment in the same house. My apartment was composed of a study, a big room of five by seven meters (fifteen by twenty-five feet), a bathroom, and a small kitchen. In addition, the house also had a balcony. Dan stayed with me for two weeks, then he returned to New York. The bed was placed in such a way that my head was against the wall which divided the two apartments. My neighbor's head was against the other side of the wall. For several nights I heard monotonous oriental music, and I thought that there was something wrong with me. Once, when I was sitting on the balcony, the teacher returned to her apartment. I mentioned that at night I heard the sounds of strange music, and I suggested that perhaps I was ill. "Oh," she said, "I just forgot to turn off the radio. You were hearing a Japanese melody. They have a holiday now in Japan which lasts an entire week. Don't worry, you are all right."

I was impressed with the kind attitude of the chief engineer. After he and his wife met me at the pier, his driver took Dan and me, along with our baggage, to the apartment. The next day I went to the office where I met my engineering colleagues who were responsible for conducting the research into new methods for developing water resources for irrigation. Among these men, each of whom possessed their engineering degrees, were six Japanese, four Chinese, and two Americans from California.

We decided to start a project in two days. On the third day, the chief engineer invited me to go and look at the water reservoirs which supplied Honolulu and the adjacent pineapple plantations with water. At one of the reservoirs he mentioned that he had spent two hundred and fifty thousand dollars to prevent leakage, but that the effort had failed since that reservoir was now empty despite having been filled a short time before by a heavy rain. "What steps have been taken to correct the problem?" I asked. He replied, "Under the direction of an engineer from San Francisco, we enclosed the reservoir with iron shields installed in a way that resembled a fence. We put these shields in place, but we did not see the anticipated results." "What a strange engineer," I said. "The soil in this area is volcanic, and when the iron shield was installed, the soil developed more cracks and became even more permeable. You would have to fill the bottom of the reservoir with a mixture of lime and sand; this would insure that any openings in the lava would be closed." "Yes, but having spent a quarter of a million dollars, we can't even consider that option," the engineer said glumly.

I should add that precipitation in Hawaii, and especially on Oahu, varies greatly from one part of an island to another. For example, on the shore near Honolulu the annual precipitation is fifty inches, while in the mountains behind the city the annual average rises to six hundred inches. The distance between these two points can be as short as two and a half to three miles. The heavy rainfall in the mountains behind Honolulu promotes the growth of lush vegetation. I remember walking over a layer of vegetation about a meter (three and a third feet) thick, as if it were the actual ground. The layer of vegetation was almost solid, and I had to tear it open in order to measure the volume of water trickling underneath.

The chief engineer was a very influential person in the territorial legislature. In fact, he had "appointed" the senators. When the police saw me riding in his limousine with him, they tried to be very helpful to me later. They even stopped traffic when I had to cross the street. I did not like it, but I could not change local customs.

My work was not difficult. I received the data on the level of precipitation, water usage, evaporation and infiltration into the ground water system—dull work. Once I went to a local tavern and ordered a beer. I sat at an oval table that was already occupied by a gentleman. He was a Russian and had been an aide of General Semenoff. We were the only Russians on the island. Of course, we became friends. He told about himself. He worked at a large store selling Oriental goods. Life in Hawaii was monotonous at that time. The biggest entertainment was the arrival of a ship. Two newspapers were published, and I became acquainted with the editor of each paper. Naturally, the two editors did not like each other.

At one point, the chief engineer mentioned that a Russian chorus was planning to visit Hawaii. It was coming to Hawaii from Japan. So, one day the Japanese ship arrived in Honolulu. Large crowds of residents gathered to look at the wonder—a Russian chorus! The pier was divided by a rope, and nobody was allowed to cross it. Suddenly I heard a voice saying, "Nicholas!"

I turned around and saw Nicholas Feodorvich Kostrukoff and Rostya (whose last name I don't remember), my old friends from Lemnos. What a meeting! When the singers settled at the hotel, I invited them all to dinner. The teacher helped me to cook and serve it. We had nourishing, tasty borscht, delicious Hawaiian fish, and so on. My neighbors cooked all the food with the exception of the borscht which I was responsible for preparing.

We told each other about our various adventures which we had experienced since 1923. The chorus gave several successful performances in Honolulu. In a week, my friends and acquaintances sailed for San Francisco.

I observed life in Hawaii with interest. My friend ordered the installation of a telephone. I should mention there are no telephone poles in Hawaii as there are no trees which could be used for that purpose. For that reason, a trench had to be excavated for the underground cable. Earlier they had dug up the same street, laid pipes to carry water, and repaired the street. Now they again began to tear up the pavement to lay the telephone cable and again the they had to cover the road with new asphalt. This process was repeated when they found it necessary to install a sewer system, and so on. I believe that selected individuals made significant profits because of this supposedly chaotic construction system.

The island laws were also interesting. Only those who had lived on the island for at least six months were permitted to vote; however, the chief engineer asked me to vote in an upcoming election, although I had only been in Hawaii for two months.

I was told that several hundred Russians had arrived as workers in Hawaii after the revolution of 1905. They were promised good wages, but purchases of food on account, as well as their transportation costs, were deducted from their wages, and they actually found themselves in debt at the end of the month. They went on strike. Later many of them died, while others moved to the United States mainland. The working conditions were terrible before 1930. The contractor, who hired the workers, did not tell them the company would supply them with food and would then deduct this cost from their wages. Usually the workers were transported in boats to the place of work.

At the end of the week the captain of the motor boat would deliver their pay envelopes to them; these envelopes were frequently empty or contained a notice indicating the worker was actually in debt. Food was very expensive, and a pack of needles cost a dollar, while on the mainland two packs cost only five cents. A gallon of paint cost twenty dollars in Hawaii, compared with a mere two dollars in California. If a customer indicated that he was not satisfied, he was told to go shopping in San Francisco.

The Woolworth chain stores were a familiar sight in America, and this corporation tried to open a store in Hawaii that would sell goods at lower prices. However, this famous corporation could not even buy a patch of land. All the land in Hawaii belonged to a small group of people who maintained rigid control over their property. At last Woolworth managed to open a store in the territory after obtaining a ninety-nine year lease. Suddenly the price of needles, paint and other goods dropped by a factor of ten. There were "tea houses," staffed by beautiful girls, among the local places of interest. The newspaper editors pointed these places out to me.

Nature is generous in Hawaii. Papayas grow on trees; they are the size of one-half of an Astrakhan watermelon. Papayas are also cultivated in Mexico, but they are much smaller. Another interesting plant is grown in Hawaii—taro. With roots weighing as much as three hundred to four hundred pounds, the Hawaiians brew a strong alcoholic beverage from the taro. They also use this plant to make a "dough" known as poi which they eat with their fingers.

The Hawaiian waters are very clear, and a large number of fish make their homes here. One can enter the sea with a spear and catch many fish. I knew a man who lived in the countryside, slept under the trees, woke when he wanted, took his spear to the ocean and took what he needed. He supplemented his menu of fish with papayas, coconuts, and so forth. As far as coconuts were concerned, they fell from the trees during the storms and occasionally killed people. In that case the government did not pay for the funerals; however, when a senator's son was killed, a law was enacted providing the family of the deceased with compensation totaling five hundred dollars.

In a similar manner, a new law dealing with the punishment for rape was adopted. Previously, if a girl was under the age of sixteen, the rapist was sentenced to prison for many years. Then a senator was accused of raping a fifteen year old girl, and the senate immediately passed a law removing the punishment for the statutory rape of a fifteen year old.

On the whole, life in Hawaii was very monotonous and low key. For a gregarious, curious person, Hawaii was not the place to permanently settle; however, life in this tropical setting would be suitable for a person who sought a tranquil existence. It's a good place to participate in sports or study nature. For example, there is an amazing island which is a refuge for numerous species of birds. One can find hundreds of thousands of exotic birds nesting there. The residents of the island are Polynesians, and only they are permitted to permanently live there. You can visit the location for a day, but are not allowed to live there. If a resident of the island departed, he could not return.

I lived six months at my first apartment, then moved to another one. It was located near the ocean, and a rather obsolete coastal artillery piece, manned by army personnel, was located not more than a hundred meters (three hundred and thirty feet) from my apartment building.

I visited the Bishop museum in Honolulu where I saw an exhibit featuring the uniform of a Don Cossack officer *(khorunzhy or junior officer of the Cossack Cavalry)*. That uniform had been given to a Hawaiian king by the Russian Tsar.

I always enjoyed swimming in Hawaiian waters, but I always had to take care to avoid a particular type of jellyfish known as a Portuguese man-of-war. It has hundreds of tentacles, and they readily adhere to your body. Later you will suffer more pain in the places where the tentacles touched your skin than you would if you had been burned in those areas.

I spent two years in Hawaii, and then I returned to New York where I began work at Columbia University, at the School of Engineering, on the study of the mechanics of fluids, including hydraulics. When I returned to New York there was no job. I had a letter of recommendation from Professor Finch, but I did not use it. I'll explain the reason later.

At that time, professor B. A. Bakhmetyev, who had been the Russian Ambassador during the Kerensky regime, suggested to me that I continue to do research on the flow of liquid through a granular media. I began working on this problem and was added to the staff of the engineering faculty of Columbia University. In 1938, Professor Bakhmetyev and I presented our scientific findings to the Fifth International Congress of Applied Mathematics held at Cambridge, Massachusetts.

Here I became acquainted with one of the most competent scientists in the field of thermodynamics and the dynamics of liquids and gases—Theodore Von Karman. I came to his apartment and knocked at the door, but nobody answered. The door was unlocked, so I went in. Underwear was scattered about on the floor, and I heard a noise in the adjacent room. I could recognize Doctor Von Karman's voice, so I entered the room which proved to be a bathroom. Doctor Von Karman was sitting in a bathtub and was rubbing his face and neck with a sock. In 1928 at the Conference on Hydraulics held in Stockholm, Doctor Von Karman introduced his new theory of the turbulence, or dynamic movement, of fluids. At that time, not many scientists accepted his ideas but today this theory is the basis for studies dealing with all dynamic currents found in fluids.

The research on the dynamics of the flow of liquids in open channels was carried out in a laboratory at Columbia University, and the results were published in various scientific journals. In 1944, Professor Bakhmetyev and I receive an award from the Society of Civil Engineer for our achievements in that field. My reports in particular were published in the journals of mechanical engineering, civil engineering, geophysics, and also in the journals of the Academy of Science of New York.

At the beginning of the Second World War, I started to teach students; they were aviators at Manhattan College and naval students at Columbia University. I was teaching them such subjects as the mechanics of fluids and construction materials, subjects which had been condensed into a brief course for military specialists. In 1941, I was licensed as a professional engineer by the state of New York, and, thus, I could practice engineering legally. Later I enrolled at the Academy of Science of New York. For some time I was the secretary of the Department of Mathematics and Engineering, and for two years I was its chairman. I received a scientific award for that endeavor. I was also given awards by the Society of Civil Engineers, the American Geophysical union and the Society of Mechanical Engineers.

Thus my teaching activities, which would continue for many years, began. These activities provided me with tremendous practical experiences, true friends, and the opportunity to learn a wide range of new information.

Many colleges and universities in America admit students from various countries. For example, at Columbia University there were many students from China, East Africa and South America. Many students who come to the big cities, like New York, Chicago, San Francisco and Los Angeles, fall under the influence of left-wing Progressives. For this reason, a number of countries stopped sending students to this country and recalled those who had been studying here.

The programs for granting diplomas are similar in all parts of the United States, but the professors' standards and assignments frequently differ. The requirements for earning a diploma at Columbia or Harvard universities cannot be compared with those in place at universities of the second or third rank; if the situation were otherwise, these institutions of lesser stature would have neither the students nor the funds to allow them to function. The differences in the quality of the various programs was especially noticeable when the graduates start the job search process.

I was fortunate to study at one of the best universities in the United States because the study of the mechanics of liquids as a scholarly discipline, or area of specialization, was only begun in 1934-35, and I was one of the first students to specialize in the field. That's why I obtained my job in Hawaii so quickly, and then, as a professor at Manhattan College, I obtained a concurrent teaching position at City University. The reader can understand that I became acquainted with the requirements in force at three very different categories of schools. Many black students, South Americans and island residents were admitted to the colleges of the second and third rank. The best students were admitted to institutions of the first academic rank where "the cream of society" studied.

Manhattan College was founded by the Catholic Society of Christian Brothers. The students were mainly of Irish, Italian or Caribbean origin. Almost all of them had graduated from Catholic high schools where, according to that tradition, all the students were treated as children by their teachers. As a result, the students lacked initiative. I remember the classes I taught for undergraduate students. During the first semester, the majority of these students received low grades. My colleagues asked why this situation was occurring, but what grades could I ethically award them if they were not properly prepared? In the middle and high schools, they had obediently memorized the material presented by their teachers, and they had never had an opportunity to develop higher-level thinking skills. How can one obtain a Bachelor of Science degree without possessing a core body of knowledge, the ability to think critically, the skill to evaluate the ideas presented by others, as well as the ability to create your own theories? The situation in the classroom improved during the second semester, and many of the students thanked me because I had revealed to them a new approach for obtaining true knowledge.

An individual who wanted to be admitted to the university had to have an interview with three professors from the history, physics and mathematics departments. These professors made their recommendations for admission based on the student's knowledge of the subject matter, but they also based their decisions on the individual's behavior and character. As a first-class university usually pays two-thirds of the tuition for the student, they don't want to waste their money on those persons who lack talent.

The top universities in the United States pay their professor's salaries from an endowment fund created over the years and funded from the contributions and bequests of the wealthy as well as less affluent alumni. Frequently these funds are specifically designated for a particular branch of scientific study. With their large endowment funds, these top-rank universities can afford to maintain a ratio of one professor for every ten students. Other universities are more heavily dependent on tuition to cover their costs, and in these schools one professor may be responsible for teaching as many as thirty to forty students. Thus there is a considerable difference in both the quality of the teaching and the degree to which the students develop true proficiency in the subjects they take.

I had a number of interesting moments at Manhattan College. Once during an examination, a student blatantly took out his crib sheets and began to consult them before he wrote his answers. Of course, I took the crib sheets away from him, told him to take a walk, and to come see me after the examination. He did not return but, instead, went to the dean to complain about the situation. The dean told the student that Professor Feodoroff would arrange for him to take a separate examination. He passed the second examination, but the student became very angry and told his classmates that he would kill me. Once he made a phone call to my apartment and said that he wanted to see me. "You may come in; I am available," I said. He arrived, and we had a long conversation. I said that he was too pampered and that he tried to reach his goals using dishonest methods. An engineer, like a doctor, must above all possess honesty and integrity. Only then can an individual count on the respect of his colleagues; only then can a person obtain a solid professional reputation. The young man cried and apologized. We became friends, but, unfortunately, he has passed away.

Another interesting event happened after the Korean War. I should say that the students who served in the armed forces during World War II and the Korean War were the best students at the university; their wartime experiences made them thoughtful, honest, and gave them a thirst for knowledge. They were the best to pass through the university system. I was teaching a course on the mechanics of fluids in the Electrical Engineering Department. I had a student who had served in the military during the Korean War. He came to me in the spring, two weeks after the beginning of the semester. The first thing he said to me was that he did not need to know the subject-matter in the course I was teaching, but he declared that he was required to take the course in order to receive his bachelor of science degree.

"Let me take your course by exemption, please." I told him to discuss the matter with the administration. He went away and I did not see him during the first half of the semester. He came to take my examination and, of course, he failed it. Next he tried to convince me to give him a passing grade. I told him, "I gave my word to the Education Council of New York that I would perform my duties as a professor in an honest manner and that I would be impartial when grading my students. You served in the army, and you know what an oath is; you know the meaning of words such as duty, obligation and discipline. Now consider that you will either diligently study my course material or you will have to spend another year in the university. The decision is up to you."

At the end of the semester, he passed his exam with a good grade and received his diploma. After the graduation ceremony, a group of students surrounded me. I saw two women among them and thought that perhaps they were mother and daughter. When I was alone, one of them came up to me and touched me on my shoulder and said, "Excuse me, are you Professor Feodoroff?" "Yes," I responded. "I am the wife of Mr.... (she named the student who had been a veteran) "and this is his mother. We would like to know what you told him on April 15th. He has undergone a considerable change since then. He has become very considerate and helps us with the housework." "Nothing special," I replied. "I just reminded him that everyone has duties and responsibilities that must be carried out regardless of personal feelings."

A son of the New York police captain who was in charge of the precinct located between 14th-and 60th streets was enrolled in one of my classes. That district is famous for its expensive shops, beautiful mansions, museums, etc., and its outlying areas were known as places where drugs were sold and prostitutes conducted their trade. Murders, abductions of girls, and loud brawls were common events there. Once after work, I was going to the subway to travel back to my home. I was living approximately a hundred and fifty blocks from the college. When I approached the station, two men suddenly rushed up to me, twisted my arm, put a handkerchief in my mouth and pushed me into a waiting auto. The car started, and we drove around the city in the early evening. The men did not say a single word. Gradually, I came to myself. What had happened?

My kidnappers were dressed in dark suits and looked like Irishmen. At that time the newspaper *Russia* had received a warning from some Jewish youths that if the paper did not stop publishing information about Soviet Jews and the methods they employed to murder the Russian people trapped in the U.S.S.R., the chief editor and other members of the board would be killed. But there was nothing Jewish in the appearance or behavior of my kidnappers. They did not reek of garlic or salted smoked fish which was a favorite food of the Brooklyn Jews at that time.

While I was thinking about the situation, the car entered Riverside Drive alongside the Hudson and stopped near a toll booth. I noticed that the driver did not pay money but showed his card to the toll collector. At that time, they untied me and removed the gag. They were still silent. We passed through the center of Manhattan and stopped near a luxurious mansion. One of the men got out of the car and opened the door on my side saying politely, "Professor Feodoroff, get out. We were ordered to take you to this house. Officer O'Connor will lead you." At that point I understood that someone had played a joke on me. But who was responsible for this play acting? I entered the house and saw my student and his father, the police captain. They greeted me and treated me to an excellent diner, having apologized for the "joke." My "kidnapping" was initiated by the student, and his father helped him to carry it out. The young man had a rich fantasy life.

The attitude of my students towards me was very good. They frequently came to me, either individually or in groups, to ask me for my advice. Once five students came to me and said,

"Our girlfriends want to have weddings in May. But we have not yet graduated from college; we have to study for a year in order to complete our requirements for a degree. We can't work and provide for our families, and we told the girls that they should wait until we graduate, work for a couple of years, and then we would be in a better position to marry them as we would have accumulated some savings." I told them that if the girls really loved them, they would wait; if not—the guys would find out soon enough. In four years, two of them invited me to their weddings. There were many cases like that. The young people often asked me for my advice regarding these vital personal matters.

The students at Manhattan College were allowed to establish a chapter of the Society of Civil Engineers known as Psi Epsilon. They asked me to become its first honorary member. Naturally other professors did not appreciate this turn of events.

Moreover, I was elected as an advisor to that organization. One of the professors vigorously protested saying, "Why was Feodoroff elected?" When I learned about that incident, I sent a letter of appreciation to the student organization indicating that I could not accept the position as advisor because of the jealous attitude of my colleagues.

A black engineer, a former student, asked me to be a godfather for his first child. Unfortunately I had to refuse this honor since I was Russian Orthodox, not Roman Catholic.

Although my relations with the students were good, my relations with the administration left much to be desired. But I don't want to dwell on that situation, since it is an everyday occurrence in academic communities.

I was head of the fluid mechanics laboratory at Columbia University. The main task of the laboratory was to conduct practical research and theoretical studies into the flow of liquids under various conditions. I met with my students only once a week. I noticed that students from India, Indonesia and Latin America were especially diligent. Seven friendly students from India attended my lectures, asking me all sorts of questions. Professor Bakhmetyev laughed at me saying, "How are you and your seven baby goats?" (*This is* a reference to *a famous Russian fairytale about a wolf and seven kids.*)

A Turk from Spain named Chingiz Uluchy studied at Columbia University during World War II. He had previously studied in France at the Institute of Transportation and

Communication. He was a talented mathematician and an excellent theorist, having obtained a Ph.D. in Mathematics in one year. Common work and scientific discussions made us friends. Once I met him near the university. It was winter, and he was wearing a light coat. He said he was waiting for his friend who had told him, "I'll see you." Uluchy understood that phrase as literal, word for word, and felt that it was necessary to wait for his friend. I explained to him that the phrase did not mean that he would have to wait for his friend, and that more likely than not he would not see this individual for a considerable period of time, perhaps even a year. The unusual idioms found in English pose genuine problems for foreigners.

One rainy day, a student of Irish extraction offered to drive me to the subway. During the drive, he mentioned that he did not like his grade and wanted me to give him an excellent grade instead of his satisfactory mark. He was an adult who worked at a corporation, and he took university courses to obtain a promotion. Usually it takes eight to ten years to get a diploma when one is attending evening courses. He also mentioned that he was the owner of a tavern and that he could make things hard for me. I understood this to mean that he had ties to the Mafia and that they could kill me. I said that I had almost died on several occasions, and that I was not afraid to face death once more. He dropped me off at the train station. I might add that he did receive mediocre grades after that incident, and I remained alive.

On one occasion, after the Second World War, the guard of the School of Civil Engineering came to me and said that a group of young men wanted to see me. They turned out to be a group of Russian displaced persons. One of them, George Trachevsky, asked me if I were really Professor Feodoroff. He had been a student at the Kiev Polytechnic Institute and a lieutenant in the Soviet Army. He asked me to help them fill out application papers and recommend a suitable university. There were about thirty of them in the group. They had left Europe and traveled to the United States and were now trying to establish themselves in this country. I recommended that Trachevsky enter the School of Mechanical Engineering at Columbia University. His life was very interesting. He was in love with a girl before the war, and unexpectedly met her in America. She agreed to marry him, but their wedding was postponed because George wanted to earn some money. Once he came to me with a black eye, looking as if he were completely drained of energy. He had received the black eye as the result of an outburst of jealousy on his part when he caught his fiancee with a rival. I tried to reconcile them; they married and named their first child Nicholas, and I was his godfather.

Student organizations bear some resemblance to Masonic Lodges having the same secret initiation rituals, meetings, and secret signs for recognition. Scientific organizations are very dull compared with these student organizations. Members are admitted on the strength of their scientific achievements, not on the basis of some mysterious rite or oath of loyalty. Membership in these fraternities can prove useful, however, when members are searching for employment or are being considered for promotion. Naturally the members of these societies help each other in these circumstances.

I cannot say that the level of education in the United States is high now, because in many colleges young people receive a superficial education and are awarded diplomas which do not reflect their true educational status. It would be better for some of these young people to study at vocational schools and become good workers, but instead they receive liberal arts diplomas of limited utility. Often these individuals are of limited value to either their employers or to American society. A similar situation existed in the U.S.S.R.

Most American students are very pampered; their parents provide them with sizable amounts of money, eager to see their children awarded good diplomas. The students are usually in good physical shape (sports are very popular in the U.S.), but their intellectual development leaves much to be desired. Children from well-to-do families often fail to develop their mental and intellectual potential. As a rule, a young man does not seriously start to think about his career until he is twenty-two to twenty-four years old. Federal financial aid, too, does not help to improve the quality of education; approximately half of the college students receive federal aid. When I entered Columbia University in 1930, there was only one grant for an engineering school that had an enrollment of one hundred students. Now an individual can complete his education for practically nothing. The federal government underwrites a system which provides unprecedented loans which do not have to be repaid until after graduation, and the repayment period can be stretched out over a period of several years.

Throughout my life I have had the opportunity to meet many outstanding people, including scientists and men with an international reputation. I would like to add a few personal details to supplement the descriptions of them in articles and biographies.

First of all, among my friends and colleagues, I remember Professor Stefan Timoshenko. He was a tall, slim individual who possessed high energy levels despite his age. He had written his excellent book, entitled *Theory of Elasticity of Construction Materials*, in 1900. This book is used as a textbook in many countries.

The misfortunes suffered by Russia deprived Professor Timoshenko of the opportunity of working in his native land. He came to the United States and obtained a position at the University of Illinois. His first dealings with the university were very peculiar. The dean of the school of engineering told him, "We have no openings, even for instructors. Maybe there is something for you to do in the construction materials laboratory. Go to the head of that laboratory and tell him that you'll conduct research." A young man, who was the head of the laboratory, asked Timoshenko, "How can I help you?" "I was appointed to conduct research," he replied. "You are just in time. We need a person to clean this place; take away those materials, remove this item, and throw away those pieces of concrete." "But, excuse me! I was appointed to conduct scientific research. I have a Ph.D. in engineering, and I am a professor. You must be acquainted with my book, for it was translated into many languages." "And we need to clean the laboratory," the young head of the laboratory said as he interrupted the professor.

Timoshenko went to the dean and informed him about that conversation. The dean summoned the head of the laboratory and talked to him. As a result, Professor Timoshenko was permitted to conduct research at the laboratory.

Timoshenko's family also achieved fame in the United States. His son became the head of the Department of Electrical Engineering at the University of Connecticut. His nephew also had a position at that university as a researcher in the field of agriculture. On one occasion, the professor met his nephew at his son's house, and the nephew started to say that he was a Ukrainian, not a Russian. The nephew also went on to say that the Russians had been oppressing the Ukrainians. Timoshenko reacted to these statements by turning his nephew out of the house and told him that he never wanted to see him again.

Professor Georgey Karelits left the U.S.S.R. before the Second World War. Under an assumed name, he joined the crew of a tanker departing Leningrad and was given a position of a common sailor. The ship was registered in Panama. He could hardly believe that he had escaped from the surveillance of the Soviet secret police. When he introduced himself to the captain, he mentioned shyly that he knew something about machinery *(Karelits was a world-renowned specialist in the field of lubricants).* The captain said, "All right. But for now I want you to be a stoker." Well, a stoker meant being a stoker, and Karelits had to shovel coal into the fire chamber.

Something happened to the ship's engine while at sea. He found the cause of the breakdown and personally repaired the engine. After that he had to answer some questions about his background. He arrived in the United States, not as a stoker, but as Mr. George. He easily found a job in America—first in the army, then at the faculty of Mechanics in the School of Engineering at Columbia University. He collected a valuable library of the scientific literature devoted to the field of lubricants. He was a genuine Russian, very sympathetic to those in need. In this respect, he was like many other Russians such as Professors Timoshenko, Ignatyeff, Kolupailo, etc.

With great love I remember my friend, Boris Vasilyevich Sergievsky, who was a famous aviator and a close colleague of Sikorsky and Sevirsky. He had been awarded the St. George Cross for valor during World War I. He was a test pilot for military aircraft in Imperial Russia. Since the second half of the 1920s, he had worked in the United States as a test pilot for the well-known Sikorsky aircraft company.

The first Cossack Stanitsa was formed in New York at that time. The Cossacks collected funds and purchased shares in the Sikorsky aircraft company. For that reason Sikorsky and Sergievsky frequently met with the Cossacks. Later, Sergievsky became a test pilot for the Department of Defense and was used as a pilot on "special missions." For example, he flew Edward, the Prince of Wales, from England to the United States and back. We became close friends while working on Russian national matters. Sergievsky was a consistent Russian patriot; he helped Russian aviators all over the world. Together with Prince S. S. Beloselsky-Belozersky he organized a "common fund" which was a charity fund designed to help needy Russians. Sergievsky donated the greater part of his wealth to this "common fund."

On one occasion I had to deliver a speech, together with Sergievsky, at a meeting of the Republican Party where we protested the attempts of the politicians to mix up the terms "Russian," and "Soviet." In addition, they failed to embrace the concept that Russia was the first victim of International Communism, and we protested the fact that they had failed to include Russia in the Declaration of Captive Nations which listed those nations which were suffering from Communist tyranny and oppression.

Captain Sergievsky also supported a church, and together with B. A. Bakhmetyev also supported a second church—the Cathedral of Christ the Savior in New York City. For some time he served as Chairman of the Society for the Relief of Russian War Invalids (White veterans). I inherited that position after his retirement.

According to American law, each test pilot must return his license on reaching the age of sixty. Captain Sergievsky was probably the only exception the authorities made, permitting him to fly until he reached the age of seventy. He had been assigned to the Don Cossack State Army in 1918. He was married to Mrs. Bloomingdale, a representative of one of the richest families in America. They were a very happy couple. Mrs. Sergievsky died soon after his death.

In 1949, I became friends with Dr. Yadoff. He had lived in Rostov-on-Don before the revolution, took part in the White Struggle, then came to France where he studied and received a Ph.D. in physics and mathematics. He emigrated to America with his wife and daughters after the Second World War. Unfortunately, he died before his time of lung cancer. I worked with him for several years. He had many inventions to his credit, including a luminous powder which did not contain phosphorus, a dynamic nozzle, and others. Unfortunately, despite their practical characteristics, these inventions were not introduced into production; the European markets had collapsed, and producers were not interested in new inventions. The military budget had been cut.

Patents have a limited life in the United States; each patent is valid for seventeen years, and during that period nobody can use the patent without the inventor's permission. He can sell it, exploit it, etc. After seventeen years, the patent for the invention becomes public domain and can be used by anyone. However, one company was interested in luminous powder; they wanted to use it in oil paints. They sent us a contract which stipulated that we had to provide them with the necessary data. But we did not sign the contract because the company wanted to make the powder without our participation. In a couple of days, we received another contract in which they attempted to hide the fact that they wanted to produce the powder without our having the right to participate in the production process; this clause had been inserted into the fine print at the bottom of the page as if by chance. Of course, we also rejected that contract.

In 1949-1954, I introduced a well-known engineer who specialized in the construction of suspension bridges, Professor D. B. Steiman, to the New York Academy of Science. David was a very interesting professor, and he had written a couple of books on the subject of suspension bridges. At one dinner in his honor, given by the Academy of Science, a beautiful young lady approached him after the meal and said, "I admire your bridges. They are very harmonious, light and beautiful." Steiman looked at her steadily and, apparently, did not hear what she had said, because his attention was distracted by her nice figure. Her dress especially attracted him. Her back was bare, and in front the dress barely covered her breasts. One could see that he was amazed.

"It's very interesting. How does this dress stay on you?" There were no straps. At last the lady felt awkward and said, "Why are you looking at me so attentively, Dr. Steiman?" "Excuse me, but I can't understand how this dress stays on you," he answered. "It's in suspension," the lady smiled, "Exactly like your bridges."

Dr. Steiman and his wife traveled to Europe in 1947. They stayed at the best hotel in Rome. There was a large bathroom in their suite, and when Steiman wanted to have a bath he turned the cold water faucet, and the faucet came off in his hand. He turned the hot water faucet and the same thing happened. There was nothing to do but to use the sink. At four in the afternoon he went downstairs where they were serving snacks and drinks. The maitre d'hôte came up and asked what they wanted to drink. Steiman ordered a martini for his wife and a vodka on the rocks for himself. The maitre d'hôte wrote the order down and disappeared.

He returned thirty minutes later with a waiter who carried a tray covered with pieces of marble. "Dr. Steiman," the waiter apologized, "we were looking for stones and could not find anything better. This is our best marble. We washed it many times." "Oh! Excuse me," said Steiman, "In America when we want to have a drink with ice in the glass we say rock, instead of 'ice.'" So ended the incident.

On one occasion, the New York Academy of Science was visited by another interesting person, Boris Julievich Pregel, who had been a lieutenant in the Imperial Russian Army and an engineer. His father had owned a big jewelry store in Kiev. Alas, the Bolsheviks divided up Pregel's property, and now Pregel's son had to earn his own living. I convinced him to become a member of the New York Academy of Science. He agreed and was enrolled. His life was very interesting.

When he left Russia in 1920, he moved to France. His father had some money in a French bank. In either France or Belgium, he met a Belgian woman who became his business partner; she had money of her own. He purchased land in the Belgium Congo and found uranium ore deposits on his property. Pregel sold the uranium to the United States, and his uranium ore was used when the Manhattan project began the development of the first atomic bomb. During the Second World War, the Soviet Union asked the United States to sell it uranium.

President Roosevelt ordered Pregel to give a pound of uranium to the Soviets, but Pregel flatly refused to do this. Then Roosevelt ordered the director of the project to give the uranium to the Soviets, who thus obtained the prize they were seeking. Later the Soviets invited Pregel to come to the U.S.S.R. to deliver lectures on techniques for mining and processing uranium ore, but he refused their offer and did not even meet with their representatives in America. Later he was elected to the position of President of the New York Academy of Science, a position he held until his death.

I would like to describe my friend Professor Parr. He was a kind man who was always available for discussions, and yet he was rather formal in his behavior and appearance. That caused many students to keep their distance from him. He an expert in thermodynamics, specializing in gas dynamics.

My contact with him involved investigations of problems of the motion of fluids and their behavior under various conditions. He developed a small, effective model that was, in fact, a visual aid which demonstrated the motion of a gas, using tetrachloride as a media. Later I modified this small model to allow it to use tobacco smoke as the media. We observed the motion of the gas passing around differently shaped objects while we adjusted the speed of the flow pattern around a body.

When I was offered a position at Manhattan College, Professor Parr had retired. He heard that I had accepted a position at Manhattan College and offered me his lecture notes on the subject of gas flow. These notes helped me when I lectured at different universities. They broadened my view about fluid dynamics for both gases and liquids.

I would also like to tell you about my contacts with Professor Luckey who was one of the oldest members of the Columbia University School of Engineering where he was Chairman of the Mechanical Engineering Department. I first met him when I was taking chemistry. While I was in the chemistry laboratory I met a student, Mr. Fisher, who, in addition to the chemistry course, took thermodynamics. When the final grades were posted, Fisher had received an F in thermodynamics. Fisher telephoned Professor Luckey and asked permission to see him. Fisher also asked if it would be all right to bring Feodoroff, a student, to this meeting. Professor Luckey agreed. Fisher expressed his surprise at receiving this failing grade. Professor Luckey asked Fisher, "Why do you think you have a passing grade? Look at your examination paper. Everything is wrong." Fisher replied, "I don't know how this could happen. I definitely know the subject matter. If you wish, you can examine me orally now. Moreover, I designed and built the power station and the water distribution system at the village of N. on Long Island. I can only say that I was ill during the week of examinations."

"Well, I can't change your grade," Professor Luckey replied. "It's already recorded. You will have to repeat the course if you want to receive your diploma." Fisher said. "I can't; I don't have the money." (This conversation took place during the Depression.) "I don't know what to do. The village I worked for also has no money, and the authorities could not pay me for my work; they could only offer partial payment for the material. While Fisher was talking, Professor Luckey opened the center drawer of his office desk, pulled out a small booklet, wrote something on it, and tore it from the booklet. (At that time I did not recognize a checkbook.) Professor Luckey handed Fisher a piece of paper saying, "Take it and pay your tuition." Fisher was holding a check for the amount of forty dollars which would cover the tuition for the thermodynamics course (four credits at ten dollars per credit). Fisher was speechless.

The next year I took thermodynamics. The general lectures were held in a large classroom. A long table was located in this classroom, and the table was divided into different sections containing whole engines, motors, and pumps. The lectures were held on Saturday from nine in the morning until noon. In those days I worked at a restaurant from four in the afternoon until four in the morning. The work was strenuous. I was not officially paid but received a dollar and was given plenty to eat which included a big sandwich. I used to take the sandwich home, giving part of it to a friend, an Armenian student who was enrolled in the Electrical Engineering Department. He had been unable to find work.

After finishing my job at the restaurant, I walked home a distance of almost two miles, from First Avenue and Eleventh street east to Ninety-eighth Street west and Eighth Avenue. By the time I arrived home, I was dead tired. Walking to and from the restaurant to Columbia University took another three to four hours. This left little time, approximately eight hours, to study and sleep. Therefore, I was continually exhausted, having slept only four hours per day.

A custodian at Columbia University was sympathetic to me and allowed me to enter the classroom at an early hour. By walking directly from work to Columbia University, I could save about three hours. I was so tired, I would fall asleep in the classroom before class started.

One Saturday I fell asleep and heard someone talking to me. After a while, I realized Professor Luckey was standing over me. "Go to my office and wait for me." I went to the office, sat down on a large leather chair, and fell asleep.

Again I was aware that someone was addressing me, rebuking me. "Why did you do such a thing?" he asked me. I told Professor Luckey I worked twelve hours a night for one dollar and food. It left me with little time for study and sleep. I had to study, for if I failed I would be deported from the country. "I am tired physically and emotionally," I said. Professor Luckey left the room, telling me to wait. When he returned, he came with the caretaker telling him to let me into his office when I came early so that I could rest. I used the office for two semesters.

Time flew. I received a diploma and obtained a job in Hawaii. In 1939, I returned to Columbia University to do research in the field of fluid dynamics. I specialized in research on hydraulic jump and undulatory motion, flow through granular media, and cavitation. One day, Professor Luckey telephoned me and told me about a large explosion that had occurred in a chemical factory in Texas. He said, "The company's chief engineer has invited me to a conference, but I think this is your problem. Therefore, we will go to the Plaza Hotel to meet the engineers from the company for discussions. The engineer told us that three two-hundred-and-fifty horsepower pumps delivered water to tanks where various chemicals were mixed. The pipe system was imbedded in a heavy concrete mass." I asked, "Please show us the blueprints. We would like to see the layout of the pipes. By the way, did anyone notice any peculiar noises or vibrations?" "Yes," he replied, "there had been a bad vibration; that's why the pipe system had been imbedded in concrete. There was also a whistling noise."

I stated that, "The blueprints indicate that the pipes had a number of ninety degree angles. Your pumps supplied liquid (water) at a very high velocity. You must understand that at a ninety degree angle, a liquid does not follow a solid boundary. In fact, it separates from it leaving pockets of low pressure." (This is a very simplified explanation.) "The pressure almost approaches zero, creating what is known as a cavitation phenomena. The force of cavitation is enormous as you have already witnessed. To protect a hydraulic structure from the effects of cavitation, you must design a pipe system with very gentle curves; this will insure that there are no sudden changes of direction—certainly not a ninety degree change in direction. With very gentle curves, the system should produce neither a vibration nor strange whistling sounds." We said goodbye.

Later Professor Luckey asked me to send the company a bill for a hundred and fifty dollars for my consultation. I did not send the bill as I thought I had done nothing to earn that fee. But two weeks later I again had a telephone call from Professor Luckey telling me that I must send the bill. He said, "You have completed eight years of high school and five years of university training and have had five years of research experience. You have to charge for that experience." Again I did not send the company the bill. One day I received a letter from Professor Luckey. When I opened it, I found a check for a hundred and fifty dollars from the chemical company. The letter also contained a note which said, "You billed the company not for what you told them, but for the time and energy you spent to acquire that knowledge. Nick, good luck! Luckey."

Professor Luckey was well known in the field of thermodynamics. The first textbook on thermodynamics in America, covering both theory and practice, was written by Professor Luckey and was used in all technical institutions. I always will cherish my memories of Professor Luckey and many other professors at Columbia University whose friendship, kindness, and highly developed professional knowledge and ethical standards sustained me through those difficult days of my life. Let the memory of them live forever!

Many of our compatriots came to America from Europe, especially from the Balkan region, after the Second World War. Dr. Vyatcheslav Sigizmundovich Jardetsky, accompanied by his wife Tatyana Feodorovna and his son Oleg, had emigrated from this area to the United States. Tatyana worked in the house of an American woman, and I helped Vyatcheslav find a position as a professor in Manhattan College's School of Engineering. Then he obtained a position in the Department of Geology at Columbia University where he wrote an interesting book about the origin and diffusion of seismic waves. Later he edited one of the most important scientific journals—*The Transactions of the Geophysical Society*. In addition, he taught physics and mathematics and, before the war, was the President of the University of Graz in Austria.

My encounter with General Count V. N. Ipatyeff, a famous chemist, was very interesting. He served at the Academy of the General Staff in Russia. He collaborated for a short time with the Soviets, being under the vigilant supervision of an uneducated janitor and a kitchen maid. A "scientist" in a leather jacket, armed with a Nagant revolver, supervised him in the laboratory. Trying to establish more normal relations with the new authorities, he told his supervisor that he had found a way of improving the quality of fuel. The commissar answered, "Show me what you've done. If you are just babbling and can't show us something useful, then shut up and just do what you are ordered to do."

The professor decided he would not show this man anything, and he even stopped discussing scientific matters with the new authorities. Once there was an international congress of chemists and physicists being held in Great Britain. The Soviets permitted him to act as their representative. He and his wife received their passports and traveled to London. Anxious to get as far as possible from the Soviet borders, they found themselves in America.

Many inventions and discoveries of General Ipatyeff have been patented in the United States. He was placed in charge of a laboratory at Northwestern University. He was a well-to-do man in America, and even established a grant to be given to a talented student who wanted to obtain a Ph.D. in chemistry. Here are some of the words found on the certificate of gratitude which Professor Ipatyeff was awarded by the American Chemistry Society: "Your research helped our bombers to end the war in the shortest possible time with the least number of victims."

Dr. Ivan Iosifovich Moskvitinoff arrived in America in about 1950. He was the only major specialist in field of hydraulics in Russia. In Imperial Russia he had worked with Professor Bakhmetyev at the Division of Communications. While in the Soviet Union, he was ready to face all the various disgusting things that could happen to any citizen at any time. But he was a quiet and unobtrusive man; that's why he was appointed as head of the Department of Electrification of the Moscow District. When the Germans approached Smolensk, Moskvitinoff managed to be captured by them. Then he was able to travel to Prague and was among those who signed the Declaration of the Liberation of Russia; General Vlasoff also signed that document.

Moskvitinoff was not extradited to the Reds. Stepan Kolupailo, the former minister of education of Lithuania, as well as the last president of Lithuania, helped him escape. Leaving Lithuania, he took the seals, stamped paper, and other symbols of state power. Using these documents, Kolupailo saved many Russians, giving them the documents which indicated that they were Lithuanian citizens.

During the 1932-1933 school year when I was a first term student, an outstanding student approached me. His name was Paul Hartman. He was working on a dissertation on hydraulics, preparing for his Master's Degree. He asked me to translate a few pages from a book by Bakhmetyev which had been published in Russia. I helped him and he obtained his degree. He had been a colonel in the United states Army during the First World War. He was an instructor and needed an advanced diploma in order to be promoted. That diploma enabled him to become a professor and later, in 1945, the Head of the C.E. Department of the City of New York.

During World War II, I taught a number of engineers sent to Columbia University by Professor Hartman who were participating in a program designed to award them a second diploma. During the war, Hartman was in Europe where he acquired a strange disease; his nails turned black and sloughed off. New nails grew and again they became diseased. The military doctors were unable to help him. I recommended that he enroll in the New York Academy of science where eighty percent of the members were physicians. Hartman followed my advice, and during one of the sessions where I was the Chairman of the Department of Engineering and Physics. I introduced him to doctors who took an interest in his disease. One of these doctors cured him completely.

With the help of Hartman, I managed to find a job for Moskvitinoff who was allowed to deliver lectures during the evening courses, and a year later he achieved the rank of professor, obtaining tenure the following year. He died in New York, and his wife returned to the Soviet Union where she had a son who was living in Siberia. I never heard any further news about her after her departure for the U.S.S.R.

I remember an interesting episode involving Moskvitinoff. Moskvitinoff, Dr. Kolupailo and I went to a conference on hydraulics being held in Montreal. A delegation of Soviet engineers was also attending this conference, and a young professor stood out from the drab background of the Soviet delegation. He was an academician, and he said to Moskvitinoff, "Ivan Iosifovich, why don't your return to the Motherland? Stop wasting your time on nonsense. They are waiting for you there, and you'll occupy a suitable position in the Soviet scientific community. Everybody remembers you and loves you." Moskvitinoff showed him his business card which read, "Professor of the University of New York City."

The Soviet academician reacted in a typical Communist fashion saying, "This is standard capitalist propaganda." I left the conference before Moskvitinoff and Kolupailo. At three in the morning, I was awakened by a phone call. Moskvitinoff was on the line. He apologized and said that he suffered pangs of remorse because the academician had wanted to talk to him before leaving Montreal. Moskvitinoff had boarded a bus in order to meet with the academician, and the driver of the bus had agreed to wait for him. The academician said he wanted to stay in Canada, but that he did not know how to apply for asylum; he asked

Moskvitinoff to help him. (Note: He also asked for the name of a person who had helped Dr. Moskvitinoff to escape from the U.S.S.R.) Moskvitinoff promised that he would contact him later, and now he was suffering from feelings of guilt. I calmed him down and said that if the academician sincerely wanted to remain in Canada, he could go to any police station and request assistance. In addition, I stated that in order to become an academician in the Soviet Union, one has to be completely, one hundred percent committed to the Communist cause.

"Do you remember another professor of hydraulics from the U.S.S.R. who was an old, depressed man? He had written a book on hydraulics, and he is not an academician. On the contrary, that guy who contacted you became an academician although he had achieved no genuine renown in the field of science. So Ivan Iosifovich, you can go back to bed and sleep with a clear conscience. It's very good that you did not help this person who undoubtedly is a thoroughly committed Communist and who most probably is also a member of the Soviet Secret Police. His mission, no doubt, was to penetrate Canada, under the guise of seeking political asylum, and to spy on American scientific projects.

Located on the campus of the University of New York City was an old military building with long hallways. One day Moskvitinoff was walking down the hallway to his classroom. Other professors had already begun their lectures. It was hot, and the doors were open. Several students joined him in the hallway. Passing by the large lecture hall, Moskvitinoff watched an instructor who was writing on a blackboard in the Russian language—writing which contained a mistake. The sentence read, "I lived in Kiev." Moskvitinoff involuntarily made a wry face.

The students noticed the change and asked him what happened. "It's written incorrectly," he said and explained the mistake. A few days later when he was passing the Russian language classroom, an instructor was waiting for him and said, "Was it you who was saying that I write incorrectly?" He answered "Yes." "So, what do you known about Russky?" "What do I know? I was a professor at the Institute of Communications in Leningrad; I possess a doctorate in science and so on." The instructor grinned and said, "But I from Kiev." (He said, ya is Kiev; the right way to say is Kieva.)

That story reminded me of another one. Colonel Druzhakin, a Don Cossack, was teaching a Russian language course for officers assigned to the British General Staff. During an examination, one of the examiners asked a captain a question, "What do you know about a male dog cable?" "You mean a field cable," the examinee pointed out. "What's the difference, male dog or field cable...just answer the question." *(In Russian, kobel means male dog while kabel refers to a wire that could be used in military communications.)* Individuals such as these became professors only with the help of patronage.

I became acquainted with Dr. Kolupailo in Iowa, at a conference on hydraulics. He was tall, a bit nervous, and constantly touching the hair on his chin (it could hardly be called a beard). He came to the United States in about 1947, and he was selected by Notre Dame University to be the Chairman of the Department of Hydraulics at their School of Engineering. Stepano, as I called him, had graduated from the Polytechnic Institute in St. Petersburg and was a Lithuanian citizen. He was a professor of hydraulics, and wrote a book entitled *Hydrometry*.

When Lithuania became independent he could travel as a foreigner to conferences in Moscow and Leningrad. He visited Leningrad on many occasions but arranged, in advance, for an old professor to meet him at the railway station. On one occasion, he bought some sausage and ham, and put it under the lining of his coat. He bought his ticket and boarded a train. During the trip, his fellow passenger was a Soviet Army colonel. As they talked, the colonel described Soviet achievements. In the evening the colonel asked, "Why don't you take off your coat? Unlike Lithuania we have law and order in the Soviet Union. I hear that they steal everything in Lithuania." Kolupailo was tightly wrapped in his coat and replied, "I like to be warm." He fell asleep. The colonel took off his boots, pants, and jacket, and said in a sarcastic tone, "Good night." Soon he, too, fell asleep. In the morning they awoke to find that all of the colonel's belongings had been stolen and also noticed that Kolupailo still had his coat. "Yes," Kolupailo said with sympathy, "It happens in Lithuania, too."

Before the train stopped at the railway station in Leningrad, Kolupailo looked out on the platform for his friend the professor. After he had seen him, he took off his belt, wrapped it around his coat, and prepared to meet his friend. He approached his friend, embraced him, and quickly gave him the sausage and the ham. The professor was also prepared for the meeting and he, too, had big pockets in his coat. He put the food into his pockets, but the militiamen were already on the spot, "Citizens! What are you doing here?" "Oh, I have just arrived from Lithuania and gave a hug to my old friend," Kolupailo answered. The militiamen replied gruffly, "Loitering is forbidden here; move along quickly." Everything turned out well, and every time Dr. Kolupailo came to the Soviet Union to take part in a conference, he brought food for his friend.

Dr. Kolupailo was a linguist. He could understand Russian, Lithuanian, German, French, English, Greek and Latin. He published his book *Bibliography of Hydrology* in which articles and books, published in many languages in many countries, were listed with accompanying abstracts.

An interesting episode occurred in Montreal at the conference on hydraulics. Stefano said that an old professor, the author of a book on hydraulics, was present among the members of the Soviet delegation. There was also a young academician who did not write anything of note except for a propaganda piece with the improbable title which read, *In Praise of the Hydraulic Sciences Founded in the New Regime and Developed by the Father of the People—Stalin*. During a break, Stefano told me that a group of Soviet men had asked him to come to a conference room. He agreed and at noon two Soviets came and took him to that room which was full of engineers and other people from the U.S.S.R. When Kolupailo entered, everyone in the room stood up and applauded.

At first he did not understand what was occurring. He saw five Soviet engineers, including the young academician, sitting at the conference table. The academician raised his hand, the applause subsided, and everyone sat down. The academician started to read a letter of honor which stated that Dr. Kolupailo, in recognition of his great services to the Soviet Union, had been awarded the Order of the Proletariat of the U.S.S.R. and the accompanying title of People's Scientist. Stefano quietly listened to his speech, stroked his chin hair (I still cannot call it a beard), and said that he had not rendered any services to the Soviet Union; he only occasionally helped his colleagues in the U.S.S.R. Moreover, after the occupation of Lithuania by the Red Army, when more than forty thousand Lithuanian citizens had been arrested and put in concentration camps, he had actively tried to save as many Lithuanians as possible.

On the whole, the Soviets had killed more than a million people in Lithuania. After he said these things he placed the medal and letter of honor on the table and proudly left the room with his head held high. The individuals at the conference table were staring dejectedly, and the people who were standing tried to leave the room as quickly as possible. The Reds had prepared refreshments which were available in another room, but nobody partook of the food and drink. I should mention that I had not been invited to the meeting, but Stefano informed me about it, and I had an opportunity to see and hear everything from the hallway.

Howard Nelson, an American married to a German woman, came to America from Berlin after the war. He had a Ph.D. in agricultural science. He contacted me because he was interested in Yadoff's dynamic tube and my name was mentioned in the patent. It was summer and, as I was preparing to go to France, my small house would be vacant for a month. I suggested to the Nelsons that they spend that month in my house.

I stayed with the Zhdanoff brothers in Paris. The elder told me that my commander was in Paris, and his wife invited everybody for dinner the next day. I could not figure out who that commander was. I had many commanders in my life, and I was a commander myself. As for the Zhdanoffs, they remained silent. When I came to the dinner, I almost fainted when *podpolkovnik (lieutenant colonel)* Vladimir Shlyakhtin met us. It was that very Shlyakhtin who was with General Popoff in Tokmak, North Tavria, and was the general who killed a fly on his head on the eve of a big battle I have previously mentioned.

Volodya was very glad to see me and told Vanya and Kostya Zhdanoff that my apples had once save us from death. Those were the two bags of apples which the Tatar children delivered to my barracks. We loaded those bags on the *Alkiviadis* and had been tossed about on the Black Sea for ten days. But nobody could solve the mystery; how could the children living in Simferopol determine when and where our ship would arrive? Our dinner was interrupted by these memories, and it was very nice to plunge again into the epoch of our fighting youth which was so dear to our hearts.

The next day was Sunday, and we went to church where I met Katy Nelson. She shrieked with amazement at seeing me. It was a miracle. Katy lived in West Berlin. She had come to Paris for the first time and decided to go to a Russian church. Such an unexpected meeting! We decided to have dinner at Maxims, a famous Parisian restaurant. Katy was with her husband Bud (Howard) Nelson. Time passed by quickly. At three in the morning we paid the bill and left a great deal of money on the table for tips. But when we came to a taxi stand, I discovered I had no money at all. Bud told the taxi driver to take me to my house and that I would pay him at two that afternoon. The driver agreed. Not only did he drive me home, but helped me to get upstairs and opened the door with my key. At two he came for his fee. I paid the amount shown on his meter and gave him a generous tip. I never encountered anything like this in other countries. Maybe Paris is different now? I met Katy and Bud after that and had many other good times with them.

After visiting France, I decided to go to Brussels where I met my old friend Chingiz Uluchy, an outstanding mathematician. He was a Turk. There I also met Soviet scientists. There were about seventy of them, and they went everywhere together. Their life revolved around a tightly planned schedule—meal, session, break, session, meal, bedtime.

There was a Cossack *stanitsa* in Brussels. General Illovaysky was the ataman. I wanted to pay my respects to him and visit with him. At that time, I was known as the Chairman of the Army Council of the Don Cossacks Outside of Russia. An invalid opened the door and described me to the general, explaining to him the purpose of my visit. After a short exchange of polite greetings, he asked me about my parents and my stanitsa, etc. Later I learned that General Polyakoff had sent a letter from the United States to General Illovaysky providing him with detailed information about me. I invited the general and everyone on the board of the stanitsa to a dinner at the hotel where I was staying. My invitation was accepted.

My hotel was composed of two buildings, one in the front with a restaurant in it, the other with rooms located off the courtyard. At a certain hour, a hotel employee came to me and reported that a group of Russians wanted to see me. I went out and was shocked at the sight of a procession moving toward me; the ataman held a mace in his hand, his aide had a battle saber. About twenty men accompanied them. The ataman addressed me with a welcoming speech and stressed that his stanitsa really appreciated the fact that, busy as I was, I still had time to meet with them. I invited them all to join me at the restaurant. Many curious people were watching our solemn meeting; this was a totally new experience for them. They decided that I was no less than a Russian prince. The hotel employees had treated me kindly before that day, but after that they addressed me with a sense of awe (I can thank the general for that).

I delivered a report at the Congress of Specialists on Applied Mechanics in Brussels. I became acquainted at this meeting with Grigory Epifanoff, a Cossack from Novocherkassk. He was married to a Belgian woman, the daughter of an engineer contractor who owned a number of hotels and who collected the finest European wines, some more than a hundred years old. He liked to entertain me, and I remember with pleasure my visits to his wine cellar.

When the congress in Brussels was over, I decided to travel to the Netherlands. I had become acquainted with Mr. Freeman and his wife in America. Ted Freeman was from England and his wife was from Holland. She gave me her brother's address just in case I ever visited The Netherlands. I took a train from Brussels to Amsterdam and called Anna Freeman's brother. We decided to meet the next day. I settled into some kind of small hotel; it was a house where the owners and the guests lived like a big family. I told the lady who owned the hotel that I wanted to take a bath.

As soon as I got into the warm water, I heard someone knocking at the door. "Do you need some help?" Somewhat confused I said, "No." In a minute she was knocking again. "Maybe you need someone to rub your back?" This happened several times. Her intrusive kindness irritated me, and I got out of the bath.

The next day I met Anna Freeman's family. Her brother and his wife were fluent in English. I told them about the reason for my arrival; I wanted to see Professor Tassy's hydraulics laboratory. They were ready to take me to Delft where the laboratory was located. In two hours I was in Delft. We arrived there before lunch, and the head of the laboratory, Professor Mosterman, was at office (they have lunch at noon in Holland). We talked to each other, and time quickly passed. We left at three that afternoon. I invited the professor and his wife and Anna's brother and his wife, Koos and Woos Voolsac, to join me for dinner.

The restaurant was small but very cozy. A small chamber orchestra was playing. We stayed until four in the morning. The bill was amazingly small. There were five of us, and we drank a great deal of cognac, paid the players in the orchestra for their excellent performance, and finally were presented with a bill for fifty dollars. If we had done this in New York, we would have had to pay about two hundred and fifty dollars for that dinner.

The next day we went to see hydraulic construction projects. About three in the afternoon, our car stopped and Woos suggested that we have a snack. She took sandwiches and beer out of her basket and asked me what kind of sandwich I preferred. I did not completely understand her, and chose the first one. It was filled with white, slightly smoked meat which was very tasty, and I ate two sandwiches. Later they told me that I had eaten smoked eel. When I lived on the Don, we thought that eels were not edible and that they were like grass snakes. And here, in Holland, they were considered to be delicacies.

I had an interesting conversation with Mosterman. He wanted to move to the United States as a permanent resident. He had been invited to work at a university and asked my advice. I told him that there was only one state professor in Holland, and that professor was about to retire. So Mosterman was a candidate for that position. Being a state professor, he could take part in both domestic and international projects and acquire recognition and prestige, as well as financial benefits. As far as his invitation was concerned, he had been invited by a private university and would hold only a second-rate, or even third-rate, position in America because he had not published anything there and was little known. There is strong competition among scientists in the United States, and he was above the competition in the Netherlands. So he had to make his own decision.

Four years later, I received an invitation from Professor Mosterman to deliver lectures on advanced hydraulics on an annual basis for a period of one and a half months. These lectures were to be given, in the Netherlands, to postgraduate engineers. I lectured for four days a week, and on Friday, Saturday and Sunday I could visit Germany, France, Belgium, Great Britain, Austria and other European countries. My business connections with the University of Delft in Holland lasted for twenty-five years. Today Professor Mosterman remains my close friend, and he visited me in South Carolina in 1992. Now he has a peculiar task; he is the head of the commission which verifies the titles and the knowledge of scientists from the former Soviet Union who are working in European countries. He determines if they really deserve titles such as doctor or academician, or if they had received their degrees or titles merely because of their connection with the Communist Party.

He is still as full of energy as he was in 1956; only his hair is grayer. I received a remarkable gift from my friends in the Netherlands, an old map of Holland painted in color in the Seventeenth Century when Holland was the dominant sea power. There are probably only two maps like this in the world, and I own one of them.

I consider my meetings with common Russian people, whose fate forced them to journey to distant and unknown lands, to be no less an important part of my life. A plain man from Minsk, Ivan Alekseevich, lived in New Jersey not far from my house. Once he had worked at a big pharmaceutical plant. When I met him, he had retired. His life was very interesting. He ran away from Russia. His father was well-to-do and owned his own land. His father also had two oxen, a horse, a melon patch, and a house with various buildings. He grew wheat.

Ivan was twenty years old when he decided to run away to America. Naturally he had no money. Then the following event occurred. His father purchased a mower and had to pay the sales agent. On the day when the agent was supposed to arrive, Ivan's father called him said, "Go to the barn; look in the right corner where the wheat is stored. You'll find a box located there containing three hundred rubles. Take one hundred rubles and bring them to me, and put the rest in the box and leave it in the same place that you found it." But Ivan arranged things in a different way. He gave one hundred rubles to his father, left one hundred rubles in the box, and took one hundred rubles for himself. Soon he traveled to America as a sailor. I told him, "Ivan Alekseevich! So you had stolen the money?" "No," he said. "I took my share. One hundred rubles was for my father, one hundred rubles was for my brother, and the final one hundred rubles was for me. I divided it equally. We had lived together, worked together, and that money had been earned by all of us."

Ivan Alekseevich came to the United States before the First World War. He had heard plenty of revolutionary propaganda about the "blood-sucking Tsar" and the glory of socialist achievements, so in 1932 he decided to return to the Soviet Union to help build socialism. He bought good tools (he had become a handyman in the United States), and came to the U.S.S.R. He was welcomed and sent to Siberia to construct roads and build cities. He was not an American citizen, though he had lived in the United States for more than fifteen years. In Siberia he saw what Soviet life was really like. Food was scarce and wages were low.

Soon Ivan noticed that more than half of his high-quality tools had been stolen. Besides that, they ordered him to do unnecessary work. When he mentioned to his supervisors that his six-month visa was about ready to expire and that he had to return to America, they told him, "You came to build? Now stay and keep on building." Ivan managed to escape—first to Moscow and then to the United States. He told me some of the details of this remarkable escape.

The railroad was a twelve hour drive from the construction site. Ivan found two Germans among the workers; they felt sympathy for his plight and informed him when the train was due to arrive. Those Germans had to take some materials and deliver them to the train, receiving food supplies in return. They left in the evening and arrived at the railway station in the morning. These men saved him. They drove him to the station where he managed to board the train which was departing for Moscow. When he arrived in the Soviet capital, he immediately went to the American Embassy where they helped him to return to the United States.

"The Tsar is to blame!" Ivan Alekseevich said when we discussed Russian affairs. "Wait a minute, Ivan," I said. "You went to the Soviet Union to construct Communist buildings for the Reds. Why do mention the Tsar?" "Why?" he asked with surprise. "And who allowed those crooks to grab the power?"

It's not easy to understand a psychology like that, but Ivan was an uneducated man. But how can one understand a Soviet historian, a professor at the Moscow State University, who told me with passion that, "Nicholas the Second was a bloodsucker." "Whose blood did he drink?" I asked. "Lenin, Trotsky and Stalin were alive, and the Tsar and his family were murdered and their bodies burned." I recommended that this good-for-nothing professor visit a library on Forty-second Street in New York and read genuine histories, not fairy tales, of Imperial Russia and the record of the enormous crimes committed by Lenin and his henchmen.

Once while living in New Jersey, I was walking home and a car stopped on the road. The driver said, "Get in, Professor. I'll drive you to wherever you need to go." I thanked him and said that I'd rather walk. He said, "Don't be afraid. I am Ivan Mikhailovich Kurovsky, from Smolensk." "Oh, a Smolensky

Cossack," I said and got in the car. He told me the tragic story of his parents and the truth about Khatyn *(Khatyn was the site of an infamous Soviet massacre)*. His father was considered to be a "bourgeois" because he had land, two oxen and two horses. He was not touched by the first wave of the communist hunt for "capitalists." But he was taken in the second wave which swept up all those who worked hard and were more or less well-to-do. His father was arrested and disappeared. Soon his mother was arrested, and he, a ten year old boy, was sent to a concentration camp in Siberia.

That camp was filled with the underaged who were forced to perform hard labor. Many of these young people died. After two years, a small group of youngsters decided to escape. Ivan was with them. They moved only at night, and slept in the day. They ate cedar nuts which they found in the taiga forest. After four weeks they saw a settlement. They knocked at the door of the first house, and came into the yard. "The dogs looked fierce, but they did not touch us," Ivan Mikhailovich told me. An elderly woman came out and asked what we were looking for. We answered, bread. She gave us two loaves of bread (there were five of us) and told us to go to another village, warning us not to tell anyone that we had contacted her. We thanked her and went away.

We hid in the forest for two days for fear that the woman would betray us to the authorities. Then we came to a village and went directly to the Communist authorities. An old man was sitting at the office. He smiled and asked to see our documents. We said we had lost them in the forest. He gave us new documents and told us to go to another village to look for a job. I think that the old man understood who we were but wanted to save us. We went to another village and were legally hired by the commune. I enrolled in a school for training electricians, but life was so monotonous there. I wanted to come home, but I knew that I would be arrested when I showed up. I really wanted to see my mother and my father. I earned some money and bought a railway ticket. I came to Smolensk at night. I went to see my friend, but I did not go to my house. My friend almost fainted when he saw me. I had to earn my living and I asked him to help me find a job.

My friend worked at night cleaning cesspools. We broke frozen human excrement with crowbars, threw it with our hands into a cart, and took it away. As if on purpose, we cleaned our first cesspool near the NKVD (*Soviet Secret Police*) building. We were cleaning the cesspool in the yard and the smell of tasty food drifted out of a window of the building (the cesspool was located near the cafeteria). I could see piles of crusty bread on the tables. By this time the crowbars had frozen to our hands, and we were very hungry. But I was patient. I saw the red, healthy faces, and I could hear them laughing as they discussed people's sufferings.

I spent a winter there and left Smolensk in the summer. Then I studied and became a railroad worker. I married in 1939, and my wife and I were waiting for the birth of our first child. The war broke out, and when the Germans captured Smolensk, I joined a Russian-German detachment. The German administration distributed food to the residents. The children and pregnant women received vegetables and chocolate. I retreated with the German army and came to the United States after the war. I worked as an electrician and a plumber here. Ivan Mikhailovich finished his sad story.

He had two daughters and two sons in the United States. His eldest son died of cancer, and one of his daughters had an auto accident and became an invalid. His wife died of heart problems, and Ivan Mikhailovich died of cancer. Another daughter and son are still living. The daughter is working and doing well, while the son is "loafing" and lives on welfare. So nobody remained from the Kurovsky family who could be of use to Russia.

Once while I was working in the yard, a stranger approached. He called my first name and patronymic and introduced himself, "I am a Cossack. I have been looking for you for a long time." I invited him into the house. He entered, saw an icon, crossed himself and knelt in prayer. Then he stood up and addressed me, "I am Ivan Aleksandrovich Tkachenko, a Cossack from stanitsa Elizavetinskaya." "Nice to meet you," I said. "How is Elizavetinskaya? Is the store at Kapustiansky still there? They sold nice cloth at that place." "How do you know about the store?" my guest asked in surprise. "There is not a trace of it now." "It's a pity; I often came to Elizavetinskaya from Novocherkassk. They had the best fish soup in the world at that place."

"There are almost no fish there now, and the water in the Don is polluted. The river is like a sewer now, and the fish taken from the Don and the Sea of Azov have the odor of petroleum and trash," my guest said. He continued, "Now I'll tell you one of my stories. Once I decided to go fishing on the lower reaches of the

Don. I obtained a mare from the *kolkhoz* (state farm), a net, and went fishing. I found a quiet spot, threw the net, and caught several carp. I gradually moved closer to the Sea. I cast the net (called a *nakidka*) and caught one and a half bags of fish after two hours of fishing (*I should mention that in Czarist times one only had* to cast a *net to obtain four or five bags of fish. I might* add that it *only took ten minutes, including the break between casting the net and dragging it on shore, to obtain a catch of this size.*) I put the bags on the horse's back and placed myself between them. At first the horse ran well, but then she slowed down. When she had to cross a brook, she lay down and died. What was I to do?

I hid the bags in the reeds, but I had to get out of that scrape. The horse belonged to the *kolkhoz*, and I had ruined the "people's property." Thus I was an "enemy of the people." I took a few fish and went to the nearest khutor, which happened to be Obukhovsky, to see a veterinarian. I gave him four big carp and told him about my misfortune. He calmed me down and promised to tell the commissar of the collective farm that the horse had contracted glanders and had died in the pasture. The veterinarian added that we would have to dig a pit, place the horse's body in it, and cover it with a thick layer of lime. I can't tell you how relieved I was. What a smart man he was! I took my catch and brought it home before dawn while everyone was asleep. I was very thankful that the veterinarian kept his word.

Ivan Aleksandrovich knew an extensive repertoire of Cossack songs which he sang with real style. It was a pleasant surprise that people still remembered the old songs from the Don region. Recently I was in Montreal, Canada where there is a strong *stanitsa* headed by Ataman I. I. Izverev. A Cossack woman from stanitsa Elizavetinskaya is living there. Her name is Cherkeshina, as I remember, and she amazed me with her knowledge of Cossack songs. I remember Elizavetinskaya with great affection. It is known for its *Kazatchy Erik*, a well-constructed channel dividing the stanitsa from the khutor Obukhovsky. The old people told me that the channel had been dug by the Cossacks in the Seventeenth Century during a war between the Cossacks and the Ottoman Empire. *(This was the war which ended with the Cossacks capturing Azov from the Turks.)* Elizavetinskaya is located about four kilometers from Azov and can be clearly seen from that city. When you are traveling by ship from Rostov to Azov and beyond, you notice that the Don divides into two branches—one passing Azov and the other khutor Obukhovsky. The Cossacks, who had been fighting with the Turks, separated Elizavetinskaya from Obukhovsky with the *Kazatchy Erik*, thus obtaining freedom of maneuver on the river.

Ivan Aleksandrovich was a very religious Cossack. He lived not far from the Alexander Nevsky church and always brought a pair of white doves to the church on Easter. The priest would let them go free. Ivan Aleksandrovich passed away recently.

I remember one phone call to my house. A man said that he was a Don Cossack and requested a meeting with me. He arrived at about four that afternoon. After our initial greeting he asked me, "Where are your sons? You have two sons it seems." "Thank you for you kind words, but I have no children," I said. "Oh, I have made a mistake," he said. "I would like to tell you, Nicholas Vasilyevich, that I am an atheist; I don't believe in God. There are many atheists in our Motherland now. We know that there is no God, so why should we believe?" Then he told me about the terrible life in Russia and the persecutions. When he finished I told him, "Each state has its laws, and each citizen must obey those laws. You must be a member of the *Comsomol (the Communist Youth League),* which means that you must also be a Communist. You may not have an official party card, but you certainly adhere to its beliefs and ideology.

"The Cossacks have a central, crucial belief; they will ask you, 'Do you believe in God?' They ask that question to every newcomer who wants to become a Cossack. If he said yes, they asked him to pray. It did not matter how he prayed, but it was important that he believed in God. Only when this question was settled was the individual admitted to the Cossack community. For that reason all Cossacks were religious. The Communists arranged everything from a Marxist viewpoint; as materialists they maintain that unless you can experience something with your senses, it doesn't exist and you can't believe in it.   The Communists steadily propagate the concept of materialism. Many people were deceived, adhering to those theories and have paid for that error with their lives.

"You were able to escape. However, you believe in a theory which clearly leads to decay in the spiritual realm; in addition, it creates envy, a desire for the property of others as well as the results of their work, and so on. You don't want to improve yourself, to love others, to adhere to all that is written in such simple words in Christ's Commandments. Thank you for telling me that you are an atheist. But try to conceal this fact in the future, for if you are an atheist or a homosexual, it's a great sin." We talked a great deal, and I hope that he changed his belief system.

As I have mentioned, I frequently traveled to Europe to deliver lectures. I visited other countries in my spare time, traveled a great deal, and met Cossacks as well as other Russian people. Colonel Druzhakin was the Ataman of the London stanitsa. Once I came to London from Amsterdam. I took a shuttle bus from the airport to the bus station where I was met by Colonel Druzhakin and Captain Pekhovsky. Captain Pekhovsky had been a Soviet aviator who flew his plane to the British zone in Germany in a daring bid for freedom. He had married a relative of General Alexander and had received a house as a dowry. He was a clever man and had a talent for fixing up property. Then he received four or five houses in the center of London as a gift. He gave rich donations to the Russian Orthodox Church and to Cossack organizations for celebrations.

The following occurrence happened to me. When I met them, I put my suitcase on the ground and held my briefcase with my documents in my hands. Then Korney Pekhovsky invited us to his house where his wife Victoria had prepared a supper. She greeted me and showed me to my room. She said that supper would be served in ten minutes. We had an excellent sour borscht, meat and dessert. Of course, vodka was available. We went to our rooms at two that morning. I opened what I thought was my suitcase and was stupefied. Located in that suitcase was a black bra and white spider. Under that I found a white bra with a black spider. (Note: Spiders were embroidered on the bra.) What is going on? I thought I closed the suitcase. Maybe I had drunk too much vodka? No. I opened the suitcase again and saw the same contents—lady's underwear, soap, powder. I pondered. My suitcase was similar to this one in appearance, and I could open it with the same key.

I went to bed, and soon heard Victoria walking in the hallway. She said it was seven in the morning and breakfast would be ready in half an hour. I was in the dining room thirty minutes later. Korney and Colonel Druzhakin were already there. I looked exhausted. "How did you sleep?" they asked. I said that I had not slept at all. "Why?" "Let's go upstairs, and I'll show you why." We went to my room and opened the suitcase. "So this is how an American professor travels!" Victoria exclaimed. Everybody laughed. We called the bus station, and they told us that my suitcase was in their office. We successfully exchanged the suitcases.

Now I would like to relate another interesting episode. I was in Delft, Holland. After a lecture one, of the professors invited me to dinner. I came to his house at six that evening. The hostess offered me some drinks. "It's so nice to be with you," I said. "I know that the phone calls won't disturb me here." I hadn't yet finished saying this when a phone rang. It was Korney, calling me from London. He asked me to meet his wife at eight that night in Amsterdam. I thanked the professor and his wife and went to my hotel where I learned that the train for Amsterdam had already departed. I did not like the idea of going there by taxi, for the distance was more than fifty kilometers (thirty miles). Then the owner of the hotel helped me. He offered to drive me to Amsterdam, and found a room for Victoria in his hotel. (It was the busy season when all the hotel rooms were occupied.) As soon as we arrived at the airport, it was announced over the loudspeaker, "Professor Feodoroff, Mrs. Victoria Perkhoskaya is waiting for you at the information desk."

On the way to the hotel, Victoria said that she had been in Italy with her husband, and that her suitcase had been lost on the trip to Holland. Finally the suitcase was located in Holland, and she asked customs to send it to England, but customs had refused to do that. They said that they had to examine its contents in her presence. That was the reason she had traveled to the Netherlands. The next day we went to customs, and the customs officer produced the suitcase. He said, however, that there was no need for the owner to travel to Holland. "What is going on?" she asked. "I requested that your customs department send my suitcase to London, but they said they had to check its contents first. And now you return it to me without an inspection. I paid more than two hundred dollars for my ticket," Victoria said. "I am sorry," the officer answered quietly. "There must be some mistake." That was a Dutch understatement.

The London *stanitsa*, named after Tsarevitch *(Crown Prince)* Alexey, August Ataman of All Cossack Armies, was very active under Ataman *Khorunzhy* (cornet) Anatoly Pavlovich Minaeff and the representative of the Don Ataman Outside of Russia, Colonel Georgy Nikolaivich Druzhakin. Minaeff was married to an Italian woman who had given birth to two sons and had died soon after. His sons were both very talented. They studied hard and graduated from a British university but did not take part in Cossack activities. At the present time, the stanitsa is headed by Mikhail Alekseevich Taratukhin, the representative of the Don Cossacks, Ataman Outside of Russia, and the Triple Alliance of the Cossacks of the Don, Kuban, and Terek Regions.

While living in the Soviet Union, Captain Pekhovsky, a Terek Cossack, was in charge of military supplies at an air force base located in Novocherkassk. When he arrived in England, he started to work as a meter reader at apartment houses. He was allowed to visit the British equivalent of our U.S.O. and had met Victoria at a canteen. Victoria loved Korney, but her mother objected resolutely saying, "Don't even think of marrying that consumptive *(the captain was pale and thin)*, ragged fellow." But Victoria married Korney in spite of her mother's protests. He was a thrifty man and an excellent manager of rental property. In appreciation of his good work, Victoria's mother gave him some more houses to manage. When Korney passed away, Victoria wrote me that she had never had such a remarkable friend as Korney. She had been the happiest wife and now she was an inconsolable widow.

Victoria was not the only woman who was happy to be married to a Cossack. Many others were equally as happy; for example, Maria Avgustovna Milova, a German by origin, was married to the representative of the Don Ataman in Germany. But I came across very different situations as well. Some of my compatriots, having spent time with their girlfriends, left them and returned to the U.S.S.R. At first the Soviets welcomed them back, and then they killed them. And the poor women were left in the West alone with their misfortune. God is their judge.

Since childhood, I have loved to travel. It always seemed to me that every person, even those with a great love for their home, dream of seeing the world. I have traveled a great deal and seen a lot. Now I would like to share my travel experiences with the reader.

I was invited to deliver reports on the dynamics of fluid motion in rivers and wide reservoirs. The lecture was held in Turkey in 1975. I returned to the United States by the following route: Delhi, Bombay, Calcutta, Bangkok, Perth (Australia), Melbourne, and Wellington (New Zealand). I took the time to see many of the sights in these exotic countries.

I experienced a funny incident while passing through customs in Istanbul. The officers placed my suitcase on the scales and spoke in Turkish, pointing with amazement at my suitcase. After five minutes I asked them what was the matter. The officer explained to me in English, "We can't believe it; your suitcase weighs exactly twenty kilograms (forty-four pounds)." Everybody laughed, and they apologized for the delay. As a matter of fact, only luggage weighing no more than twenty kilograms is allowed to be taken on board, and I was the first person who had complied with regulation for many years.

After departing Ankara, where I successfully delivered my scientific paper, I flew to Teheran on a Turkish plane which had been made in the U.S.S.R. It was a heavy, rough and noisy aircraft. Fortunately, the trip was short. I spent two days in Teheran and continued on to India. The Society of Engineers in Bombay and Calcutta had been informed of my arrival. I landed in New Delhi at three in the morning, but a car was already waiting for me.

The representatives of the Society of Engineers of Delhi drove me to a hotel located about twenty miles from the airport. On the way there I asked him, "What happens if we meet cows lying in the road?" *(It is a well-known fact that cows are sacred animals in India.)* "Oh no! There will be no cows," the driver said with conviction. Five miles down the road we saw several cows lying across our path. What were we to do? We could not push them away or shout at them. However, the driver was inventive and "played" with the headlights, turning them on and off. The cows became irritated, and approximately thirty minutes later got up and wandered away.

The hotel was excellent. I could order anything I wanted at any time and have it delivered to my room. I decided to order tea. I should mention that I never drank unboiled water during my journeys. I applied the same rule to fruit, rinsing it with boiling water and peeling it. That's why I never fell ill.

The Minister of Agriculture came to visit me at eleven in the morning. He was interested in the problems associated with irrigation and the design of channels for flood control. He was accompanied by two Indians who were former students of mine at Columbia University.

Our conversation was very friendly and, I hope, proved advantageous to the Indian government. I recommended they invite Dr. Nelson who was well acquainted with the climate of

India, Indonesia, and the other countries of that region. I delivered a successful lecture at the local Society of Engineers. I spent only two days in Delhi. It is a very interesting city, and you would have to spend years to thoroughly understand it.

Arriving at the Bombay airport I was met by two engineers. One of them was my ex-student, one of the group of seven students. Bakhmetyev had liked to joke, "How are your seven kids? *(I hope the reader remembers the tale about a wolf and seven kids.)* He had turned into a respectable gentleman having been a thin, curious student.

My program consisted of presenting two days of lectures at the Polytechnic Institute and one day of lectures at the Institute of Engineering. My ex-student warned me, "When the lecture series at the Polytechnic Institute is over and you return to Bombay, stay where the train stops." *(The Polytechnic Institute was located forty miles from Bombay.)* I left the hotel in the morning and took a taxi to go to the railway station. I figured that it was not far away. The porter who carried my suitcase said to the driver, "Americano." Soon I realized that we were going in the wrong direction. I made a remark, but the driver snapped, "Oh, Efendy! I am driving you to the railroad station." We drove for about two blocks when I saw a policeman.

I figured out that I should have arrived at the railway station twenty minutes earlier. The policeman took down the tag number and the driver's license number and ordered him to take me to the station as soon as possible. I think the story ended at the police station where the scoundrel was taught a lesson. I went to buy a ticket at the railway station. A tall, slender man who had an appearance similar to that of the tribesmen who lived in the Caucasus Mountains stood in my way. "Efendy, let me carry your suitcase," he said. But I was an experienced traveler and knew that even in London or Amsterdam this was a way to have your luggage stolen, so I refused his offer.

I went to a counter to pay for my ticket, but the cashier sent me to another register. Different classes of tickets are sold at different counters in India. The young Indian followed me and offered his help again. He was a decent-looking chap, and I allowed him to follow me. He took my suitcase and went ahead. There were huge crowds of people in the station, and the large space was covered with thousands of people of different age, sex and social class. My companion cleared the way skillfully, and I would not have been able to take a step without his assistance. He led me to the train, then to my railway car, and said goodbye to me politely. I gave him two dollars which at that time equaled fourteen rupees *(in 1975 you could buy one kilogram of rice for two rupees)*. The Indian thanked me and asked when I would return. I said that I did not know.

The dean met me at the railway station near the Polytechnic Institute and drove me to my temporary apartment. It was a huge stone house which consisted of a large room of incredible size and a bathroom. The ceiling was about twelve meters (forty feet) in height. The room was furnished with a bed which was covered with a canopy. The house had possibly been built at the time of Muslim rule.

My lecture was a success, and I returned to my apartment in the evening. I had the only air-conditioning unit at the institute. The dean came to see me, and we talked until three that morning. I went to bed with the lights on. Something worried me. I opened my eyes and saw many lizards running down the canopy. I discovered a huge spider, larger than a hen's egg, in the opposite corner. I could not sleep for the rest of the night. What were those monsters going to do? At dawn I went out on the porch. One of the professors was sitting there. We talked to each other. He lamented that the British were to blame for the poverty in India. It's easy to blame somebody," I told him. "But you still have castes, in particular the Untouchables. You'll never shake hands with them, and these people are doomed to do dirty work all their lives." He did not say anything.

The second lecture was more interesting. The next day I left for Bombay. I arrived at the railway station at six in the afternoon, and the lecture began at eight that night. I went to the ticket counter to place a phone call to the chief engineer having forgotten his words, "Don't leave the place where the train stopped. Soon I understood that I had lost my way.

It was nine that night when they finally found me. But the audience, more than three hundred people, had been waiting for me patiently. I delivered my lecture in a luxurious mansion, a former residence of the British viceroy. The tables were loaded with various Indian dishes, and I sampled many examples of the national cuisine. The lecture started at ten that evening and finished at midnight. The discussions continued long after midnight, and at three in the morning the chief engineer invited me and two of his assistants to come to his house. When we arrived at the house, he wanted to turn on the light, but there was no light. The moon was shining, and he looked up and said thoughtfully, "They stole the light bulb again." The light bulb was at the level of the third story.

"Let's go in," he said. We entered and saw that his house had huge rooms, covered with carpets and furnished with vases—all luxury items. "I've heard that you like whisky. We have some," the owner said. A servant was standing behind each chair, and three servants were distributing drinks and refreshments. As if by magic, all kinds of food appeared on our plates. As we finished sampling each plate, it disappeared without notice. It was interesting for me to watch the servants. One of them had a countenance that suggested that it would have given him great pleasure to have choked all of us.

We drank and ate, and the chief engineer invited us for breakfast at five in the morning. The table was set up on the ground in front of the palace on the shore of the Gulf of Bombay. The table contained a rich variety of dishes, but I was most attracted by the sight of the Gulf; there was not a ripple on its surface, and it was shimmering with all the colors of the dawning day. One could view a strip of water reddened by the rising sun, and then the fireball appeared; but the air was fresh and clear, and, oh, what silence! The divine silence filled one with amazement at the creation of God—again what silence! Large bushes covered with blossoms bent down to the level of the sea, and nature was fragrant with the joy of life. We had a long breakfast. Everything good has to end, and I said goodbye and went to the hotel. Later in the morning I flew to Calcutta.

Calcutta is a city of contrasts. I was not a tourist and had no opportunity to see all the places of interest, but still I saw something of the city. The streets, except for the central parts of the city, are very narrow and crowded. The population of India is approximately a billion people, and many live in the cities creating huge crowds. I saw a group of people in the street who discussed something in a lively manner. A cow went by and left its dung there. One of the Indians cleaned up the cow dung with a piece of paper and fell asleep almost in the same spot where the cow excrement had been deposited. Maybe he wanted to be closer to a "sacred substance" *(cows are sacred in India),* or perhaps he just did not care.

I witnessed a tropical shower while I was in India. My hotel was in front of a bank. I went out, intending to cross the street and cash my American Express check. I only needed to take two steps, for the street was very narrow. Suddenly the sky opened, and the rain completely drenched me. The sight of three young Indian girls was much more impressive; it reminded me of the pictures from *One Thousand and One Nights*—their beautiful bodies were tightly wrapped in wet saris.

I entered the bank, wet but impressed, cashed the check, and continued to observe the street life. I had an opportunity to visit the suburbs of the city. Here there were many lakes filled with crocodiles. In fact, I could not see the water—just crocodiles. When I asked why they didn't use the crocodiles as food, they answered that the crocodiles were sacred, too.

The Calcutta airport is very large. I was sitting in a reception area which contained long leather sofas on both sides of the entrance. There was no crowd in this area, and I became aware of a sweet odor and the sound of singing which originated from the street. Soon a procession appeared which consisted of three Buddhist monks followed by a group of dancing women. The monks were dressed in saffron-yellow robes and the women covered their path with flowers. The procession entered the reception area. The head monk sat on a sofa with two women sitting on either side of him. Other women knelt and kept on covering the floor around him with flowers. Two other monks were standing. People started to crowd around this group. They knelt and moved toward the monk who was sitting in that position. He took flower garlands from one of the women and put them around the necks of his kneeling followers. The women formed a passage with the chief monk sitting at one end and two monks standing at the other end. All the surrounding area was covered with flowers. The procedure took about an hour. Then the flow of worshipers stopped, and the chief monk opened an English-language newspaper, turned to the section containing the comics, and started reading.

Soon the departure of my plane for Thailand was announced. I took a Japanese plane to Bangkok where two Thai engineers met me and drove me to a hotel. They told me not to drink unboiled water or eat raw fruit. I had to deliver two lectures the next day one at the Institute of Technology and the other at the Institute of Engineering. The majority of the people living in Thailand today are descendants of tribal groups which moved south from China to escape the despotic rule of the Chinese Emperors. These tribes settled in many areas of Southeast Asia with a particularly large contingent moving into the Menam Chao

Phraya river valley. The Thais are Buddhists, and their temples, known as *wats*, are famous for their great beauty, especially the majestic main *wat* in Bangkok where they keep a golden statue of Buddha.

The temple is covered with light blue mosaics about which there is an interesting story. Long ago the Thais had ordered blue chinaware from China, including cups, saucers, plates, and so on. The Chinese filled the order and loaded the goods on a barge. As the barge was sailing to Siam, a storm broke out and almost all the chinaware was broken. At first they wanted to throw the shards away, but the chief monk ordered them to cover the face of the temple with the broken pieces. Anyhow, after many years of hard work, the temple is one of the wonders of the world. Two statues of Siamese cats with their mouths wide open are standing at the entrance. A lady wanted to have a picture taken while she was standing next to the cats. I took the picture of her, and it looked very nice.

The next day I went down the Menam Chao Phraya river in a motor boat. I have never seen such a dirty river. Even the famous Red River in the United States, which carries a burden of up to eighty percent of diluted clay during the rainy season, seemed crystal clear when compared with the Menam.

My lectures were a great success, and on the next day I flew to Australia.

Thailand and India are countries with great contrasts. Life is relatively slow and quiet there. Nature is rich. I saw many crocodiles, working elephants and buffaloes, resting in the water. I saw very poor people who lived on a handful of rice and encountered very rich people who were living in luxury. I also saw hard-working Indian craftsmen, porters, tailors, and people engaging in various other trades. I witnessed solemn festivities in Thailand where an exotic royal armada, covered with various decorations, performed ceremonies for the benefit of the crowds gathered along the banks of the river. I watched young candidates for the monkhood, whose main task was to learn the virtues of patience and meekness. I had seen a lot, but my journey was not finished yet—Australia lay ahead.

Seamen have an ancient custom; when the ship crosses the Equator, they dunk the uninitiated in the ocean, and then they celebrate by giving special certificates and serving a good dinner. Alas, I crossed the equator on a plane and could only dream about the old custom. I arrived in Perth at three in the morning. I noticed a sign attached to a glass wall in the customs area: "Prof. Feodoroff, welcome! Go to the information desk; we are waiting for you." The dean of the School of Engineering and the driver were waiting for me. In a few minutes we were in a hotel.

It was a small, cozy hotel which could accommodate ten people. To my surprise, the door was not locked. We entered a small hall and saw a note on a table: "Welcome. Your room is number four. The key is here." My room was big and bright and the windows opened onto the garden. I wanted a drink. The dean asked me if I would be present for breakfast at his house at noon. I gave him a positive answer and he left. I was thirsty. I was used to drinking only boiled water and did not comprehend that Australian water was very pure and that one could drink it from the tap. At ten in the morning, I went downstairs, and the hostess served me a tasty breakfast which consisted of fresh eggs and bacon, coffee and fresh rolls. At noon the dean and the driver came to pick me up.

Three professors and their relatives had been waiting for us at the dean's house. They showed me my suggested schedule. During the first two days I was to deliver my lectures and make a report concerning my research. However, I wanted to tell them about politics, about Soviet deception and propaganda techniques, and about the truth that was being revealed by individuals who had managed to escape from the U.S.S.R. I planned to present three lectures with the first being on the subject of the truth about life in the U.S.S.R. This would be followed by a lecture on education in Europe and America with the concluding lecture to be on the subject of flood control in the United States and the attitude of the U.S. Congress towards scientific projects. The dean discussed this proposed schedule with the professors, and they decided that my lecture about the realities of life in the Soviet union would be held on the third day and would have a time limit of one hour.

I did not need time for preparation. I was ready. I might add that my lectures were well received, and the lecture on the true nature of conditions in the Soviet Union lasted for three hours instead of one. The audience asked me many questions. An article was published in a local paper that stated, "In spite of the fact that Professor Feodoroff is a victim of the Communists, his lecture was very unbiased and interesting."

I became acquainted with Mr. von Miller there. His father had been an officer in His Majesty's (Russian) Guards

Regiment. He had a factory in Australia where purses, wallets, and other products were made from kangaroo leather. I remembered that there were other Russian people living in Australia who liked to hunt. They were a nice group—a White Army veteran, a Polish man and a German who had served in the Wehrmacht. On one occasion they decided to go on a kangaroo hunt.

After a long search they spotted a kangaroo. The Russian brought his gun but did not shoot, the German aimed without shooting, and the Pole fired a shot. The animal fell down; the Pole approached it and covered it with his jacket. Then he stepped aside to take a picture. At that moment the stunned animal came to life, jumped into a forest, and disappeared. The Pole screamed excitedly, "Shoot! It has my jacket!" But there was not a trace of the kangaroo who had jumped away with the man's jacket. The Pole was in despair, for there was two thousand dollars in the jacket. They only found the piece of clothing some two hours later. The Pole asked the Russian why he had not fired. "When I was aiming, I saw his sad, olive eyes. I had fired many a shot under combat conditions, and I never missed my target. But here...." The German said the same thing; he could not shoot an animal with such beautiful eyes.

I met a Russian priest in Australia. He had a rose *nalivka (a type of brandy)* of remarkable quality in his house; nothing could be compared to it. Unfortunately that priest and his wife have passed away, and the recipe is lost forever.

After five days I flew to Melbourne to deliver lectures there. Melbourne is an industrial city, and its buildings reminded me of America. I was invited to answer questions on television, but the timing of the program was inconvenient for me as I had to travel to New Zealand. There was a Cossack stanitsa in Melbourne, headed by Ataman Aleksander Efimovich Kunakoff. I attended a dinner there, after which I delivered a lecture. Bishop Savva of Australia, residents of the stanitsa, the Russian church Cossack chorus, and guests were present at the dinner which was opened with a prayer and the singing of the Russian National Anthem. Several speakers addressed the audience. I remember a gentleman whose sister worked at the library of the Soviet Consulate. He had arrived in Australia two years previously. I was told that whatever we said would be known in the Soviet Consulate within an hour. So that gentleman began, "Comrade...excuse me, Mister Ataman." Then the standard wishes for health, success and so on followed. The chorus performed the anthems of the Don, Kuban and Terek regions and also performed several Cossack songs. It was very nice to listen to the excellent singers, and it was a pity that we had to leave.

Instead of broadcasting on television, I spoke over Australian radio. The format for the program consisted of the host asking us several questions and the four guests providing the answers. The other guests were a disciple of the blind Indian philosopher Bati-Bati, the winner of the Miss Asia contest, and an English professor. One of the questions concerned our attitude toward homosexuals. The Englishman said that it was a normal variant of human behavior, while the Indian stated that, on the contrary, it was abnormal. I replied that it was a disease, and that it was necessary to treat homosexuals in psychiatric clinics. The girl said that she was incompetent to answer that question. Then the host asked a question about the situation in the U.S.S.R. Everyone except for me stated that the situation in the Soviet Union was good, and when I began to tell about the horrors of life in the U.S.S.R., the broadcast was terminated. In an hour I departed Australia on a flight to New Zealand.

On a map, New Zealand looks like two large fish. I landed in Wellington and was met and driven to a hotel. In a couple of hours I was traveling along the shore in a motor boat. Two engineers who accompanied me suggested that we have a look at the exotic places found in New Zealand. We went ashore at a secluded beach, and soon heard marvelous singing. The Polynesian fishermen were the ones who were singing. We spent some time in their village and returned to my hotel in Wellington.

I gave a lecture at the university and flew to the United States the next day. En route the airplane stopped at the island of Fiji. The people have unusual customs there; their clothes are very scanty, just covering the most important part of the body. Men are tall, about two meters (six and a half feet) in height. Women are, as a rule, plump and short, about a meter and a half (about five feet) in height. Our next stop was in Hawaii. I could hardly recognize the island; I could not locate places that I had seen in 1937-38. Multi-story apartment houses, condominiums and luxury hotels had replaced the one-story houses which had resembled Cossack bungalows. But the beauty of nature had been preserved, and I enjoyed smelling the fragrance of the flowers that grow on Oahu. So America lay ahead. The weather favored us. We flew the last three thousand miles over the glassy surface of the ocean under the cover of the blue tropical sky. It was easy for me to travel from Los Angeles to New York.

Many times in my youth I was offered to tell my fortunes. I kept refusing. I did not want to know what is in the cards for me. But I know for sure that my life is going to be very unusual. Artist: Nadya Karnov.

Chapter 5

COSSACKS OUTSIDE OF RUSSIA

Whatever happened in my life, no matter how interesting and fascinating my scientific and teaching activities had been, I always recognized that I was a Don Cossack. In my heart I was always concerned for my Motherland, and I was deeply worried about the fate of those Cossacks who remained under the heel of the Communist dictatorship. I was equally concerned about the conditions of those Cossacks, like me, who lived in exile. Our journey of many years, which had started at the time of the evacuation from the Crimea, is still going on. Its end can be clearly seen now, for almost all of the White veterans have appeared before the Throne of God, and their children have grown up on a new soil. I am convinced that, despite all the horrors of the Twentieth Century that have been visited on the Cossacks, they will revive, and the strength of the revival will appear in their native land, in the souls of the young Cossacks who are now raising the Cossack banners in the Don, Kuban, and Terek regions, and in Siberia. We'll not return to our Motherland physically, but we never left it spiritually.

I always took an active part in Cossack affairs in the United States and in Europe, but I never thought my senior friends would nominate me for the position of the Ataman of the All-State Army of the Don Cossacks outside of Russia, and that the elections would reaffirm the nomination. I always realized how "heavy the Ataman's mace was" and understood how difficult it would be for me, being busy with my scientific work, to manage the Army affairs effectively. And the situation of the Army in the Sixties was very complicated.

In 1965, Ataman G. Polyakoff declared, without my knowledge, that I was appointed as the deputy of Ataman V.V.D. I was surprised. To begin with, I went to General Feodor Feodorovich Abramoff to clear up the situation. Usually Ataman General Polyakoff informed me ahead of time about any orders which he was preparing. And now I wanted to tell General Abramoff that I was unable to hold that position because I was very busy at the university and was engaged in scientific work. I wanted to send my refusal to the newspaper. But Feodor Feodorovich convinced me not to refuse the position. I told Ivan Alekseevich Polyakoff that I agreed, but that I could not give much time to Cossack affairs. But General Polyakoff persisted, and I accepted the position.

The elections were held in 1965. Russian Cossacks of all the political wings participated, except for the Anarchists and Communists—the demolishers of the family and the state. In addition, the Cossack separatists, who were under the control of the Papal authorities and who belonged to the Uniate church, also did not participate. *(As can be seen, the Vatican provided assistance to the separatist Cossacks.)*

Mrs. Baikalova-Latysheva, who resided in Nice, told me about that new formation established by the separatists. Her husband, Baikaloff-Latysheff, was an outstanding artist and had won many awards at international expositions. He spent his last years in Spain where he found shelter in a peaceful country ruled by General Franco. Other European countries had been disturbed by the Second World War and by Soviet influence. Before she came to France, she had lived in Yugoslavia and worked for a Serbian newspaper. She was fluent in Serb, Italian, French, English, and, of course, Russian. She was considered to be a excellent worker at the newspaper.

Once a Papal nuncio came to the editorial office and asked for information about local Cossacks. The editor-in-chief said that he could only provide him with superficial information, but that there was a lady. The nuncio asked Mrs. Baikalova to invite the local president of the Cossacks to the residence of a Catholic priest, and when the Cossack leader arrived there he gave him a large sum of money. Later the nuncio realized that he had made a mistake and had given the money to the wrong organization. *(He had intended to give the money to the separatist Cossacks.)* We knew that the separatist Cossacks were also not squeamish about obtaining money from the Reds.

But I'll return to the election procedure. The Army Council consisted of people who were well-known to the émigrés. It was headed by a Colonel of the Imperial General Staff, N. A. Hoklacheff. His aide, Lieutenant Colonel of the General Staff V. M. Azhogin, Lieutenant of His Majesty's Guards Regiment E. A. Samsonoff, architect N. D. Popoff, and others, were members of the council. The representatives of the Russian émigré press were invited to record the voting process. Included were representatives from *Russkaya Zhizn, Russia, Novoe Russkoe Slovo, Nashi Vesty, Pereklichka,* and other newspapers.

A church service took place in honor of the newly elected Ataman at the main synod of the Russian Orthodox Church Outside of Russia. Vladyko Nikon prayed at a special service and blessed me with an icon. A dinner was served after that event at Columbia University's faculty club. It was a beautiful gathering of those who came for the celebration. I was also elected the President of the Society for the Relief of Russian War Invalids because other candidates refused to take part in the election. It's easy to understand why because our opponents slandered and defamed us. The created endless lawsuits; their slanderous publications were like a nightmare.

I devoted all the time that I could spare from my university activities to my service to the Cossacks. Sometimes I had to sacrifice my time, leaving my scientific research and rushing to a meeting or a session, solving urgent problems connected with the Cossack community. Ataman I. A. Polyakoff was giving up his responsibilities as his disease, asthma, was progressing.

Cossack life, like that of other Russian organizations, was rather monotonous. We had the balls where the Queen of the year was elected—on Tatyana's Day. As a rule they were organized by the Society of Engineers and the Society of the *Rodina* (Motherland). There were balls held in honor of the St. George Cavaliers, and in honor of the veterans of the Army Corps. I think that now I must be the only St. George Cavalier who is still alive.

My work mainly consisted of writing letter to American newspapers in order to expose the so-called "achievements" of the Soviet "paradise." The articles were published in such newspapers as the *Asbury Park Press* (New Jersey), and *The State* (South Carolina), and others. Letters to senators and congressmen were frequently sent. The activities of our board were not always consistent. Sometimes our good intentions produced no results, and all we to show for our efforts were the memories of the energy and the money that had been wasted in vain.

In 1967, esaul (Captain) Vladimir Nikiforovich Testin decided to create the Charity Fund in memory of P. N. Krasnoff. He invested the major share of his personal funds, a couple of thousand dollars was collected, and a house with ten acres of land was purchased in Howell, New Jersey, about a mile from the Aleksander-Nevsky church. It seemed that the Fund had no future, but Testin did not give up. The taxes on the land and the house "devoured" the scanty sum of money provided. The Fund received no donations. I lived in New York at that time.

Testin suggested that I buy, for a moderate price, a neighboring house with five acres of land. "It would be nice," Testin told me. "The members of the Army Council under the chairmanship of Lieutenant Colonel of the General Staff V. M. Azhogin asked me to buy the adjacent land and give it for use as a cemetery. And the priest, Rev. Valery Lukianoff, agreed to use the land as a cemetery. "It should generate a sizable income." Rev. Valery Lukianoff gave his approval. About two thousand graves could be placed on one acre. The law required that there be no less than a sixty-meter (two hundred foot) separation between a cemetery and a neighboring house. That requirement was fulfilled on three sides of the outlined cemetery, and we had to buy the old estate on the fourth side; otherwise the city would not allow us to arrange for the establishment of a cemetery.

Members of the Army Council convinced me to buy that land. I did not have enough money, but I had good credit. I sold my house in New York, borrowed money at the bank, and purchased the land with the house. Two years passed while we were waiting for a final decision. Then Testin passed away, and the Army Council decided to sell the Fund's estate and donate the money for the construction of the parish house—a place for meetings and several rooms for a Russian school, and a place for the library named in honor of P. N. Krasnoff. So it was accomplished, and now there is a bronze memorial plate at the entrance with an inscription on it that this library is dedicated to honor the memory of Ataman P. N. Krasnoff.

I was left with the house I had purchased. I never intended to live at that location which is about a mile from Lakewood, New Jersey, the largest Hassidic center in America.

Many Russians had settled there at the turn of the century because there were many Jews who owned poultry, yards and hired Russians as laborers. That's why there are many Russians in Lakewood now. With the arrival of the Russian emigrants after the Second World War, life was in full swing there. The Russian community supported a White Army veterans organization, a union of Pupils of the Gymnasium in Serbia, a Union of Russian Engineers, and an organization for Guards Cossacks. There were army and regiment celebrations; all the church holidays were celebrated; balls, lectures, meetings, and concerts were held in this area.

I remember a good deed which was accomplished during my tenure as Ataman—the presentation of the Cossack Memorial Cemetery in Lients, Austria. The history of that cemetery is as follows. On the initiative of the General of the General Staff Svyatoslav Denisoff (we called him "Svetik" being pupils of the Novocherkassk Gymnasium), the deputy Chief of Staff under Ataman General I. A. Polyakoff, a call was sent to all countries to collect money for a memorial dedicated to the preservation of the memory of the atrocities committed in Lients in 1945. *(This is the site where the British and other Allied forces forcefully returned White Russian personnel to the Soviet authorities. These White Russians were then executed.)* An especially large sum of money was collected in the United States and sent to Innsbruck in care of Nicholas Alekseovich Hokhlacheff. Generals Polyakoff and Denisoff, Colonel Rogozhin and Lieutenant Colonel Hokhlacheff took part in creating the design of the memorial. Gordienko, a Ukrainian, was taking care of the memorial and the cemetery. His son had been killed at the time of the tragedy and was buried there. And his other son had become insane as a result of the massacre committed by the British against the defenseless Cossacks. Gordienko and his wife spent the rest of their lives taking care of the cemetery. Cossack Lyashenko has taken care of the cemetery in recent years.

So one day in the early 1970s, the Austrian Ministry of Roads decided to "remove" the cemetery under the pretext that it was necessary to construct a road that would pass through the site. I wrote a petition to the governor of Austrian Tyrol asking him to preserved the memorial and the cemetery, for here the tragic events had occurred. The Ataman of the Kuban Cossacks, Colonel Tretyakoff, together with the Ataman of the Terek Cossacks, signed the petition. I sent copies to the mayors of

Innsbruck and Lients. I asked Goluboff to see the governor and schedule an appointment for me so that I could meet him and present him with a medal of the Don Army in commemoration of the Fiftieth Anniversary of the great tragedy of the Cossacks (their life in exile). We had that ceremony; it took place in a luxurious hotel in Innsbruck.

After the dinner I addressed the governor (Goluboff translated my speech) with words of gratitude for his kindness and asked him to preserve the cemetery. He promised to do everything possible and said, "Your grief is our grief because one of the ugliest events in the annals of civilization occurred on our land." We also raised the question of giving a special status to the cemetery—it had to be under the authority of Black Cross Society, because all the Cossacks who had perished there had served in the German Army in separate anti-Communist detachments. Russians, together with Austrians and Germans, fought against the Communists. The mayor of Innsbruck, who was present at the ceremony, gave me a book dealing with the history of the city. A year later I received notification that the cemetery, indeed, had been placed under the jurisdiction of the Black Cross Society and was being cared for in an appropriate manner.

F. Shcherbakova, wife of a White Army veteran, provided invaluable assistance in helping me bring this project to a successful conclusion. She owned a car which enabled me to travel to Innsbruck very quickly, even though I was delivering lectures in another country. I had paid all the expenses, including the dinner for the governor, because the ataman's treasury was empty then (when Ataman I. A. Polyakoff was alive, the membership fees from the stanitsas already had been reduced to zero).

I am very grateful to all those who helped to preserve the site of the tragedy for the education of future generations, and I am especially grateful to the Governor of Tyrol for his assistance. He kept his word, and now the Black Cross society maintains the cemetery.

There was another gratifying deed that I wish to describe. On the initiative of Dr. Oleg Yadoff, with the assistance of Captain of Aviation Boris Vasilyevich Sergievsky and Professor N. V. Feodoroff, General Denikin's memorial was established. The monument, a heavy granite six foot cross, was erected near the St. Mary Church at Vladimirskoye cemetery in New Jersey.

Later Professor N. V. Feodoroff and Captain Sergievsky set up a monument to the hero of the Don Army, Lieutenant-general Feodor Feodorovich Abramoff. The memorial, two meters (6.6 feet) in height, resembles a rock.

The press has a very important to play in influencing public opinion. The White Russian press in the United States reflected all facets of life in exile—from heroic deeds to unfortunate confrontations. A great many magazines and newspapers were published, and I would like to mention the most prominent.

The newspaper *Novoe Russkoe Slovo* (*New Russian Word*) has been published on the East Coast since 1910. It was founded by a Socialist-Revolutionary, Victor Shimkin. It was then the favorite newspaper of Russian Jews.

Another newspaper, Russia, had been founded by Mr. Rybakoff, an ethnic Russian. Its circulation is limited, and one can easily count the number of its subscribers. It is a Russian national newspaper.

The Russian Voice, was under the total control of the Soviet Union.

A number of magazines were published by patriotic organizations: *Pereklichka* (*Roll Call*), the journal of the military high school organization; *Nashy Vesty* (*Our News*), the journal of the White Russian veterans organization; *Donskoy Ataman Vestnik* (*Don Army Herald*), the journal of the Don Cossacks. *(This is but a sample of the publications sponsored by the Russian émigré community.)*

Russian Life was published on the West Coast. Mrs. Delianich, a Serb woman, was its editor-in-chief, and it remains a true Russian national newspaper.

Some magazines existed for a little over a year and then ceased publication. As a rule, the success of the publication depended on the personality of the editor as well as his persistence and ideological persuasion.

Nicholas Petrovich Rybakoff, the editor of *Russia*, passed away in 1962. Georgy Borisovich Aleksandrovsky, a warrant officer in the Russian Imperial Navy, carried on his work. But first he had to pay off debts which remained after Rybakoff's death, and pay a certain sum to Rybakoff's son. Only Prince Beloselsky-Belozersky and Captain Sergievsky could give that amount of money, but Mr. Aleksandrovsky had to convince them of the necessity of publishing the newspaper. At that moment I appeared on the scene. I talked to G. B. Aleksandrovsky (he was a mining engineer, and the similarity of our professions drew us together). He agreed to keep on publishing the newspaper. Then I sent invitations to all Russian organizations asking them to send their representatives to a dinner at Columbia University. Every one of them responded.

I arranged the menu, approved by a representative of the All-Russian Alliance, Colonel of the Imperial General Staff S. N. Rasnyanky, who had been a participant in the Bykov siege and later was a participant in the Kornilov Ice March campaign. The food was delicious, and after dessert I explained the reason for our meeting and asked Colonel Rasnyansky to explain the details for meeting the publication costs. B. V. Sergievsky promised to donate ten thousand dollars, and Prince Beloselsky-Belozersky also promised to help. He was absent but left his phone number. We called him, and said he would donate ten thousand dollars (five thousand at once and five thousand in two weeks). G. B. Aleksandrovsky was appointed the editor-in-chief. I thanked everyone for their support. S. N. Rasnyansky proposed we drink to our intimate friendship. *(This is a Russian custom permitting one to use the informal "you" or "thou" form)*. "But I am not a cadet, and I am more than twenty years younger than you," I said. But he insisted, and we had a formal drink together. *Russia* was published until 1976; G. B. Aleksandrovsky passed away on March 6, 1981.

Russia published complete data about the dominant position of the non-ethnic Russians in the U.S.S.R., the extermination of the Russian intellectuals, the deportation of many scientists to the bleak Siberian mines in Kolyma, the creation of fake scientists equipped with Communist Party membership cards, etc. The Jewish Defense League sent letters to the editorial staff threatening to kill them if the newspaper would not change its attitude. In addition, the newspaper *Russian Voice* accused Russia of Fascism. *Russia* published that the Masons work to achieve their goals of the destruction of Christianity, because Christianity contradicts their Masonic ideology. Christian priests and believers had been massacred in Russia by the direct instigation of the Masons who wanted the people to be like submissive sheep whose wool could be easily sheered. The Masons want to be the elite organization of the world. They harassed Aleksandrovsky, the editor of the newspaper *Russia*. Usually he worked at the printing-house after his job at the editorial office was completed, returning home after midnight. He lived about eleven miles from the printing house on the outskirts of New York.

The newspaper had many subscribers. We hoped that it would pay for itself in a year, and maybe make us a profit. But the inevitable had happened. G. B. Aleksandrovsky had a car accident; his car had a head-on collision with another vehicle which had been moving at a speed of sixty to seventy miles an hour. The crash was so violent that Aleksandrovsky's car flipped over, and he suffered severe brain damage as a result of the accident. He lived several years after the accident but became an invalid. The newspaper ceased to exist. We published several issues after the accident but ran out of money. We, the remaining members of the editorial staff, G. Voitsekhovsky and I, appealed to the Russian public but received only thirty-five dollars and fifty cents. At the same time, *The New Russian Word* received donations of more than eighty thousand dollars.

Colonel Vladimir Ivanovich Tretyakoff, officer of the Imperial Army, published a magazine about the *Pervopokhodnyky (the participants of the Kornilov campaign—their history and their struggles)*. He also published a book about General Kornilov. He was a soft-spoken, kind man. We renewed the activities of the Triple Alliance of Cossacks from the Don, Kuban and Terek Regions.

But when Mr. Bublik, an engineer, was elected as Ataman of the Kuban Army, the situation deteriorated. Bublik was under the influence of Glazkoff, an adventurer and a scoundrel. A group of Kuban Cossacks, linked with Don and Terek Cossacks and other Russian national organizations, broke with Bublik. This new group was headed by true descendants of the White Russian Veterans, the sons of *Pervopokhodnyky*—Ataman esaul (Captain) Evgeny Andreevich Baeff, and the editor of the *Kubanets* magazine, Colonel Aleksey Dmitrievich Shilenok.

Aleksey Dmitrievich occupies a special place in the history of Cossack emigration. He grew up in a cultured family and received a good education. He had come to the United States after World War Two and occupied high positions in American industry. He was the chief engineer at a number of machine-tool companies, and the President of the Philadelphia Branch of the American Society of Engineers. Many times he received awards from scientific organizations and the U.S. government. He is a member of the New York Academy of Science. He is also known as one of the most active members of the Russian émigré community.   For a long time he was a teacher and a board member of the Russian parish school in Philadelphia and was an elder in the Russian church.   Together with his wife, Svetlana Aleksandrovna, he was a sponsor of the cultural society *Beseda (Conversation)*. For many years he was the permanent editor-in-chief of the most popular Russian magazine—*Kubanets*. It is very gratifying that *Kubanets* is now published not only in the United States but also in Russia.   Aleksey Dmitrievich and Svetlana Aleksandrovna made reports on the Day of Sorrow *(on November 7, 1917, the Communists seized power in Russia, and this has become known as the Day of Sorrow)*.

The group, headed by A. D. Shilenok and E. A. Baeff, is called the Kuban Cossack S*oyuz (union)*. It is the only effective Cossack organization outside of Russia worthy to represent the émigré community because it takes a firm anti-Communist position and resolutely defends the cause of the White Struggle. Now, in the era of post-Communist chaos where ultimate loyalties are in question, it is especially important to fight for the purity of the ideological heritage of the White Movement, and for the preservation of the memory of the heroic deeds of the Russian warriors in their struggle against the forces of Communism.

Of course, I worked mainly in the United States and had a better knowledge of Cossack affairs in this country. But visiting Europe and other parts of the world, I tried to collaborate with my fellow Cossacks. I would like to devote a few passages to my Cossack brothers living in Europe.

In Munich, Bavaria Colonel Boris Nikolaevich Miloff was the representative of the Don Ataman. He was an honest, loyal officer of Imperial Russia. Not only did he know how to fight, he was a talented orator and organizer. At one time he headed a large Cossack stanitsa in Munich, but in the 1980s only a few members were still alive. Time takes its toll.

Leonid Ivanovich Baratoff, a Cossack from the stanitsa Starocher-kasskaya *(he also held the rank of colonel in the United States Army and was wounded in combat),* and Boris Nikolayevich Miloff cheered up the Russian community at the Tolstoy Foundation with their interesting reports. It's all over now. Miloff has passed away, and Baratoff is in the Veterans Hospital in California. He had been wounded in the hip while fighting at the front and now is paralyzed. It's a great pity, because he used to be so active. He wrote many historical articles about Imperial Russia which were published in such émigré magazines as *Tchasovoy* (*Sentinel*), *Atamansky Vestnik* (*The Ataman's Herald*), *Kubanets*, and in the newspapers *Russian Life*, and *Our Country*. He was a serious and sincere researcher concerning the historical truth about the high quality of life enjoyed by the citizens of Imperial Russia, and he consistently conveyed the sense of grandeur found in the Russian culture before the Revolution.

There had been several Cossack stanitsas in Germany during Miloff's lifetime. The old people have passed away by now, and the young ones are assimilated. Our descendants, with rare exceptions, have not joined the Cossack family.

The most prominent Cossack unions existed, undoubtedly, in France. First I should mention the Museum of His Majesty's Guards Regiment—the spiritual center which united Russian officers and Cossacks who had served the Emperor. It's a miracle that the regiment managed to deliver its regalia to Paris and preserve it up to the present time. The most valuable exhibits from the regalia collection have been given to the Royal Museum in Brussels, Belgium, for safe-keeping. I met officers loyal to Imperial Russia such as General Pozdneeff, Colonel Dubentsoff, Generals Zuboff and Pozdnysheff. The latter had been the Chairman of the Society for the Relief of Russian War Invalids for many years.

I also met Cossacks of the leftist political persuasion in Paris; they were Socialist Revolutionaries such as Melnikoff, Ulanoff, and others. As a rule, Cossack political factions represent small groups of people at odds with one another. On the one hand, political passions facilitated the acceleration of the process of dissolution of the Russian Cossack emitter community; on the other hand, it gave life to numerous magazines and newspapers, many of which had a lively content and were very popular. For example, Melnikoff's *Rodimy Krai* (*Native Land*), if we ignore the pages devoted to the moral decay of the leftist opposition, is an excellent magazine which published many literary masterpieces created by Russian emitter writers. But I did not like the accusations made in that magazine against the Don Ataman, General I. A. Polyakoff; I considered these criticisms to be irrelevant. By now all the arguments among the Cossack émigrés are of no importance as the community has passed on to another existence, but at the time these disputes promoted the destruction of Cossack unity.

A small group of *Atamantsy* settled in Cannes, France. They participated in the cultural life of the Russian community and visited areas where Russian émigrés had settled in sizable numbers. Cannes is a wonderful location. Everyone has a genuine feeling of happiness there among the fragrant flowers, singing birds and pleasant weather. Nicholas Feodorovich Poluboyaroff headed the Russian community in this location. He lived in a home for senior citizens where he had a bedroom, a small stove, a living room and a bathroom. Meals were served in a common dining room, but if the residents invited guests the kitchen took their orders, and the food was delivered to the apartments. In case a resident wanted to cook for himself, the kitchen supplied him with all that he needed. Senior citizen homes in Europe are like first-class hotels. I visited Russians and Cossacks who lived in those homes not only in France but also in Germany. I remember my visit to the Colonel of the Imperial General Staff, Erast Shlyakhtin *(he was a Cossack from* stanitsa *Kamenskaya)*. His wife cooked delicious borscht and Russian cutlets. Of course, there was also vodka and snacks. Erast and his wife knew many Cossack songs. The songs were the highlight of the visit. His nephew Vladimir Vasilyevich was present there. So there were four of us and we made a quartet. How we sang! The neighbors listened to us with their hearts sinking. The concert lasted for two or three hours, but unfortunately we had to part. Anyhow, our life is composed of meetings and partings.

While visiting His Majesty Guards Cossack Museum, I had the pleasure of meeting the best representatives of the fighting Cossacks such as Ilya Nikolayevich Opritzcheff, General Konstantin Rostislavovich Pozdeeff (we met as old friends in 1960 because we had met before in 1918 when we captured Novocherkassk; he was the commander of my regiment). The general had a very nice wife, Olga Feodorovna. I remember an excellent dinner in the dining room of the museum. At the end of the dinner, Ilya Nikolayevich told Pozdneff, "Kostya, don't forget our Cossack dessert!" And a genuine Astrakhan watermelon appeared on the table. It was unforgettable!

While giving lectures at the University of Delft in Holland for more than twenty years, I had an opportunity to visit France and other European countries which were places of dispersion for the Cossacks and our fellow veterans. I had very friendly relations with the Guards Treasurer, Colonel Boris

Feodorovich Doubentsoff. I cherish his letters. They are full of thoughts and concerns about Russia.

Once while in Paris, I visited the Cossack museum again and received an invitation to a banquet arranged by Mrs. Fisher to be held on a Sunday at a local rest home. Mrs. Fisher, a White Army veteran's daughter, had been married to a very rich gentleman. He left her a considerable fortune, and she decided to buy two old estates in the suburbs of Paris and Nice which she intended to use as rest homes for White Army veterans. Each month the Board of the Russian All-Army Alliance sent a group of elderly Russians there who needed rest and medical care. They lived there free of cost and had all their needs provided.

The reception was held in one of those houses. I came there with General Pozdnysheff. There were many guests—more than a hundred—and the tables were ladened with food and drink. Mrs. Fisher was very cheerful and looked very nice. The dinner began, and then the speeches were delivered addressing Mrs. Fisher and others—dead and alive. I remember how General Pozdnysheff began his speech: "So now, after having eaten tasty snacks, I can say a few words...." I was shocked at such a beginning, but my neighbor at the table, a lawyer, told me having noticed my reaction. "This is not so bad. Did you know about the beginning of his speech at the 150th Anniversary of the Union of Institute Students (The Union of the Ladies who were former students at the Institute)? He appeared on the stage, rubbed his head and said, 'Oh, my God, what do I see? When I last saw you, you were young and shapely. What happened to you?'"

The meeting was over late, ending after midnight. It was joyful and pleasant. I refrained from delivering a speech because there had been enough speeches given on that occasion.

I left Paris and went to the Valley Of Flowers—the gem of France. Famous French perfume factories are located there. There was also a boardinghouse for elderly Russians at that place. I wanted to see Nicholas Feodorovich Poluboyaroff. They were waiting for me, and the administrators of the home served a dinner. The menu was organized by Poluboyaroff. We had a very good time. Alas, now there is not a single Russian at that home; all of them have passed away.

While in Paris I visited Sofia Feodorovna Shatilova, wife of General Shatiloff, the head of the General Staff under General Wrangel. She enchanted everyone. She sparkled with inner tranquillity, warmth, and a depth of feeling. I should also mention Olga Feodorovna Pozdeeva and her daughter. Their attitude towards me was full of delicate understanding, and the memories are still warming my heart, even now many years later. I met many Cossacks who worked as taxi drivers. I had a rather low opinion of the French, but I should admit that they had some nice features which are not often encountered when dealing with Americans; for example, they work together with a more cooperative spirit. My good friend, a Cossack, Ivan Ivanovich Zemtsoff, had his own cab and earned his living as a taxi driver. The rules prohibited him from driving paying passengers on Sundays. Unfortunately I needed to make a purchase on a Sunday at a location in a distant section of Paris; it was located far from his house. He said, "I'll arrange it." We went to the taxi parking lot. He talked to a driver and invited me into a car. An unknown driver took me to the store, waited for me, and drove me back. Naturally, I asked him, "How much do I owe you?" "Nothing," he said. "I drove you at the request of my colleague." I was deeply touched and gave him a few dollars as a gift. Something like this would most likely never happen in America.

I should mention that the Cossack organizations, especially the Don Cossacks, in the United States gave considerable attention to anti-Communist activities. One of them, the most festive and traditional, was the Day of Sorrow. We observed it on the same day when the annual Communist celebration of the "October Revolution" took place in our Motherland. The Board of the Russian Organizations in America, which included the Don Cossacks, was the initiator and organizer of the observation of the Day of Sorrow. For that purpose we rented the school building in the center of the Russian settlement in New York. The board was headed by Prince Beloselsky-Belozersky and Colonel Rasnyansky. The program was as follows: a prayer was given *(the Metropolitans of the American Russian Church and Russian Orthodox Church Outside of Russia were present);* then the reports reflecting the urgent problems were delivered; and finally the main performance took place. At first there had been many people at the ceremonies marking this tragic event, but each year more and more Russian people passed away.

Once, on the eve of the Day of Sorrow, Colonel Rasnyansky made a phone call to my apartment. He was very excited because we could not use the school building on the next

day which was the Day of Sorrow. So we decided to visit the
district Chairman of the Board of Education and talk to him.
However, we failed to convince him that he had made the wrong
decision. Koltypin, George Feodoroff and Rasnyansky talked to
him. I was silent. But at the moment when my friends were at a
loss and did not know what to do, I spoke to the Chairman. I
introduced myself as his colleague, the professor of the School of
Engineering and Architecture at the University of the City of New
York. I found out that the reason for the refusal had to do with a
letter sent by a certain Mr. L. which misrepresented the propose of
our organization. Mr. L. was angry with us and was slandering
our organization. But we did not have a political organization,
and the district Chairman of the Board of Education was
determined to insure that this was, in fact, the truth. "Wait a
minute," the chairman interrupted me, seeing my university card.
"Why, my fellow professor, did you not tell me about your
organization before? Of course you can use that building on the
seventh of November." We thanked him and said goodbye. The
Day of Sorrow commemoration was a success.

Fewer and fewer people came to our meetings as time
passed by. During the last years we, the members of the Don,
Kuban, and Terek Cossacks Triple Alliance, and the Board of
Representatives of Russian Organizations in America, observed
the Day of Sorrow with a memorial service. Ex-Soviet Jews came
to join us on that day in recent years. They declared that life in
the U.S.S.R. was normal, and that the socialist society was very
successful. But when we objected they only shrugged their
shoulders saying that our objections to their descriptions of life in
the Soviet Union were nothing more than capitalist propaganda.

Being the Ataman of the Don Cossacks, I always
maintained connections with Russian organizations on the basis of
national unity. Not only Cossack organizations in the U.S.S.R.
are decaying—the American-Russian Aid Association headed by
Vasylieff, Rumel and Shantykhoff was also undermined. These
individuals facilitated the disintegration of the Society, pushing
aside Prince Beloselsky-Belozersky. Prince Beloselsky-
Belozersky, Rasnyansky and I urgently gathered the members of
the Society (about a thousand people) to discuss the management
policies of the present leaders of the Society. The results of the
discussion, as well as the documentation of the financial situation,
were submitted to a judge in New York. The court approved our

appeal, and we were authorized to lead the Society, thus saving it from disintegration.

The Society exists up to the present time. Rasnyansky was elected the Chairman of the Society, I was elected as his First Vice President, and *Porutchik* (Lieutenant) Tomashevsky became his Second Vice President. Prince Nicholas Koadasheff, N. Vysokovsky and others were the members of the board. At the beginning, the meetings were quiet, but later Prince Koadasheff interrupted everyone who spoke, behaving in a childish manner. Finally Colonel Rasnyasnsky lost his temper, put aside his papers, and left the room with these words, "I resign as Chairman." The situation was critical, and I rushed after him. He was sitting downstairs, dressed in his coat and shivering as if from a cold.

I brought him a glass of water and said, "You, Sergei Nikolayevich, will not leave now. You are a *Bykhovets* veteran *(Rasnyansky had been put in Bykhovsky prison together with L. G. Korniloff. N. F.),* and the *Bykhovets* veterans don't leave their posts. Excuse me for saying that to you. I am a veteran *Tchernetsovets* partisan; *Bvkhovtsy* and *Tchernetsovtsy* would rather die than leave their posts. Now there is silence upstairs, and it will last until you come back." He went upstairs together with me, returned to presenting his reports, and the meeting continued in a quiet and peaceful manner.

Our activities for normalizing the American-Russian Aid Society were going on successfully. We had to elect a new chairman after Rasnyansky's death. I could not be the chairman for two reasons—I lived seventy miles away from the House of Free Russia, and I was the Chairman of the Organization of Russian Immigrants, the Chairman of the Society to Aid Russian War Invalids, and Ataman of the Don Cossacks Outside of Russia. I was also an active member of the American Society of Engineers as well. But the Chairman of the American-Russian Aid Society was supposed to be present in the office for three days a week, and I could not afford to do that. For that reason, I proposed to elect Sergei Sergeevich Ziloty. He was retired by that time and could spend long hours at the office of the Society talking to his fellow countrymen. At the same time, Mikhail Aleksandrovich Romash, being diligent and having a good understanding of the affairs of the Society, conducted the business of the organization.

I don't know who told M. A. Romash about me, but about thirty years ago I received a map of the Ukraine with a note:

"Here is what the Galicians are doing, wasting the money of both the United States and New York State." The map portrayed the territory of the Ukraine as stretching as far as Moscow. Having received the map, which was distributed legally in the United States, I sent a letter to the Chairman of the Historical Museum of New York City (whose employees made the map) describing what his employees were doing during their working hours. But I never received a reply.

Later I met M. A. Romash at the Society *Otrada (Joy)*—Russian cultural/educational organization. He was a very kind man. After the death of S. S. Ziloty he was elected as the Chairman of the American-Russian Society for Relief in October of 1992.

There were difficulties in the Organization of the Representatives of the Russian Émigrés of which I was the president. This organization received twenty-eight thousand from the proceeds of a will. The "wheeler-dealers" who wanted to start a publishing business appeared at once. These were Mr. Vysokovsky with his friend. These persons had no experience at all, and they wanted to launch a complicated business. I remember a session when a Kuban Cossack woman, Zinaida Efimovna Kharkovskaya, gave Vysokovsky a good dressing-down, and he, being unable to endure any more of the proceedings, left. However, the organization is functioning up to the present. It arranges performances, meetings, renders help to invalids, and observes the Day of Sorrow.

ALL-RUSSIAN COSSACK CAUSE

There are fewer and fewer Cossacks left. N. F. Kostrukoff's chorus does not perform any more. S. A. Zharoff passed away. Geography, too, is playing its destructive role; nothing separates more than long distances. Correspondence helps to maintain connections to some extent, but our particular "ethnic" group is dying gradually as well. At the beginning of the Sixties, we had been sending out up to four hundred copies of the *Donskoy Ataman Vestnik*, and now even twenty copies are too many. I should add that many of our readers made no contributions to the magazine. No, I don't mean the money. I mean information, family stories, memories. Now we send seventy-five copies to Russia, and they ask us to send them more. But here—just silence.

Two years ago, we made an appeal to a cadets meeting to create an information center, unite all Cossacks, and so on, and only twelve Cossacks responded. At present I am in contact with only two of the twelve. Ten of them stepped aside. H. N. Protopopoff takes care of the unification, but who listens to him? And so it is everywhere—a light sparkles and then dies away. There are no people.

In 1975, a group of Russian patriots decided to save the House of Free Russia in New York. Colonel S. N. Rasnyansky collected about five hundred voting members from the Russian Army union of Gallipoli; I collected about five hundred voting members—the Cossacks and their relatives. But in reality, in 1992 only sixty-seven people voted in the election for the new president, and only fifteen people were present at the meeting of the renovated Board of the American-Russian Aid Society located at the House of Free Russia.

More than a half of that thousand have passed away by now, and the others are spending the rest of their lives in senior citizen homes or are living with their children. The dispersion continues.

Of course we can reinforce the ranks of patriotic organizations, admitting new members, whoever, just to show that these organizations are alive and active. One of the Cossack organizations is acting in such a way. But regeneration is regeneration.

I would like to give particular praise to two people—the Ataman of the Kuban Cossack Alliance in America, Evgeny Andreevich Baeff, and Anatoly Vasilyevich Lukinoff, who had rebuilt a chapel (which was falling to pieces) at the Vladimirskoye Cemetery and who built a parish house at the Memorial Church in New Jersey.

Russian people are moving out of New York. Many of them moved to small towns in Maine, New Jersey, and St. Petersburg, Florida. Our ranks are growing thin, and the Russian Army at the Throne of God is increasing. We were born to die. That is our destiny.

Cossack activities now mainly occur in making arrangements for the Day of Sorrow commemoration and serving at requiems for the Cossacks and all the Russian people who were victims of extradition to the Soviet Union by American and British authorities after World War Two. We celebrate the Army festival on the first Sunday of October. But not many people come for these celebrations now.

Only thirteen men from an American regiment survived during World War One. They meet every year. Last year the thirteenth of them came to the restaurant where they used to meet and saw only empty chairs. He sat down, ordered his dinner, ate it, sat for a while and fell asleep in an eternal dream. A remarkable story.

I retired in 1982 but continued to work as a consultant for the Grigg Engineering Company. Almost all my friends who were Cossacks have passed away. I am the only one who is lingering. But there are no young people.

CONCLUSION

The long journey of a Russian White Army veteran and emigrant is over. How much pain and patience, and how many tears streamed down a battle-hardened face. And now, in my declining years, I remember those Russian patriots who took up their arms without hesitation and followed the road of armed struggle with International Communism. I remember those heroes and heroines *(especially Russian girls in soldier's coats, white kerchiefs and with rifles in their hands)* who perished in the boundless Russian fields defending Russia. I remember our courageous youth who reinforced the ranks of the White Army, placing their young lives on the altar of Russia. In those days of moral degradation, cowardice, self-interest, breaking of the military oath, not many moved to the oasis of faith and loyalty to Russia—to the White Army.

The White Warriors did not succeed. They became exiles, but we should remember the words of the founder of the White Army, General Alekseyeff, that they have ignited a flame in the midst of total darkness. And that light has not died away. It is flaming up at the present.

A thought often occurs to me—why we should live, struggle, and suffer? But my parents' self-reliance and strength and the blood of my ancestors told me, "Be patient, it could be worse." And, summoning up fresh energy, I followed the straight path, the way of honor and love of Russia. I used to think and say, "Oh my God! For what purpose are these tribulations occurring? All the sufferings fell on us, on the Russian people." But when I remembered that it has been even worse "there," I gained new power to follow my thorny path. There is nothing worse than moral illness. The Cossacks spent all their lives in their saddles. As for our generation, it has no saddles. Through all their history, the Cossacks "endured." And in the Twentieth Century they had to endure unprecedented sufferings. They had to suffer and endure. There is a well-known Cossack proverb, "Be patient, oh Cossack, and you'll be an ataman." Never in my youth could I imagine that I would be, at first acting, and then a full and equal Ataman of the Don Cossacks Outside of Russia; that I would endure all those squabbles that had been so alien to me in the university and everyday life. But it was my destiny. I endured and investigated, and now I paraphrase the old proverb. "Be patient, Ataman, you'll be a Cossack." So I am patient.

We are the true sons of the Russian land, and we traversed a hard path. I remember how we waded through the mud from Rostov to stanitsa Novopashkovskaya, how we miraculously arrived in the Crimea, how we opposed the overwhelming forces of the Reds, and I think that there is no force which can subdue us. The Cossacks go to the Court of God with their heads held high.

We went into the unknown. It started outside of Russia. The first crucibles were Chilingir, Gallipoli, and Lemnos. The Allies "took care" of us, trying to drive us back to the U.S.S.R. like cattle for the slaughter. But even hard labor in mines and road construction projects, the intrigues of the Soviet agents such as Ageeff, Lebedeff, and others, or government leaders such as Stambolysky, could not break us. The mines and roads in Bulgaria, Serbia, and France were developed with the sweat of White Army veterans who survived due to the moral strength of their leaders, especially General Baron von Wrangel.

Further dispersion created centers of old Russian culture in many countries. The churches, built with hard-earned money, became the meeting places, inspiring our steadfastness of purpose as well as our love and respect. Wherever fate brought the Cossacks, they built churches and opened schools.

None of us could predict that thorny path which awaited my generation. Almost all of us have gone to the Throne of God, and those who are alive are thrilled to see the double-headed eagle, the tri-color flag of the Russian Empire, the St. Andrew's ensign of the Russian Imperial Navy, soar over the territories of a hopefully free Russian state. Self-denial and the heroism of the Russian man will save Russia. God, save and preserve.

APPENDIX

A COSSACK
AND A COSSACK OFFICER

None of the military groups, none of the military assemblies, none of the armies of the world have something like a Cossack army, in the sense of an almost family unity of the rank-and-file men and the officers. It was facilitated by the fact that the Cossack regiments were formed on the basis of the villages. The only exceptions were the guards and the special units. But the Cossacks found their common relatives even there and maintained related connections. Besides that, the spirit of military service was well known to every Cossack since his early childhood, and a Cossack could accustom himself to the service easily. As a result of such a strong unity, there were no deserters. A deserter could never return to his native village.

The officers often not only knew their subordinates, but also their families, relatives, and their life in the village. A *Khorunzhy* (junior officer) was often of the same age as his rank-and-file Cossack and they knew each other since their childhood. That's why their relations were friendly. An officer was a friend, a father and a brother. Vasily Mikhailovich Azhogin

Voiskovoy Starshina (lieutenant colonel) Vasily Mikhailovich Azhogin remembered how, during World War One, on the Rumanian border, a *Vakhmistr* (Cavalry Sergeant Major) came to him and said that two horses were missing in the reserve regiment.

Vasily Mikhailovich asked if anybody in the regiment was drunk. "Yes! There is a drunk Kalmyk." "Send him to me as soon as he comes to himself," Vasily Mikhailovich ordered. At noon, Tseden the Kalmyk arrived, clicked his heels and stood at attention. "Where did you get the money for vodka?" Vasily Mikhailovich asked him, "and where did you put the commander's horses? They should be returned at once." "Me did not take..." the Kalmyk tried to justify himself. But Vasily Mikhailovich interrupted him: "Either you bring the horses in the morning, or you'll be court-martialed and hanged for stealing." Death by the sentence of the court-martial was always considered to be the most dishonorable. "When you bring the horses, come to me and I'll slap you in the face—that will be your punishment. I will not tell anybody what happened, though I myself should be court-martialed for concealment of the theft. But this is my own problem."

Early in the morning the Vakhmistr reported that the horses at their proper place. Later Tseden came. "So," Vasily Mikhailovich said, "before you get a slap in your face, you must tell me how and to whom you sold the horses." A Rumanian village was located across the river. "Your nobleness," Tseden said, "at night me took the horses, crossed the river, sold them to a Rumanian, bought vodka. And now me went to a big stable, took my horse and swam home—as you told me."

Vasily Mikhailovich gave him a big slap and said: "Go and don't tell anybody what happened."

However, it came out. The next day, the Commander of the regiment called Vasily Mikhailovich: "Why didn't you tell me about the that?"

"I promised the person who stole the horses that I not report him," Vasily Mikhailovich said.

"Then you'll be court-martialed," the Commander snapped.

But the revolution started and the incident was forgotten. I think that the Commander understood that Vasily Mikhailovich was right and did not want to discuss the matter in public.

During the Civil War, Vasily Mikhailovich went on Stepnoy Pokhod (the Steppe March) from Novocherkassk in February of 1918. A man on duty came to him during a halt and reported that a Kalmyk wanted to see him. To his great surprise, Vasily Mikhailovich saw Tseden. "How did you find me, Tseden?" "Me found your nobleness," Tseden answered joyfully. "Do you have your horse?"

"No", Vasily Mikhailovich confessed, "I have no horse."

"What is a Cossack without a horse? Me bring you a horse." Tseden disappeared and returned in a couple of hours with two horses.

"Tseden!", Vasily Mikhailovich exclaimed, "You stole again?"

"Why stole? The Red ran away, me got the horse," the Kalmyk objected.

Vasily Mikhailovich often remembered that story. He lived to a venerable age. For a long time he was the elder at Alexander Nevsky Church in Howell, New Jersey. He was a typical Cossack—honest, staunch, religious. As many other officers, be had to save many people during his life, regardless of their religious or political views.

There was a custom in Russia during the good old times—to put a wreath of immortelles—little golden flowers—on a grave of a deceased. At some places these flowers are called "podorozhnyk."

Let us weave a wreath in our thoughts and put it on the head of a White Warrior who had fought courageously against the enemy of all mankind—the Communists.

A HORSE — THE COSSACK'S FRIEND

Horses and dogs are noble animals, true friends of man. One can say that a Cossack was born with a horse, as well as an American is born with a car.

The South of Russia, like all Russian territory, is favorable for animal breeding. There is plenty of grass, and, therefore, plenty of fodder. In winter, cattle and horses stayed in the stables and in summer they grazed. The Cossacks always had a lot of hay stocked for winter in huge hay-stacks. The Reds especially liked to put it on fire—the blaze was bright.

The horses which were not needed for everyday work, were sent with the drovemen to distant pastures, where they stayed from early spring to the autumn frosts. It was interesting to watch the horses brought home in autumn. We, the children, were impressed. Usually a stand for the priest, honorable residents of the village, members of the board and guests, was built near the church.

Well-trained drovesmen tried to lead the horses right in front of the stand. It was not easy because the horses got wild during the summer. There were rarely less than two thousand horses in a drive. Later each owner had to bridle his horse and take it to a stable. When the horses were passing the stand, the priest sprinkled them with holy water and delivered a thanksgiving prayer. That ritual had a deep meaning of the unity of a Cossack and Nature.

The Cossacks used horses more than other animals. A Cossack could not manage without a horse at his household, and also went to military service with his friend. Very often his life depended on the endurance and agility of his horse. He always took care of his horse. There is popular Cossack saying: Even if you don't eat yourself, cherish your horse."

In the Imperial Army they called the Cossack Cavalry "light," as distinct from the "heavy" cavalry which consisted of cuirassiers, houssars, and the others. The Cossack cavalry and the scouts ("plastny") were also called "irregular," opposing it to the Russian "regular" army.

The drovesmen were held in great honor. They were welcomed in every house. Children climbed the trees to see the horses. Imagine several thousand horses, rushing to the village and suddenly stopping. The horses who hadn't seen a human dwelling for a long time became confused. One can hear them snorting—they dilate their nostrils and raise their tails. It seems that in a moment they will rush in a roundabout way across the Cossack's gardens and fields, destroying everything in their way. Then the droveman comes forward and the horse—leader of the herd—recognizes him. With a fluffy tail, he stands near the man and follows him. Then, as if by magic, the other horses follow him. The land trembles under the hooves of numerous horses and the air is filled with their snorting. An experienced droveman leads them to a place where the owners with lassoes are waiting. When all the horses were taken to the stables, the celebration starts.

I'll never forget my brother Peter's horse—a beautiful Don horse. Nobody but my brother could saddle and ride it. It would buck off anyone. I could only clean and wash it. My uncle was a riding instructor and he taught my brother to ride. Once he decided to ride my brother's horse. My brother tried to dissuade him, but he wouldn't listen. The horse was saddled and my uncle rode from Novocherkassk in the direction of the stanitsa Aksaiskaya. The horse was quiet, even tender. It took sugar from my uncle's hands. But about four hours later, the horse returned by itself, and then my uncle came—dirty, limping and scolding the horse in all possible ways.

Once I heard an interesting story about horses. It took place in 1900. A Cossack regiment was in China. On a clear, quiet day, the Cossacks were riding along the Great Wall of China. They saw white horses in a distance. "What's that?" they asked the Chinese interpreter. "These are the wild horses of our Bogdykhan," he said. "They are known throughout the world as pure-blood horses."

The Cossacks asked for permission to catch a few horses. Soon each of them was leading a beautiful white horse. "What are you going to do with them?" the Commander asked the Cossacks. "We are going to break them in," they answered. They saddled the horses, having them hobbled and on the ground. A Cossack stood over a tied horse with his legs spread. When, after a signal, the lassoes were taken away and the horse jumped from the ground, the Cossack was already in the saddle. The horses "danced", dashed aside, made incredible turns, but the Cossacks sat firmly in their saddles as if they became rooted to them. Strong, firm Cossack hands controlled the horses skillfully. And the horses quieted.

The Englishmen who had seen the white horses asked the Cossacks to sell them, but the Cossacks suggested that the Englishmen should catch the horses themselves. Finally the Cossacks agreed to catch the horses for a fee. The Englishmen flatly refused to break in the horses. The captured horses were supposed to be carried to the special riding houses for training.

"Are you going to carry them on flat platforms in the open freight cars?" our Commander asked his British colleague, "Don't do that. The wild animals will kill themselves and crush everything around." But his reasonable voice was not heard. One day the Cossacks heard a strange noise and then shots. Several Cossacks were sent to find out what was going on. They reported that the Englishmen put the horses on the platforms and tied them. When the train whistled, the horses burst out. They tore the ropes and started to jump from the platform. Many of them broke their legs and were shot by the Englishmen. The Cossacks were crying while listening to that report. Beautiful animals were destroyed as a result of stupidity and obstinacy.

I heard another terrible story about horses, related to the Patriotic War of 1812-1813. French Cavalry of Marshal Murate, having broken the front line, rushed to the hill where three emperors—Alexander I, Francis I of Austria, and Frederick III of Prussia—were standing. At that critical moment, Colonel Efremoff—a Cossack officer from the personal guard of Emperor Alexander I—suddenly attacked the enemy's cavalry from one side. Cossack sabers broke against the iron armor of the French. Then Efremoff ordered: "Hit the horses!" The Cossacks began to hit the French horses who threw their riders. Three Emperors were saved by resourcefulness of the Cossack.